THE OTHER WIFE

DANIELLE RAMSAY

Boldwood

First published in Great Britain in 2024 by Boldwood Books Ltd.

Copyright © Danielle Ramsay, 2024

Cover Design by 12 Orchards Ltd

Cover Photography: Shutterstock

Every effort has been made to obtain the necessary permissions with reference to copyright material, both illustrative and quoted. We apologise for any omissions in this respect and will be pleased to make the appropriate acknowledgements in any future edition.

A CIP catalogue record for this book is available from the British Library.

Paperback ISBN 978-1-83751-108-2

Large Print ISBN 978-1-83751-109-9

Hardback ISBN 978-1-83751-107-5

Ebook ISBN 978-1-83751-110-5

Kindle ISBN 978-1-83751-111-2

Audio CD ISBN 978-1-83751-102-0

MP3 CD ISBN 978-1-83751-103-7

Digital audio download ISBN 978-1-83751-104-4

Boldwood Books Ltd
23 Bowerdean Street
London SW6 3TN
www.boldwoodbooks.com

To my sister, Paula Elizabeth Ramsay

We can never go back again, that much is certain. The past is still close to us. The things we have tried to forget and put behind us would stir again, and that sense of fear, of furtive unrest, struggling at length to blind unreasoning panic – now mercifully stilled, thank God – might in some manner unforeseen become a living companion as it had before.

— DAPHNE DU MAURIER, *REBECCA*

Who is it that can tell me who I am?

— *KING LEAR* (ACT I, SCENE IV)

1

Do you know what you've done to me? It's not the girl, not the girl. But I loved this place and you have made it into a place I hate. I used to think that if everything else went out of my life I would still have this, and now you have spoilt it. It's just somewhere else where I have been unhappy, and all the other things are nothing to what has happened here. I hate it now like I hate you and before I die I will show you how much I hate you.

— JEAN RHYS, *WIDE SARGASSO SEA*

The ocean crashed ever closer to the castle walls as the storm whipped itself up into a frenzied hysteria. I looked out of the lead-paned windows at the blazing glow off to the right, disrupting the black of the night. I watched and waited as it grew brighter and more defiant, undeterred by the rain. Hissing sparks from the fire were now rising, intense and furious as it spread. Hypnotised by what swiftly became a raging ball of blue, red and orange within the large Victorian conservatory, I watched as it began to devour everything in its wake: feasting, I imagined, on the dried-up oil paintings and dusty charcoal sketches of Lady Isabella Langdon stored there. Not that there were neighbours who could raise the alarm, as there was no one else for miles and miles around. Soon, there would be no escape when the fire reached the castle's ground-floor rooms and the impressive columns and central stone staircase that led up, dramatically branching off in two directions. I envisioned the waves of feverish flames consuming the interior walls adorned with their imposing hunt trophies, ornate brass decorated targes and swords, centuries-old tapestries and portraits of lairds and ladies long gone as the thunderous waves of the ocean engulfed the rocks below, reaching higher and higher up the sheer cliff face towards me. My only way out would be to leap from this room to the jagged boulders waiting beneath. Startled, I jumped back as salty sea spray hit the old lead windows, tapping to get in like the ghosts of the dead with brittle fingers at the glass.

To save you? Or stop you?

Again and again, the howling wind beseeched me to let the wildness in. To allow it to take me. To take everything. To pull me down into the cold blackness. I knew the scorching fire would destroy what the ocean couldn't reach.

I felt the weight of the Cartier sunray gold-plated vintage cigarette lighter in my left palm. My fingers delicately touched the names engraved along the side. Her name – Isabella Langdon. And his – James Buchanan Langdon. It was a present from him to her.

To his love – his first wife.

'What are you doing in here?' questioned a distant voice.

I didn't respond as I stared at the approaching devastation.

'I asked, what are you doing in here?' the voice repeated, this time louder, more authoritative. 'You should be in bed.'

I instinctively flinched as the words cut through my thoughts, drowning out the screech of the screaming Atlantic Ocean as it hammered at the walls, the windows and the doors, seeking revenge.

Revenge? Or refuge?

'I asked you what you are doing in here. You're not allowed in this part of the castle. Are you even listening to me?'

I now recognised the voice. Turning, I kept my head down, too fearful to look up. For this was Laird James Buchanan Langdon. The owner of this doomed medieval castle and the last of his ancestral line.

He flicked a switch, immediately dispelling the dark shapes lurking in the corners as the exquisite and intricate crystal chandelier in the centre of the ceiling burst into life, illuminating the large, impressive bedroom.

I had contemplated turning on the reading lamp on the writing desk, but I was more terrified of him finding me than of the shadows and the distorted forms that lurked within them.

I wondered how he had known to look for me here or if he came every evening when I was in bed and sat in the blackness waiting for her – his first love – to come back to him.

I found myself edging further against the deep stone windowsill. My back was dangerously close to the rattling panes and the bony fingers outside so desperate to reach me.

I turned and looked out, expecting to see some ghostly figure. But no one was there. There was only the waiting abyss below and the rising phoenix of fire in the distance, unfurling its wings of orange and yellow flames, tentatively stretching towards the main building. It hadn't taken long for it to take hold, to be reborn out of the ashes of the past.

His past. Her past.

'This is her bedroom. Isn't it?' I dared, my voice barely above a whisper.

I glanced over at him. He was unaware that a fire was spreading.

But not for long. I only had minutes left, if that. The screeching storm disguised the exploding windowpanes of the art studio as it cracked and buckled under the intense raging flames.

'Isabella's,' I whispered, scared to speak her name out loud.

You didn't imagine her. She does exist. Her cigarette lighter in the palm of your hand is real. All of this is real...

I looked across at the monstrous, ornate antique four-poster bed, shrouded in heavy, cloying, intricately detailed fabric. It had been left waiting for her return: Lady Isabella Langdon.

His other wife.

The countless pillows and scatter cushions were all plumped, stiff and full. The centuries-old, thick, gold-threaded throw partially covered the soft, downy goose-feathered quilt and the deep-filled mattress with its white, pristine Egyptian cotton sheets, waiting for her cold body to seek refuge for the night.

This was their bed... Before he...

I couldn't bring myself to acknowledge it.

Laird James Buchanan Langdon, my husband – or so they told me – had been her husband. She had been his other wife, the one before me, who had disappeared without a trace.

Just as he's trying to make you vanish into nothing: stripping you of your sanity until all that is left is a husk. Intimating that you have lost your mind, allowing him to defend his abhorrent and unlawful treatment of you.

'This was her bedroom,' I dared to venture.

He didn't move, as if too fearful to step into the room.

Her bedroom.

'Do you remember?' he questioned.

He waited for a response.

But how can you remember? She, Isabella Langdon, was before your time here.

I stared at him, not understanding.

He shook his head. 'Of course you don't remember,' he said, his voice barely audible.

I couldn't tell if he was sad that I didn't remember, his expression lost to me.

He then stared at me as if seeing me for the first time.

'What in God's name are you wearing?' he questioned, his voice abrasive.

I flinched.

'And what's in your hands?'

I instinctively hid them behind my back.

'I'm serious. What do you have?'

Again, I didn't answer.

Then he saw her – his other wife. 'Oh my God! What have you done?'

I followed his gaze to above the fireplace. To the portrait of Isabella Langdon.

'Why? Why? It's all I had left...'

He suddenly broke through whatever unseen barrier had prevented him from crossing the threshold into Isabella Langdon's bedroom. He strode across the polished wooden floors and antique Persian rug, his eyes only on me, as if unable to look at the furnishings and all her belongings which still adorned the room. I had often wondered why he had never stripped it bare of her existence, so no one would ever know she had once lived here. Instead, he kept it as a shrine. Nothing had been moved or touched since that fateful night when she disappeared. Someone still polished the furniture and plumped up the pillows and the scatter cushions, and aired the room as if expecting its owner to return.

Everything was as Isabella Langdon had left it.

I looked at her writing bureau with the antique oxblood Chesterfield captain's chair positioned in front of me by the window. It was awaiting its mistress to sit back down and resume her duties as she gazed out at the expansive ocean beyond.

A rewired vintage 1920s black and bronze candlestick phone sat on the desk. I had called the emergency services to alert them about the fire. I wanted them to know about him – my husband – to know what he had done. For I knew about her, his other wife, and soon the police would as well.

I had scoured every inch of Isabella Langdon's room, searching for clues about what had become of her. I could feel her gaze upon me. I glanced over at the hearth, prepared for a fire that would soon burn when the flames from the conservatory finally reached here. I looked above the extravagant marble fire surround and to the portrait dominating the chimney breast – at her. Isabella Langdon, once proud, defiant and beautiful, was now unrecognisable. Her features and body slashed beyond repair. Her dazzling emerald-green ball gown ripped to pieces.

I smiled as I turned away from the sabotaged painting and looked down at the emerald-green ball gown – the same dress Isabella Langdon had posed in for the portrait.

I knew my husband – her husband – had made arrangements to make me disappear. I had overheard his words to his housekeeper earlier this evening:

'*I intend for every trace of her to be gone from here by the morning... I made a mistake bringing her here. I should have realised that she could never be Isabella.*'

Unlike Isabella Langdon, he wanted everything that reminded him of me gone. My bedroom had been emptied of all my clothes, toiletries, aside from my favourite book that I took like a talisman everywhere. All vanished without warning. The housekeeper had packed it away to be forgotten about or destroyed. So I had run, and knowing all the external doors were locked, I had hid from what I expected to follow – my disappearance. This was the last place I expected him to find me.

And yet, he has found you. Are you really surprised he knew you would hide in here?

'And why are you wearing that dress?'

I didn't respond.

I recoiled as he surprised me by dragging the protesting, heavy writing bureau out of the way, blocking my exit with his tall, athletic physique. I clasped my hands tightly behind my back, trying to hide their contents from him.

'Please, hand over whatever you're hiding and take that silly dress off.'

I shook my head.

'Why? Why would you wear it? Why are you doing this to me? All I have done is try to help you. This has all been for your own good and you do this to—'

I stared at him, waiting for him to finish. Instead, he dragged a trembling hand through his dark, unruly hair as he seemingly forced himself to look at me.

I wanted to scream in retaliation – how could what he had done to me be for my own good? He was the one who kept me here, isolated and cut off from the world; everything he did was for my benefit, my safety – or so he said. I could hear his oft-repeated reassuring whispers enveloping me like a snake, coiling round and round my body, suffocating me until it felt like I couldn't breathe.

He lied to you! His loving words... They were all lies.

My mind threw me back to her – Isabella Langdon. His other wife. The one that he had kept secret. Had he whispered the same declarations, the same threats to her? But I knew the answer. For I had found her diary and read her scrawled entries. Her suspicion he was having an affair, followed by her realisation that he wanted rid of her – forever.

For he threatened to kill her...

She had written about it. Her fear that he would act out his desire.

And he did it. He made her disappear. For no one knew that she had ever existed.

Not even you. Not until you found this room and her diary.

My eyes darted to the comfortable brown leather Queen Anne armchairs on either side of the large, cold, dark fireplace. I wondered whether that was where he and Isabella had sat together in the evenings as the wild winter nights wailed outside.

'Are you even listening to me?'

I was jolted back by his voice.

I dragged my attention back to him and away from her.

His eyes bore into mine. I kept my resolve. I had to...

'And wipe that red lipstick off.'

He waited a beat.

'Now!' he demanded when I failed to act. 'You look...' He faltered, as if unable to say it.

Not that he needed to, for I knew I could never be her – his first wife.

'You look ridiculous,' he finally said.

His words cut through me. But I knew they were the truth. I did look ridiculous, despite wanting to appear beautiful – like Isabella Langdon.

I became aware my body was trembling as I clenched the evidence of her existence, that I wasn't insane, even tighter in the palm of my hand. Not that he needed to see what I was holding.

Evidence against him.

He knew well enough what I had discovered. After all, I was wearing his other wife's emerald-green ball gown.

I didn't answer. I couldn't. Nor could I bring myself to look him in the eye. I avoided his gaze, too fearful that he would break my nerve.

'Christ!' he again cursed. 'Mrs Taylor?' he called over his shoulder. 'Mrs Taylor? I need some assistance here. Please?'

I waited.

'I can't take this any more...' he said, unable to look at me. 'I tried to help you...' He faltered, shaking his head. 'I'm not some monster,' he uttered as if for his own benefit as he turned away.

But he is. He is a monster. He killed his first wife.

'You killed her. You murdered her the night Isabella told you she was pregnant with your child,' I accused without thinking, my voice barely audible.

But he heard it.

He swung back around to me.

The chandelier light suddenly went out, throwing us into abrupt blackness.

'What did you say?'

I swallowed. It felt as if his hands were around my throat, suppressing my defiance, my words.

'You killed her and her unborn child,' I repeated.

'You don't know what you're saying,' he replied in a low voice.

I stared up at his face, unable to read his expression in the dark.

Then he caught sight of the glowing light outside.

'What the hell have you done? WHAT HAVE YOU DONE?'

'You killed her!' I threw back at him. 'Now the police have no choice but to come. And when they do, they'll find out what you did to her.'

'STOP! FOR GOD'S SAKE, STOP! I CAN'T TAKE ANY MORE!'

I watched as he fumbled in his trouser pocket before pulling out what I realised was his mobile phone when the screen lit up. However, there was no signal, so I knew he couldn't call for help. Instead, he switched the torch app on and shone it on the desk. He then rested the mobile against a silver photograph frame, its light casting an eerie glow as he grabbed the old phone and dialled 999.

'It's an emergency. I have a fire at Dunstrafne Castle,' he replied when someone answered his call as he watched the blaze outside. 'The conservatory. But it will spread to the main castle. Tell them to hurry. I have no staff here to contain the fire. No... No, I don't know how... What? You've already received a call about the fire? How?'

He suddenly looked at me, his expression frozen.

'No... NO!' he shouted as the receiver fell from his hand.

I gasped as the coldness cut through me. Swift and decisive.

'Oh God... No... no...' he murmured as he stared at my dress illuminated by the torchlight from his mobile phone.

Her dress.

However, the ball gown that had fitted her perfectly curvaceous body was too large for my thin, shapeless frame.

You look ridiculous... Just like he said.

'Mr Langdon?' the housekeeper questioned breathlessly as she entered the room.

I could see Mrs Taylor's gaunt, skeletal face accentuated by the light from the candle she was holding.

'The power has gone out,' she informed him. She then looked at me. 'Mrs Langdon? What are you—'

'There's a fire in the conservatory. You need to get the boys out. Mrs Taylor!' he insisted, turning to the housekeeper when she didn't move.

'No, please? Mrs Taylor? Don't leave me with him,' I pleaded. 'He's... he's going to—'

'Mrs Taylor? The boys? Get them and take them outside and wait in the grounds until help arrives.'

She hesitated. 'But what about you and Mrs Langdon?'

'I'll take care of her. Go!'

'But Mrs Langdon? Why is she wearing...' She stopped as her

gaze fell upon the ball of orange and yellow illuminating the blackness outside.

'I'll carry Mrs Langdon downstairs. Get the boys before the fire spreads, Mrs Taylor. PLEASE!'

'Is she... Is she hurt?' she questioned as she looked back at me.

'I think so. You can take a look when I get her outside. Now, please, get the boys before the fire spreads.'

'Yes... Yes, of course,' she answered before disappearing.

He turned back to me.

I heard myself gasp.

Or was it him?

I looked up at his face, but he was staring at my dress. I followed his gaze.

I could see the exotic juniper-wood handle belonging to my husband's blade-and-corkscrew pocketknife protruding through the emerald-green silk dress. Engraved on the slim, folding, polished stainless-steel blade with the iconic, signature Laguiole bee, her words to him were immortalised forever:

To my love, forever yours, Isabella x

I then saw blood spreading outwards on the emerald-green ball gown.

My bandaged right hand fluttered over the handle, unsure of what to do.

'NO! DON'T! LEAVE IT!' he cried out as I gripped the handle and pulled with what strength I had until I prised it out of my abdomen.

I watched as it fell from my damaged hand, spraying blood across the hem of the green dress and the wooden floor. Surprised I felt no pain, I slumped back against the windowsill before my legs gave way, and I slid to the floor. Panicking that the stolen pages from Isabella Langdon's diary and cigarette lighter had fallen from my grasp, relief coursed through me when I felt her white-gold wedding ring, which was too large for my fingers, still in place on my left fourth finger. I had somehow managed to keep hold of it. Her name was inscribed on the inside, intertwined with my husband's name, along with the date of their wedding, nine years ago. I leaned against the wall and closed my eyes, holding on to her wedding ring with what fading strength I had left. Someone would find it when they found me, and they would start asking questions.

'They'll think you stabbed me,' I whispered.

I smiled at him. I knew he was trying to figure out how I had managed to take his precious pocketknife, which he carried everywhere.

'It's over,' I said, my voice barely audible.

'No...' he uttered, dropping to his knees. 'God... What have you done to yourself?'

'So, they'll know what you did to her,' I muttered. 'They'll believe you tried to kill me, just like your other wife. The one you murdered.'

I could hear sirens in the distance.

I had won.

I tried to fight the heavy darkness obscuring my thoughts.

You've destroyed him, your husband – James Buchanan Langdon. They'll know what he did to her, that he made her disappear two years ago. His first wife – Isabella Langdon – the one you know he murdered. The police will search the castle and the grounds for her body. And they'll find her... And you...

2

FIVE DAYS EARLIER: THURSDAY

I braced myself, then opened my eyes. A flash of agonising pain overwhelmed me. A cautionary reminder not to move. The pounding, excruciating torture where even breathing was intolerable came back to me. I shut my eyes and lay perfectly still, not wanting to stir it. I could still feel it there, my migraine lurking deep in the recesses of my mind. But it was quiet – for now.

I waited and waited until curiosity forced me to try again. I had no idea of time or how long I had been lying there. I tried opening my eyes again, ever so slowly, not wanting to awaken it. I blinked a couple of times as I took in my surroundings. The high pure-white ceiling merged seamlessly with the blank, indistinguishable white walls.

Panic started to stir as I realised: I had no idea where I was or why.

I waited. Nothing happened. No memory came out of the confusion.

All I knew was that it was too bright, too white. There was no colour anywhere: no paintings or prints on the walls or flowers in a vase on the white chest of drawers. I caught sight of the long white linen dress hanging outside the white wardrobe. Even my bedding was white. It was as if I had awoken in a world bleached of all colour.

Where are you?

I breathed in, held my breath and listened as I lay on my back staring at the ceiling, allowing my brain to acclimatise to my new surroundings. My only thought was not to trigger the debilitating pain that had wiped me out.

For how long? How long have you been lying in this bed?

I had no idea.

I could hear my heart beating again and again, faster and faster as my anxiety built.

Then I heard an external noise crashing in above the pummelling of blood inside my ears. I followed the sound, gingerly turning my head towards what I realised was a window. Heavy white curtains filtered the light, but it still squeezed through the material.

I pulled my legs up, slowly rolling onto my side, bracing myself for an explosion of pain, but nothing happened. Relieved, I sat up and placed my bare feet on the cold wooden floorboards. I readied myself for some form of reprisal for this movement, but it didn't come. I looked down at the old-fashioned, long white cotton sleeveless nightdress I was wearing. I didn't recognise it. The cool air around me kissed my shoulders, savouring my bare skin. I stood up, navigated my way over and pulled the heavy curtains back, revealing a large window divided up with small leaded panes set back in impenetrable stone.

I looked beyond the panes at the cast-iron black bars outside the rain-smeared window which prevented it from opening out. I stared at the bars beyond the trails of rainwater, like tears cascading down the glass.

Why are there bars?

But I had no memory why, aside from the fact I was high up, perched on a cliff. Maybe thirty feet or so below rocks waited to break my fall, and then dangerous dark-grey tumultuous water stretched far beyond my imagination. I had an overwhelming desire to jump and let the crashing waves take me as far away from here as possible.

I inwardly gasped, surprised by this thought.

Could that be why there are bars on the window? To stop you from...

Then I spotted a tall figure walking along the pebble beach beyond the rocks, throwing something for two red fox Labradors.

A man.

There was something familiar about him. About the dogs.

Do you know him?

I studied him, fascinated as he walked in my direction, head down against the ravaging wind and driving rain. He was wearing a long brown wax coat with the collar turned up, a dark brown bushman leather hat, dark trousers and walking boots.

As if sensing my presence, he suddenly looked up.

I stepped back, hoping he hadn't seen me. But I was too late. He stopped, waved and waited for me to respond.

I watched as he dropped his hand when I didn't acknowledge him. He bent down and picked up some driftwood and threw it into the water.

I jumped as the door scraped open. I turned to see a tall, erect woman in her late fifties walk in.

'Mrs Langdon, you're awake, I see,' she affirmed.

I didn't answer. I simply watched as she entered the room with an air of authority.

She was carrying a tray with a delicate porcelain Dresden tea set, small slices of triangular-shaped toast and two boiled brown eggs. There was only one cup and a saucer. I also noted the glass of water and a small paper cup. I didn't need to see the contents of the paper cup to know that it contained a cocktail of medication.

I recognised the paper cup. I also recalled the multiple tablets contained within it. The ones I had to take whenever I awoke.

Is this why everything feels so confusing and it is so difficult to remember anything? Are you being drugged? If so, why?

'How are you feeling this morning, Mrs Langdon?' she questioned.

Her tone was gentle, but something was off.

Again, I remained silent.

'Your migraine?' she added for clarification.

'Gone,' I whispered, surprised by my own voice.

'Good, good. Maybe you could manage to come downstairs later. I think the change of scenery would do you the world of good.'

I nodded, unsure of who she was and how she knew me. 'Mrs Langdon?' I repeated.

I watched as, ignoring me, she placed the tray down on the antique French bedroom bench. I recognised the style as Palais de Versailles. The same with the matching antique white linen upholstered bed with its gold frame, the wardrobe and chest of drawers. I looked around the room with more confidence. The white Mulberry bed linen felt familiar, whispering to me that I had slept here before. It was as if the neurons in my brain had suddenly started sparking and reconnecting with one another, forming a vagueness where nothingness had existed.

'Are you all right, Mrs Langdon? You look confused.'

I turned to her. 'Who are you?'

She looked at me. I couldn't tell if she was surprised or not by my directness. 'I am Mrs Taylor.'

'Mrs Taylor?' I repeated back, waiting for my brain to play catch up.

Nothing happened.

I stared at her, feeling a sliver of fear at her presence. She was wearing a long, old-fashioned high-neck grey dress with sleeves. Her flat black Oxford shoes and thick nylon tan tights matched her sensible, no-nonsense dress. Her black and silver hair had been scraped back into a tight, knotted bun, accentuating her sharp, pale features. A silver chatelaine was attached to the belt around her narrow waist. A series of chains hung from the Victorian-style decorative belt hook with keys, scissors, a watch, a pen and other items. I stared at the appendages, particularly the silver notebook. Did she write things down about me in that notebook of hers?

Who is she to you? And why are you here?

'Do you remember me now?' she questioned.

I shook my head.

There was something about her that scared me. It wasn't the fact she looked as if she belonged to a bygone era. It was more than that. There was a sinister, threatening air to her, despite her gentle voice.

'Would you like to get back in bed for your breakfast or would you care to sit at the table? If so, you'll need a cardigan on to keep you warm.'

I then noticed the white-and-gold-edged table and chair in the corner of the room. There was a book on the table. It was mine. The acknowledgement surprised me.

Not that I knew what the book was, only that it was important somehow.

'Who is the man on the beach with the dogs?' I asked, turning my attention to the window.

Mrs Taylor began pouring my tea. 'Mr Langdon, I presume,' she stated without looking at me. 'Now come along. How about you get back into bed while your tea is still hot?'

'The dogs. What are their names?'

She turned back to me with a faint smile. 'Henry and Jack. Remember? You like the dogs.'

'I do?' I mumbled, watching them bound along the pebble beach chasing sticks, unperturbed by the stabbing rain or the thrashing waves hitting the shore. 'The man? Mr Langdon?' I repeated, staring out of the window at him as he bent down again, retrieving something from the pebble beach to throw for the dogs.

'Laird James Buchanan Langdon,' she replied.

'And I'm Mrs Langdon?' I questioned, confused.

'Yes.'

'I'm married?' I asked as I held up my ringless left hand to the light. There was no telltale mark on my finger.

'You lost it, remember?' she stated in response to my confusion.

'No... No, I don't remember,' I mumbled.

'It will come back to you. It always does,' she assured me.

'It does?' I asked.

'Yes. Give it time. You're still suffering the effects of your migraine. It lasted three days this time.'

I stared at her. 'Three days?'

She nodded.

'Was I awake?'

'You took your migraine medication, which thankfully helped you sleep.'

'I see,' I murmured.

'Can you tell me what day it is, Mrs Langdon?' she asked as she busied herself pouring milk into the scalding liquid.

It was an odd question. 'I don't understand.'

'The day?' she repeated, now standing upright and facing me.

I shook my head.

'Today is Thursday,' she answered. 'You became unwell on Monday.'

'Where am I?'

'Please look at the whiteboard. Remember? That's what you do when you can't remember things.'

'The whiteboard?' I repeated, confused.

'On the wall opposite your bed,' she replied.

I turned from her and looked at the wall.

She was correct. On the opposite wall was a large whiteboard.

'Where am I?' I mumbled as my eyes tried to decipher the harsh black words that refused to be pinned down.

She waited, watching me as I studied the board.

'Where am I?' I repeated, turning back to her.

'Home,' she replied with a sigh.

I wondered whether I had asked this question before. 'Home?' I questioned.

'Dunstrafne Castle. It's on the whiteboard, Mrs Langdon.'

I looked back at the whiteboard and shook my head, scared. 'The words don't make sense to me.'

'They will in time, Mrs Langdon. This is the effect of the migraine.'

'Where is...' I faltered.

'Dunstrafne Castle?' she asked.

I nodded.

'Argyll.'

I frowned.

'The west coast of Scotland,' she answered as she walked towards me.

It struck me that she had answered these questions many times before. It felt familiar this routine of ours. An odd ritualistic toing and froing until my mind hit reset.

And if it doesn't? What happens then?

'Why is everything white?' I asked as the thought popped into my head.

She was now by my side and looked at me smiling. I somehow

knew that the smile was insincere. It never quite met her eyes which she now fixed on mine. In that instant, I felt that those penetrating, sharp raven-black eyes of hers never missed a trick.

'Because this is what you requested. Remember? White helps you keep calm.'

'Calm?' I repeated, unsure of what she meant.

'Your nerves, Mrs Langdon.'

I stared at her, again not understanding.

'You get easily agitated and the colour white soothes you. And then, there are your migraines.'

'I thought a soft blue promoted calmness?'

Her smile slipped from her thin lips. 'Yes, but you insisted on white. Remember?'

Are you irritating her?

'And the bars on the window?'

Again, she sighed. 'They are there for your safety. We wouldn't want you falling out, would we?'

'We?' I muttered.

She looked down at the rocks and then to the beach. 'Your husband and I.'

I turned back and looked at the double bed. It was evident only one person had slept there. Nor were there any personal items in the room which suggested he shared this room with me.

'Where does my husband sleep?'

'He sleeps in another room.'

'Why?'

'Because you need peace and quiet to recuperate, Mrs Langdon. You've been unwell. Exhaustion. Mental exhaustion. You had a...' She faltered as she looked at me, as if unsure of what to say. 'A mental breakdown. So, Mr Langdon brought you here to rest.'

I stared at her. 'Brought me here?' I mumbled to myself. 'What is this place?'

'Dunstrafne Castle has been in the Buchanan family since the thirteen hundreds.'

'The Buchanan family?' I questioned.

I felt as if I should have known the answer. But I didn't.

'The Buchanans are a Highland clan. Laird James Buchanan was Mr Langdon's grandfather,' Mrs Taylor began as she continued watching the tall figure with the dogs continue along the beach. 'He had three children, but only one survived to adulthood and that was Mr Langdon's mother, Moireach Buchanan. She married Mr Langdon's father, Douglas Hamilton Langdon. Your husband is the last remaining Buchanan of his line. When Moireach Buchanan passed away three years back, Mr Langdon inherited the castle and five-thousand-acre estate.'

'Did you know his mother?' I asked.

'No. That was before my time here. Mr Langdon decided to return with you here to help you get better and asked me if I would work for you both.'

'Return here?' I echoed.

She suddenly looked at me as if she had disclosed too much. She cleared her throat.

'Yes, from your residence in London.'

A sudden flash of an image of a Victorian house overlooking Hampstead Heath flooded my mind, saturating me with a feeling of security. Of safety. Unlike now.

'I want to go home,' I said, starting to feel a familiar trope of anxiety take hold.

Something didn't feel right. I had awoken in a foreign land. It was an unknown terrain. But I could vaguely remember a place before here. Somewhere without the man below on the beach and Mrs Taylor, the housekeeper of this fourteenth-century castle.

This prison...

The thought surprised me. Terrified me.

'Come, come, Mrs Langdon. You are home. Remember? We have been through this before.'

She rested her hand on my arm.

I inwardly gasped at her cold touch. It elicited a familiar feeling but in a frightening way.

Be careful. She's hurt you before. Remember? Try! Try to remember!

But I couldn't remember. I just knew this woman who called herself Mrs Taylor was dangerous. So was the figure on the beach. Laird James Buchanan Langdon – the man she called my husband.

3

'No! I don't want to—'

'Please, Mrs Langdon!' she insisted, cutting me off. 'Come along, let's get you back into bed. Once you have had something to eat and drink, then you can get back up and take a walk,' she suggested, supporting my elbow to guide me.

I yanked my arm away from her touch and backed away from her.

'Mrs Langdon, please. I am trying to help you,' she insisted.

I had a feeling that if I didn't do as she wanted, I would regret it. It was a tenuous memory, something I couldn't reach in the far-thrown corners of my mind, but I was sure I had resisted her before only to be punished. I couldn't say what that punishment was, but I knew she had hurt me.

'Thank you,' she said, smiling at me as I relented and allowed her to lead me over to the bed.

I felt like a child fearful of the repercussions if I didn't comply.

I sat on the edge of the bed, rubbing my arm where she had touched me as she fussed, plumping up the pillows.

I suddenly noticed the sporadic, days-old mottled bruises covering my skin.

What the...?

'What happened to me?' I mumbled, staring at them.

Some of the marks were fading, but some were very recent. I then caught sight of the purplish and black discoloured band of skin as if I had been restrained.

Oh my God... What did they do to you?

Without even looking at me, she replied: 'You occasionally hurt yourself.'

Her voice was now flat, factual and emotionless.

'I hurt myself? How?' I questioned, incredulous.

'You just do. You bang into things and—'

'My hand?' I queried, cutting her off. 'Why have you done that?'

I stared at the criss-crossed white bandage strips covering a cannula inserted into the back of my hand.

'You needed fluids, Mrs Langdon. Otherwise, you would have become dehydrated. As I said, you have been asleep for three days.'

'Where's the drip, then?' I challenged, not quite trusting her.

'I removed it earlier this morning as you were starting to stir. I expected you to wake up and be able to take some food and liquid.'

I stared at her. I had no memory of her coming into my room earlier and removing the intravenous drip.

'Come along,' she instructed, signalling to my legs.

I watched as she lifted them and carefully placed them on the bed. They also had bruises and weals. She then pulled the duvet over them, hiding the injuries from view.

I kicked it off.

'I'm not cold! Tell me how I hurt myself!' I demanded.

'Mrs Langdon, please do not talk to me in that tone. As I said, sometimes you accidentally hurt yourself by banging into things or falling down. Your coordination is affected by your migraines. At times, you can be known to pass out from the pain.'

'I can?' I hoarsely questioned.

Is she lying to you? Is she? If so, why?

I stared at her, trying to read her face, but it was inscrutable.

'I want to talk to Mr Langdon,' I stated.

'All in good time,' she assured, smiling at me, oblivious of my distress.

'NOW!' I yelled.

Her black eyes bored straight through me as she folded her long, slender hands together.

'Mrs Langdon, do I need to remind you of what will happen if you start to get distressed? Now, please, let me help you before you cause your migraine to resurface.'

You have every right to be distressed! You have no idea what the hell is happening to you! Or who she is!

But there was something in her quiet voice which silenced me. Or was it the faint whisper of a shadowy memory, a bad feeling, of something that had happened to me before when I had been 'distressed', as she called it?

'I know you feel somewhat disorientated, Mrs Langdon. You always are when you have suffered one of your episodes. As I said before, things will get clearer as the day continues. It takes time for your memories to come back.'

'Episodes?' I numbly repeated.

'Your migraines,' she clarified.

'Oh,' I muttered, confused.

'As for Mr Langdon, he is walking the dogs on the beach. You know that,' she pointed out.

I watched as she lifted the tray up and brought it over to me.

'Can I trust you with breakfast?' she questioned as if talking to an infant.

I nodded.

She gently placed it down on my lap.

'Thank you,' I whispered.

Thin-lipped, she nodded. Then smiled.

'Now, take your tablets first. Then you can have your tea, toast and eggs. I boiled you two this morning as I imagine you must be famished.'

She imagined wrong. I had no appetite, which surprised me if I had been in bed for three days.

She handed me the small paper cup. I took it from her and peered inside. There were six tablets – all different.

'What are they?' I asked, frowning.

'Three are for your migraine,' she explained.

'My headache... I mean migraine has subsided,' I stated staring at the medication.

'For now. Your doctor has prescribed a single dose of zolmitriptan, naproxen and domperidone daily,' she answered.

'My doctor?' I mumbled. I couldn't recall a doctor.

'Yes.'

'I'd like to see my doctor,' I requested, not trusting her.

I didn't know her. So how could I believe what she was telling me?

'I'm afraid that won't be possible,' she answered.

'Why?'

'Because your doctor is based at a clinic in London. As I reminded you earlier, we are in Argyll in west Scotland, Mrs Langdon.'

'What about a local doctor?'

'I'm afraid that isn't possible. Mr Langdon insists on you being treated by the UK's leading neurological physician.'

'Surely a local doctor could see me. To help me understand what is happening to—' I abruptly stopped as she cut me off.

'Professor Alex Walker specialises in the brain, and the nervous system. As a neurologist, Professor Walker has expertise when it comes to migraines that other doctors, such as your local general practitioner, cannot possibly offer.'

'Professor Alex Walker is my consultant?' I suspiciously questioned.

It felt odd that I didn't remember them. Nor did I recall ever seeing a neurologist.

'Yes, Mrs Langdon.'

'For how long?'

'How long what?'

'How long has Professor Walker been my consultant?'

'I can't answer that question. However, I am sure Mr Langdon will be able to tell you.'

'How long have I suffered from migraines?'

She sighed as she looked at the paper cup in my hand.

'For as long as I have known you,' she answered. 'Now, that's enough questions. Please take your medication before your tea gets cold.'

I stared down at the tablets. 'The other three. What are they for?'

'Diazepam to help lessen your anxiety. The other is an epilepsy tablet and finally, one to lift your mood.'

'I don't suffer from epilepsy!' I asserted.

Mrs Taylor sighed once more. 'I am simply under strict orders to make sure you take your medication.'

I looked back down at the drugs, unsure of what to do.

'Professor Walker is insistent that they are taken every day without fail.'

'The recent migraine attack. How did that happen if I take medication daily?'

'Because you refused to take your medication on Monday morning, Mrs Langdon.'

'Oh,' I mumbled.

The excruciating pain that had made me want to jump out of the window to end my suffering came back to me. A cautionary reminder of what lurked in the darkest part of my mind, biding its time.

'The sooner you take your medication, the sooner you can have a refreshing cup of tea.'

She picked up a starched white napkin off the tray and positioned it under my chin.

She then took the small paper cup from my hand.

'Now open your mouth,' she instructed.

I parted my lips ever so slightly.

'Please, Mrs Langdon?' she said, bending over me and raising the thin paper cup to my lips.

I reluctantly opened my mouth enough for her to tip the contents onto my tongue.

'Now take a drink,' she said, handing me the glass.

I took it from her and gulped back a mouthful. As I did so, I felt as if I was going to gag, but I somehow managed to swallow all the tablets.

'That wasn't so bad now, was it?' she said, smiling at me.

I didn't reply.

'Here's your tea,' she said, offering me the cup and saucer.

'Thank you,' I whispered.

I felt violated. I didn't trust her because I didn't know her.

But you do know her. Don't you? She knows you.

I took a tentative sip of lukewarm water.

'Thank you,' I said again, placing the tea back down. I pushed the tray away. 'I've had enough.'

'You need to eat some toast. Or at least some boiled egg,' she suggested. 'You need some nourishment, Mrs Langdon.'

I watched as she offered me the plate of toast. I didn't react.

'Mrs Langdon?'

'I'm not hungry,' I replied, pushing the plate away.

'At least take a couple of bites,' she insisted, taking a slice of toast and lifting it to my lips.

I shook my head.

'I can stay here all day, if you so wish. However, I am sure Mr Langdon will be saddened to hear that you're not trying to get better. He's been terribly worried about you.'

'Why isn't he here, then?' I retaliated.

'He's been sat in that chair by the table for the past three days and nights watching you. He's exhausted. I suggested he get some fresh air with the dogs and that I would come and sit with you. Then, when I checked on you, I saw that you were starting to surface and so, I brought you some breakfast.'

And drugs...

'The sooner you eat, the sooner you can get dressed and go downstairs and see Mr Langdon. He'll be returning soon from his walk, I imagine.'

'I can?'

'Of course,' she assured me.

Still, I didn't trust her. A vague, unformed memory gnawed at me that I had been held prisoner in this room for—

I stopped myself. I had no idea how long I had been in this room. *Days? Months? Oh God... Years?*

'Come along, Mrs Langdon,' she persisted, forcing the toast between my lips.

I bit a piece off, and automatically chewed, then swallowed.

'It's tasteless,' I mumbled.

'Okay, let's see if we can make it more palatable,' she said as she cut off the top of one of the boiled eggs.

I watched as she sliced the toast into soldiers and placed one into the soft egg.

'Hopefully this will be more appetising,' she said, raising the dipped toast to my mouth.

I conceded, opening my mouth, unsure of what game we were playing. Again, this performance on both our parts felt oddly familiar.

I chewed, then swallowed. Again, it tasted of nothing, despite the addition of the rich yellow yolk.

'Another one,' she said.

I complied.

'Good,' she praised, smiling at me before repeating the process.

Finally, there was only one soldier remaining. Mrs Taylor plunged it into what was left of the soft-boiled egg before offering it to me.

I opened my mouth and allowed her to put the final piece on my tongue.

'See? That wasn't so difficult, now, was it?' she said, again smiling.

Satisfied I had eaten, she lifted the tray off my lap and returned it to the bench at the bottom of the bed.

'I need to use the bathroom,' I admitted. 'Where is it?'

'Of course, Mrs Langdon,' she answered.

She came over to me and took my elbow, helping me out of bed.

'Thank you,' I mumbled, standing up. 'Why is there nothing personal in my room?' I asked, noticing, as if for the first time, the odd bareness of the room. 'No paintings. No photographs. I mean, there's nothing here. It's completely bare. So, so impersonal. It's like a hospital room.'

'This is what you requested,' she answered.

'It is?' I asked, puzzled. 'Why?'

'You wanted the room minimalistic and white, void of colour and objects. You explained that colour and clutter aggravate your migraines. Also, when you did have photographs and paintings in your room, you destroyed them. Remember?'

I shook my head.

Why don't you believe her?

'Can I have a phone to call my... my doctor? I need to speak to them about what is happening to me. I can't remember anything.'

'Of course. But, let's get you to the bathroom first.'

She guided me to a door opposite the one she had entered. I had assumed it was a walk-in cupboard, but it led into a deceptively large room, transformed into a stylish en suite. I looked around the modern, bright space. There was a Victorian-style bathtub with claw feet by the lead-paned window. Again, there were bars on the outside of the window. The bathroom also consisted of a spacious walk-in shower cubicle with a large rain showerhead, a white hand-basin with a contemporary single tap, and a close coupled toilet. The floor was a pale beige marble with matching walls. White luxurious bath towels rested on the edge of the bath. A variety of Jo Malone toiletries sat on the marble counter next to the sink alongside hand towels. I walked over, compelled to pick up the Orange Blossom Cologne by Jo Malone. I sprayed some mist in the air, hoping to ignite the flicker of a memory. But no seductive scent came out of the bottle. I replaced it and pumped some Orange Blossom Body & Handwash into my palm. I sniffed it, but again, it lacked any scent. Aware that Mrs Taylor was watching me, I washed the soap off.

As I did so, I looked up at the beige marble above the sink. Something was missing.

How odd.

'Why is there no mirror?' I asked, turning to her.

A memory that was so delicate, so ethereal that it physically hurt to try to untangle it, eluded me. Somewhere burrowed, deep inside my mind, was the answer.

Why? Why don't they want you to see yourself?

'You broke the mirror above the sink,' she explained. 'Mr Langdon didn't think it safe to replace it. At least, not yet.'

'I broke the mirror?' I repeated. 'Why? Why would I do that?'

It made no sense. Again, I questioned why they wouldn't want me to see myself.

'I believe you were having one of your episodes,' she answered.

'A migraine?' I questioned, unable to keep the scepticism out of my voice.

'The pain you experience can make you lash out,' she explained.

I didn't believe her.

I tentatively touched my face, scared of what I would feel. I was seeking confirmation of scars or physical injury, evidence that something terrible had happened to me. But as my fingers took in the contours of my features, I couldn't feel any obvious disfigurement. I then reached up to my hair. My fingertips delicately touched my abrasively cropped scalp.

'My hair? It's so short,' I murmured, struggling to find some recollection of what I looked like.

'You've always had short hair,' she explained.

I stared at her, confused.

'You have always had short hair, Mrs Langdon,' she again assured me.

'But...' I faltered. 'No... This isn't right,' I argued. 'What have you done to me?'

'Mrs Langdon, please do not raise your voice at me,' she said quietly.

Wary, I stepped back from her.

Do you remember?

I didn't remember, but I had a feeling that I would regret it if I didn't listen to her.

'Can I have some privacy to use the toilet, please?' I asked, acknowledging her unspoken threat.

'Of course.'

I watched as she stiffly turned, back erect, and walked out of the en suite.

I walked over to the door and closed it. I looked for a lock, but unsurprisingly, there wasn't one.

I turned and stared around the bathroom. There were no cupboards or cabinets. I walked over to the bathroom marble counter where the towels were stacked and the various scentless, fake toiletries. I could feel tears stinging my eyes as I tried to recall what had happened to me.

I ran my fingers through my hair, groping at the short locks, trying to visualise what I looked like.

Words from Lewis Carroll's *Alice in Wonderland* came to mind:

I knew who I was this morning, but I've changed a few times since then.

But I didn't even know who I was this morning. Or yesterday. Or the day before.

Who are you?

4

'Mrs Langdon? Mrs Langdon?' she called out, knocking on the door.

The bathroom door then swung open.

I turned to see Mrs Taylor.

'What are you doing? I've been waiting over ten minutes for you to come out,' she said.

Did I detect concern? I couldn't say.

Without answering, I looked back out of the window at the shimmering water stretching to the unknown horizon and beyond.

'Mrs Langdon? Did you hear me?'

I nodded.

'Then, please come away from there,' she instructed.

'Why? In case someone sees me and they know that you're keeping me here against my will?' I fired back as I continued staring out of the paned glass and the black bars at a world beyond my reach.

I heard her sigh, followed by the clicking of her black Oxford shoes on the marble floor as she approached me.

'You are not here against your will, Mrs Langdon. Please stop saying such things. Mr Langdon and I are doing everything we can to help you recuperate. Once you are well enough, you can return to London and resume your old life. Until then, Professor Alex Walker insists that being away from the noise and stress of city life, will hopefully lessen your migraine attacks and help you after your —' She stopped abruptly.

I turned to her.

How can you believe her? What proof do you have that she's not lying to you?

'It should also ease your neurosis and nerves, which have been fragile since your breakdown,' she added as if reading my mind.

Or did you say it out aloud?

I didn't know what was real or not. I had awoken into a nightmarish world where I couldn't remember where I was, let alone who I was any more. I couldn't trust this woman standing in front of me. Worse, I couldn't trust myself.

Have you always been like this?

I slowly breathed out. I had no idea. The thought of not knowing whether I would remember my husband – *if he is your husband* – or this place, and even the housekeeper, if that was what she was, terrified me. My life was in their hands, and I didn't know if that meant I was in danger.

What if they kidnapped you and are drugging you to keep you here against your will? And if that is the case, how do you escape?

'Dunstrafne Castle is flanked by the north Atlantic Ocean on one side, with forests and mountains on the other. Quite remote,' she explained.

Her statement was disconcerting, as if she was inside my head.

Or maybe she is anticipating your thoughts. Have you had this conversation countless times before? Perhaps...

'Which means you can take as long as you need to get well without anyone bothering you,' Mrs Taylor continued.

If she was trying to reassure me, it had an adverse effect. She had just confirmed I was being held prisoner by people I didn't know in some remote medieval castle with bars on the windows, surrounded by thousands of acres of trees and mountains. No one would ever know I was here.

So how are you going to get help?

'I want to talk to this Professor Walker,' I replied. 'I want to talk to someone other than you!'

'All in good time. Mr Langdon will need to arrange it.'

'Arrange it? Just call this professor! Or better still, give me their number, and I can tell them what you're doing to me!'

'Professor Walker is very busy, Mrs Langdon. You must be able to appreciate that. I am sure Professor Walker will explain everything to you in due course.'

Her words failed to appease me.

I could feel my 'nerves', as Mrs Taylor called them, becoming frayed. I was trying to keep as calm as possible to prove her wrong, but I was falling apart, bit by bit.

I suddenly felt the floor throw me off balance. I grabbed on to the roll-top bath to stop myself falling and shakily breathed out.

What is happening to you?

I could feel the toast soldiers dipped in the soft-boiled egg I had eaten churning in my stomach alongside the cocktail of drugs I had taken.

'The drugs?' I muttered, closing my eyes as the room started to dangerously close in around me. I could feel the blood suddenly drain from my head as a clammy coldness took hold, clinging to my skin.

'You're in the final stage of the migraine, known as the postdrome. This has happened before to you, many times, Mrs Langdon. Unfortunately, you can't remember, but you will,' she assured me.

'I... I... don't feel...' I faltered. I couldn't grasp the word. It eluded me.

How can that be possible?

It was there a second ago, and now it was gone.

I winced. I raised a trembling hand to my forehead. My head felt heavy and...

'I can't... I can't find the word. I... I...'

The word had disappeared and felt lost to me forever.

'Do you feel unwell?' Mrs Taylor questioned.

'Yes... And I'm dizzy and I'm feeling... I feel discombobulated. I... I...'

I shook my head. I couldn't find the word. That too had vanished in a fog of confusion and panic. I could feel it there, as if it was hiding from me, enjoying my suffering and frustration as I tried to force it into view.

I risked opening my eyes. The world was still as disturbing.

'What's happening to me?' I asked as Mrs Taylor placed an arm around my waist to help steady me. 'I... I can't even remember words now.'

'Shh, Mrs Langdon. Come along. Let's get you back into bed. You need a few hours more rest.'

'But, what's wrong with me? Please? You need to tell me,' I pleaded.

'You're experiencing cognitive symptoms related to your migraine,' she explained.

'Cognitive symptoms?' I questioned. 'I... I'm drugged. You drugged me?'

'No, Mrs Langdon. I administered prescribed medication. Your thinking, reasoning and remembering have all been affected by your migraine. This is, as I said before, the postdrome stage of your migraine. You're simply suffering from temporary memory loss and brain fog, which can last up to twenty-four hours after the pain of a migraine ends. Both are common and aren't unique to you, as I am sure Professor Alex Walker will again explain to you.'

'The room is... It's spinning,' I said, clutching hold of Mrs Taylor's arm with both hands for support.

'You're experiencing dizziness. That's normal,' she stated gently.

'And the memory loss? I mean, I am losing words now! Words! Does that mean that I might lose the ability to converse?' I asked, panicking.

'Now you are catastrophising, Mrs Langdon! This state is temporary. It will pass. As I said, you have brain fog, which is linked to cortical depression in the brain.'

'I don't know what the hell that is!' I muttered through clenched teeth as I tried to navigate, with her help, my way out of the en suite and back to bed without falling down. 'And I don't care! I just want to know what you've drugged me with!'

'Cortical depression is when the cells in the cerebral cortex, also known as the grey matter, are affected by the electrical and blood flow process spreading from the back of the brain, where vision is controlled, to the front of the brain, where thinking is controlled. You are not feeling the effects of being drugged, Mrs Langdon. As the cortical depression moves over your brain, it can slow your thinking down or make it hard to find words. These are the symptoms you are experiencing.'

'Why are you telling me this? You're talking gibberish!' I hissed, finding myself reduced to shuffling for fear of losing my balance.

'I am following your orders. You told me that whenever you found yourself in this state, to remind you of Professor Alex Walker's explanation so you wouldn't be so frightened.'

'It's not working! You're making me even more frightened than I already am,' I accused. 'For all I know, you are talking nonsense to me to make me feel like I am going mad.'

'Yes, that may be. But as I explained, I am following your own instructions.'

Is she? Or is she trying to convince you that she's not drugging you?

Finally, I reached the bed and, with Mrs Taylor's aid, lay down.

'Can you close the curtains, please?' I said, placing a trembling hand over my eyes.

'Of course.'

'Thank you.' I shallowly breathed in, then out, trying to ignore the dizziness that had taken me captive. Even lying down, I felt as if the bed was tilting and the walls were bending down towards me. 'I want to see Mr Langdon,' I whispered. 'I... I need to see him.'

I could feel a tear in the corner of my eye start to slowly roll down towards my left ear, followed by another. Then another.

Why are you crying?

'What is his name, again?'

'James, Mrs Langdon. Your husband's name is James,' answered Mrs Taylor in her quiet voice.

I heard the sudden swish of the long, heavy curtains as she closed them, bringing welcome respite from the unbearable light.

'James. I like that name,' I replied. 'Is he nice?'

'He's a good, kind man,' she simply answered.

At least, that's what I thought I heard.

'Good,' I murmured, feeling my body sinking into the mattress, deeper and deeper.

It was as if I was disappearing.

'Will my memory come back when this ends?' I heard myself asking.

'Yes. Your condition isn't dementia. So, your memory will return.'

I didn't know whether that was good or bad. How would I know if I couldn't remember what my life had been like before I awoke this morning?

* * *

The door opened, followed by: 'Mrs Langdon?'

I didn't reply. I didn't want her here. I wanted to be left alone.

'How are we feeling?'

The dizziness had passed, but the confusion had not.

'Mrs Langdon?' she repeated.

'Better,' I lied, hoping she would go away.

'Good.'

I watched the housekeeper's austere, grey, unchanging figure with the tight black and silver knot of hair twisted in a severe bun at the back of her head as she walked over to the curtains and pulled them apart.

Sunlight flooded into the room, loudly bouncing off the stark white walls.

Everything was too bright. Too white.

'No,' I objected. 'It's too bright. I want to...' I faltered.

What do you want to do?

The decisive thought cut through me like a cold blade:

You want to die.

'I want to sleep,' I lied.

'I'm afraid not,' she replied. 'Mr Langdon has requested your company at dinner this evening.'

'No,' I mumbled, turning away from her and pulling the duvet over my head.

'Come, come, Mrs Langdon! You've languished in bed now for three days.'

Three days? How? It was...

'This morning you said it was Thursday,' I challenged. 'How can I have lost three days?'

She started to pull the duvet down.

'No!' I cried out, holding on to it. 'Answer me!'

'Please, Mrs Langdon, I am only trying to help you. Now come along, time to get up.'

'No,' I replied, refusing to let go of the duvet.

'You have stayed in bed for long enough. You have no excuses, as your post-migraine symptoms will have passed by now. It's Saturday late afternoon, after all.'

'It can't be Saturday! You said this morning that it was Thursday,' I argued.

'Yes, I did say that on Thursday, Mrs Langdon. Today is Saturday. Please look at the whiteboard. I have sat with you for the past three days. I have fed you as best I could, and I have taken you to the bathroom when required. Aside from toilet visits, you refused to leave your bed. Now it's Saturday, Mr Langdon insists you get up and have a change of scenery. He is worried about you languishing up here.'

'I don't remember!' I cried out. 'You're lying to me! You're trying to make me think I am going insane!'

'Please? Look at the whiteboard,' she again advised.

'The whiteboard?' I repeated, confused.

'On the wall facing you,' she replied.

I forced myself to sit up. I squinted as I allowed my eyes to adjust to the white room.

She was correct. On the opposite wall was a large whiteboard.

'Oh...' I mumbled, surprised. 'When did you put that there?'

'It's always been there, Mrs Langdon,' she answered.

I stared at it. Why couldn't I remember?

'No, it hasn't,' I replied. 'I would have remembered.'

'Clearly, you are still having problems with your memory.'

'I am?'

'Yes,' she stated.

I stared at the heavy black writing on the whiteboard. It didn't make any sense to me. I struggled to remember if I had seen it before today.

'I remember feeling unwell on Thursday and having to lie down,' I said.

Mrs Taylor didn't reply.

'But I don't remember three days passing or you coming into my room,' I declared, turning to look at her.

'I know this is frightening for you, but it will pass. Your memory will come back,' she explained.

If she was trying to make me feel as if I was losing my mind, she was succeeding.

'And why is it there anyway?' I questioned. I had the faintest of feelings that I had seen it before. Or had I? Was I simply absorbing Mrs Taylor's words as my own?

'Please read it,' she suggested.

'What?'

'Please read the words, Mrs Langdon,' she repeated in her quiet way.

'Why?'

'It will help you remember,' she explained.

'But I do remember,' I argued.

'You are still struggling to remember what day it is,' she pointed out.

'Am I? Or are you lying to me to convince me that I am going insane?' I retaliated.

'Read out the first line,' she again recommended as she folded her hands, ignoring my question.

She waited.

'Saturday, the twenty-sixth of August,' I reluctantly read out.

'Good. See? That wasn't that difficult, was it?'

It was now the end of August, but I had no concept of the month passing.

Or of the summer passing.
Shocked, my eyes drifted down the whiteboard:

Q: Where am I?
A: Dunstrafne Castle, Argyll, West Scotland.

'How long have I been here?' I asked as fear uncoiled itself in the pit of my stomach. It was a familiar, unwelcome feeling.

Mrs Taylor walked over to the board and pointed to the third question:

Q: How long have I been here at Dunstrafne Castle?
A: 46 days.

I gasped. 'I have been here for forty-six days?'
Oh God... How?
'Yes.'
'Why can't I remember?'
'We've already had this conversation. Many times. Look, it is written down here to remind you,' she said, the tip of her long finger touching the fifth question:

Q: Why do I struggle remembering things?
A: I suffer from migraines. They affect my memory. But my memory always returns. Don't panic. Trust that it will come back. In the meantime, I can trust Mrs Taylor and my husband, James. They are not trying to hurt me. They are trying to help me get better.

'It does?' I questioned, looking at her. 'My memory will come back?'
'Yes,' she said, giving me a reassuring nod.

I then looked back at the whiteboard and at the fourth question.

Q: Who is James Buchanan Langdon?
A: He is your husband. You have been married for two years.

'We've been married for two years?'

Oh God! You have lost two years of your life! TWO YEARS!

'Look at the fifth question again, Mrs Langdon,' Mrs Taylor instructed.

How does she know what you're thinking? How?

'The fifth question,' she gently insisted. 'Read the answer, please.'

I did as she said, mumbling the words aloud as I read them: 'I suffer from migraines. They affect my memory. But my memory always returns. Don't panic. Trust that it will come back. In the meantime, I can trust Mrs Taylor and my husband, James. They are not trying to hurt me. They are trying to help me get better.' I shook my head. 'Why did you write that? It's all lies!'

'I didn't write it, Mrs Langdon. Those are your words.'

I didn't believe her. 'That isn't my handwriting!' I asserted.

It was too hard and angular, crude even. The letters were all pointed, jagged, lacking any softness or subtlety, as if a young child learning to write had painstakingly copied out the words.

'I can assure you that it is,' she replied.

'I wrote that date this morning?' I sceptically questioned. 'Why can't I remember?'

The writing was ugly and infantile.

'Yes. After your breakfast of porridge. You managed a few spoonfuls—'

'I had soldiers and a soft-boiled egg for breakfast,' I interrupted.

She smiled at me. 'That was on Thursday morning. Today is Saturday. Remember?'

I struggled to accept what she was telling me. Behind the smile were lies. I felt as if she was gaslighting me, telling me time had passed when it hadn't. Trying to convince me I had lost entire days, with no memory of simple functions like eating and toilet visits.

The question was why.

'We have a routine. I ask you the day, and you write the answer down. It's a way of keeping track. The same with the days you have spent here. You erase the old date and number of days and replace them with the new ones.'

Why can't you remember? Is it possible that someone is erasing your memories? Your very existence?

I searched her inscrutable face for answers, but it held none.

'I can't do this...' I mumbled, terrified.

I felt I was being pulled into a place from where I would never find my way back. I looked at her, but she seemed so far away. The room was somehow disappearing on me. I closed my eyes against the ensuing darkness as horrifying thoughts assaulted me.

You've lost two years of your life! How? How is that even possible?

It was as if I had lost my way in Dante's Underworld and had drunk from the Lethe – the river of unmindfulness – eradicating all my memories. The question was whether this state of oblivion would lift. Would I ever find my way back from this death-like state of barely existing?

'You can do this, and you will. What you are experiencing will pass,' Mrs Taylor stated. 'It always does.'

I could feel the tears pressing up against my closed eyelids, trying to escape.

Will it pass?

I thought of the Greek goddess of truth, Aletheia. Mrs Taylor was my Aletheia, pulling me up from the shadowy Underworld and revealing a world I had long forgotten.

The question was why I was in such a state of oblivion. Was it –

as she said, and as the words on the whiteboard screamed at me – that I suffered from debilitating migraines that wiped my mind, or was it something more sinister than a neurological disorder? The drugs I remembered taking this morning – or on Thursday, if this really was Saturday – could have been responsible for my confused state.

'I believe that seeing Mr Langdon will help you,' she continued. 'You've been in this bed for nearly a week now. Come on, Mrs Langdon. A warm shower will lift your spirits. I'll help you put on your favourite dress. The change of scenery will do you good, and the company. Being alone with your thoughts all the time isn't good for you.'

What thoughts? You don't have any! At least, none you can remember.

I tried to swallow, but failed: fear of the unknown had me by the throat.

'Why is my memory like this? Why is this happening to me?' I whispered.

'Your husband will explain everything to you,' she reassured me.

I nodded. I needed to try my damnedest to stay present. I needed to see this man whom Mrs Taylor called my husband, to understand what was wrong with me. I opened my eyes. But all I could see in front of me were the crude, childish black words on the whiteboard that represented my life.

Or what is left of your life... One you don't recognise.

All that exists are fragmented pieces scribbled all over a whiteboard.

But who wrote it down? You? Her? Or him? This man she claims is your husband: James Buchanan Langdon?

5

I shivered, unable to dispel the accusatory eyes staring down from the imposing portraits, calling me out for being an imposter. I had no right to be here, in their ancestral home, with the last of their proud, defiant line – James Buchanan Langdon – pretending to be his wife. I felt intimidated by their bold and arrogant presence as they watched, silently judging me as I sat at the long dining room table with the current laird. My skin pricked with their disapproving, haughty glares for forgetting my life with them – with him. Worse, for not wanting to remember him, my husband. Instead, I was desperate to escape from this castle – this prison – filled with ghosts of a past I no longer recalled or cared to remember.

Or was I trembling from the cool evening breeze lingering on my bare skin from the open French doors that led out on to the garden and the water beyond? I could hear the waves, gentle and seductive, lapping against the pebble beach below the low stone wall at the bottom of the garden. The candles on the table suddenly flickered and hissed out at the gust of air blown in from the north Atlantic Ocean. My last memory before Mrs Taylor came into my room to help dress me for dinner was three days earlier – Thursday morning. I recalled when I awoke for the first time in my mind in Dunstrafne Castle, the rain hammering at the windowpanes in my bedroom and watching James Buchanan Langdon walking with two dogs, hat on, collar turned up against the harsh weather. And now... Now, it was calm. The evening sun had lingered with us for a while, reluctant to let the day pass until the shadows of darkness had forced its retreat.

But, if I were to believe Mrs Taylor, the sudden change was because days had passed. I had lost the time from Thursday morning until Mrs Taylor entered my room, announcing it was late Saturday afternoon and that my husband desired my company at dinner.

'You're cold,' he noted.

He scraped his chair back and stood up.

I allowed myself a furtive glance at him – my husband.

Do you recognise him? This man who calls himself your husband.

I did, and I didn't. He was familiar to me and paradoxically unfamiliar.

Curious, I watched as his tall, muscular figure strode over to the French doors, followed faithfully by the two red fox Labradors, and closed them against the sudden darkening skies. The sun had left us to the mercy of the night. I assumed it must be about 8.45 p.m. Not that I had any means of telling the time apart from the changing skies.

I had passed a tall chinoiserie longcase clock in the grand hallway with its tall stone columns. I had paused, mesmerised by the four oriental gold-painted dragons on the wood around the clock face. Below, on the long door, the oriental carvings continued with a young woman in a beautiful gold and black kimono and, beneath her, a mountain towards the bottom. I had stared at the brass face with its black numbers and hands, waiting for them to move. Only, for some reason, time had stopped in Dunstrafne Castle at precisely 11.11.

Why?

I had a feeling that this time was significant – to me. But why that would be eluded me.

W. H. Auden's poem, 'Stop All the Clocks', came to mind.

I had shivered as I remained there, waiting for the hand to move, but death held it tight in its cold, lifeless grip. There was a sadness, an unspoken grief that clung to the claustrophobic air, skulking in the shadows.

Why has time stopped here?

I had asked Mrs Taylor, but she had shaken her head and said she had no idea. That perhaps there was no significance, that the clock's mechanism was simply faulty.

But that wasn't the only anomaly.

Why are there no mirrors anywhere?

It wasn't just my bedroom and en suite that didn't have mirrors. There were none on any of the walls. I had noticed the bare spaces where something had once hung along the corridors as I walked by the first floor, down the stone staircase to the main hallway, and then to the dining room.

Again, I had questioned Mrs Taylor, who shrugged off my paranoia. To her knowledge, the paintings, now being professionally restored, were affected after storm damage in the west wing had caused significant dampness in the castle. She reasoned that there were mirrors, in her quarters for example, as there had been one in my bathroom until I had smashed it in a fit of...

A fit of what? And why can't you remember?

What is your husband trying to hide from you? And why doesn't he want you to see yourself?

As if feeling my questioning gaze, he turned and looked back at me.

'Darling, put your cardigan on. It's hanging on the back of your chair. Shall I help you?' he asked, walking towards me. 'It's getting cold in the evenings now that summer is coming to an end.'

I looked down at myself and realised I was wearing the long, sleeveless white linen summer dress I had seen hanging on my wardrobe door. That was when I had first woken up here three days ago. But, instead of just three days passing, apparently forty-six days had disappeared since I arrived at Dunstrafne Castle. Not that I had any empirical evidence – only the word of Mrs Taylor, my husband's housekeeper, and a whiteboard with fragments of my life scrawled on it.

I shook my head, unaware of feeling cold.

'You were trembling,' he said. 'Please? Let me at least drape the cardigan over your shoulders.'

'I'm fine now you've closed the French doors,' I replied.

'Shall I light the fire, then?'

'No,' I replied, noticing the large fireplace and the mantelpiece above it. Something was missing, either a large painting or mirror, leaving behind a section of the wall that was in stark contrast to the sun-bleached wallpaper surrounding it.

Storm damage as well?

He nodded reluctantly and returned to the table.

'Why are there no mirrors?'

He sat down and looked at me.

'Why?' I demanded.

'You...' He faltered.

'I what?'

'You smashed the mirror in your bathroom,' he answered. 'I haven't had time to replace it yet. But I will do.'

'What? Why would I do that? It makes no sense.'

Unable to look me in the eye, he ran his large hand through his dark hair.

'Why?' I repeated.

'I don't know,' he replied. 'I... I don't know. You were angry.'

'And is that why there's no mirrors anywhere else? Have you hidden them from me in case I break them as well?' I challenged, not believing that was the reason why there were no mirrors.

Why would I break a mirror? It made no sense. I thought of the ancient Romans and their belief that the mirror reflected the soul, which would renew every seven years. Consequently, breaking a mirror would mean waiting seven years for a new one to dispel the gods' punishment of bad luck for violating such a portal to the soul.

Is that what they don't want you to see? That you're soulless now.

I stared at him, but he still refused to look at me.

He's lying! You can't trust anything he tells you.

Do you even recognise him?

I recognised his clothes, but not him. The light blue cotton Ralph Lauren shirt and navy chino trousers that he favoured when it was just us for dinner.

Just the two of you? Isn't it always just the two of you? The two of you alone in this mausoleum, waited on by a housekeeper who looks as if she has been here for centuries.

'Did we ever entertain here?' I asked, looking at the empty chairs, seated around the grand, long table more appropriate for banquets than for two people thrown together out of...

Out of what? Why are you even together?

I didn't belong. The knowledge that I wasn't supposed to be here coursed through my veins. I knew I had been brought to this place against my will.

'Yes, we used to host some wonderful dinner parties. That was when you were well, of course,' he said.

But you haven't been yourself of late...

I could hear his unspoken thoughts as if they were my own.

Then I heard something familiar. It dispelled the feeling of fear that had followed me, hungry and vengeful, since I awoke here on Thursday morning.

I listened, trying to understand what I was hearing.

It's music... Oh... It's so beautiful!

I could hear the piano keys, delicately floating in the air. Despite being so faint, I could still recognise the sombre piano piece as Chopin's Prelude in B Minor, Op 28.

How do you know it?

But I did. I knew it, felt it as if this piece of music had always been with me.

I expectantly looked across to the heavy double wooden doors that led out to the cavernous stone-flagged hallway, with its high stone walls adorned with countless weapons, barbaric hunt trophies with spectacular, stabbing antlers.

'Can you hear it?'

'Hear what?' he questioned, frowning at me.

'The music?' I asked.

Instead of answering me, he picked up his knife and fork and resumed eating.

Have you said the wrong thing?

'Eat something. It's your favourite,' he encouraged, glancing at my plate. 'Here. Take my napkin so you don't stain your white dress,' he offered.

'I have mine on my lap,' I replied.

He ignored me, reaching over and tucking it into the collar of my dress as if he didn't trust me not to spill my food.

I resisted the urge to yank it off and throw it back at him.

Instead, I looked down at my plate, surprised to see bloodied fillet steak, grilled asparagus and delicate buttered and seasoned new potatoes. I picked up my fork, then paused. Did I even eat meat? Let alone a fillet steak so rare that it was oozing blood.

I couldn't remember.

Seeing I didn't move, he reached over and caressed my hand.

His lingering, wanting touch burned my skin. My silver fork clattered loudly on the dinner plate as I threw it down and snatched my hand away, hiding it on my lap.

I stared down at the delicate hairline crack in the red and blue Victorian Royal Crown Derby plate, unsure whether it had always been there before or if my act of resistance had fractured it. I recognised the antique plate as part of a dinner set used for generations in the Buchanan household.

How do you know that?

But I did know it. I also knew without looking at the wall behind me that the glass display cabinet held a rare 1813 Nantgarw porcelain dinner set with finely painted bouquets and gilt scrolls and ribbons around the edge, decorated and overglazed in London, rather than the factory in Nantgarw, in Wales. It had been gifted to the Buchanan family in 1814.

I had no understanding how I knew these facts. I just did.

And yet, you can't remember the day of the week or what led you here – to Laird James Buchanan Langdon.

'Darling?' he said, interrupting my thoughts. 'I... I would never hurt you. You don't think I would, do you?'

I kept my head down, unable to look at him. My eyes rested on the numerous faded and fresh angry bruises on my arms. But they were also accompanied by scratches and cuts as if someone had torn at my flesh.

You don't know what he would do to you. Or what he has already done to you. You don't know him. You don't know if you ever did know him.

'Darling? Please? Look at me. Stop scratching at your arms. Please? Stop it! Your skin will never heal if you keep picking and squeezing at your skin.'

I glanced up at him.

You barely remember him... But you know he's lying to you.

'You did this to me,' I accused. 'These bruises, these scratches—'

'God, no! Darling, how could you even think that?'

I looked back at my plate. The pooling, stomach-turning liquid seeping out from beneath the bloodied steak horrified me.

How can that be your favourite food? Do you even have a favourite dish?

I had no idea.

'Stop it! Please! Stop hurting yourself!' he cried out, grabbing my hands and holding them still.

I stared at him, willing him to hurt me. To prove me right. But he didn't. Instead, he rested my hands down on the table.

'Please? Just eat with me. That's all I want. One night together without any...' He stopped himself and shook his head.

I couldn't read his expression, his dark brown eyes a mystery to me. But there was a melancholy to his voice that resonated deep within me.

I suddenly realised the music had ended. I couldn't hear it any more, regardless of how hard I strained. I looked up towards the double doors leading out into the main hallway.

It's gone... Or did it ever exist? Or maybe it was a memory.

'Please, look at me. I love you...'

Does he?

'I know you don't want to be here, but give it time. Things will start to improve, I promise you. And your memory will come back.'

I didn't want to admit to him that some details had started to come back. But I didn't trust them. Nor did I trust him.

I looked up at the man sitting next to me.

James? Your James?

I recognised the black, unruly, curly hair and the proud, chiselled features from some past life. He was much older than I last remembered, still as handsome but lined, which I suspected was from the battering winter winds and the caustic summer rays. And his hair had a peppering of silver strands, suggestive of years passing.

Years that you can't remember...

But it was his intense, dark eyes that took me by surprise. I didn't recognise them.

He looked at me as if feeling my questioning gaze before turning away.

Why? Why can't he bear to look at you?

'Please? Try one mouthful. For me,' he again persisted.

I stared back down at the food.

'Here, let me,' he said, leaning over and cutting up my food as if I were a child.

'I've missed you these past few days,' he continued. 'You had me worried.'

I didn't know how to respond and found myself awkwardly nodding, aware he was expecting a reciprocal response.

You can't remember him, so how can you have missed him?

I pushed what was on my plate around with my fork as if I was selecting something to sample. But I had no appetite.

I waited until he reached for the bottle of wine to top up his glass before spearing a chunk of fillet steak that he had diced up for me with my fork and then dropping it furtively into my napkin. Then another. And another.

'Ahh, that's what I like to see,' he said, glancing at my plate.

I waited until he resumed eating before tipping the contents of my napkin onto the floor. I heard the two red fox Labrador dogs now under the dining table scramble for the food.

I then watched him eat. He stopped after a few mouthfuls, and looked over at my plate.

'Please, don't do that,' he said.

'What?' I questioned, placing my fork down and hiding my hands on my lap.

'Feed your steak to the dogs. I can see what you're doing.'

I stared at him.

'Henry! Jack! Get out from there! Out!'

I felt one of them lick my hand before reluctantly following the command.

They both came out, tails and ears down, and lay down on the rug next to his chair.

'Stay,' he muttered, glancing down at them. 'Just a little bit more,' he implored, now turning back to me. 'You need to eat. You've gotten so thin, darling. I'm worried about you.'

Is that why there are no mirrors? Does he not want you to see what he sees when he looks at you?

I shook my head and pushed my plate away.

I heard him mutter something under his breath before taking another sip of wine.

'Can I have some?'

'Red wine?' he asked, looking at my untouched glass of water.

I nodded. Waited.

'You know you can't drink alcohol with your current medication,' he explained.

'Who prescribed my medication?' I questioned.

'Professor Alex Walker. You remember Alex, don't you? Alex has been your neurologist for two years now.'

'I've had this condition for that long?' I asked, surprised.

I noted his cheeks flush.

Was it from the wine or is he lying to you?

'Where am I?' I demanded.

'You are home,' he replied.

'Home?' I repeated.

'Yes. We came back here from London to help you get better. You know that. This has always been our home.'

Do you?

'And the boys were so excited to come back. You know how much they love roaming around this place.'

'We have children?' I asked, shocked.

He laughed at me. At my reaction.

'The boys are our dogs, Henry and Jack,' he said, reaching out and ruffling one of the dogs who raised his head in response to his name.

'Oh,' I mumbled, realising that they were the red fox Labradors whom I had just fed.

'Remember, we bought them for your birthday when they were eight weeks old. You couldn't choose between the brothers, so we decided to take both of them.'

Numb, I shook my head, accepting from his smile that it must have been a good memory.

If it really is a memory.

I watched as my blank response led him to take another mouthful of wine.

Maybe you should lie. Like him...

'How old am I?' I questioned.

'You're thirty-two,' he replied.

'No...' I faltered.

How can you be? You're... you're only... How old are you?

'You're wrong, I'm thirty,' I asserted.

Unable to look at me, he took another sip of wine.

'Mrs Taylor says we've been married for two years,' I stated.

He cleared his throat as he put his wine glass down. 'Yes, that's correct.'

Yet, he looks uncertain.

'You're still wearing a wedding ring?'

'Yes,' he answered.

'Where's mine?'

'You lost it,' he replied.

'How? How did I lose my wedding ring?' I sceptically questioned.

'Darling, please?' he said. 'We've been over this countless times. You lost it. I don't know where. If I did, I would have given it back to you to wear.'

'How did I lose it?' I repeated.

'For God's sake! I don't know!'

I stared at him. His outburst didn't surprise me. It confirmed my suspicion that this was all an act.

I heard one of the dogs whine in response to his raised voice.

'I'm sorry... I shouldn't have shouted,' he apologised.

He reached out to touch me. I pulled my hand away from his.

'I want to go home,' I stated.

'You are home, darling.'

'No! I want to go back to my real home in Hampstead Heath. This isn't my home,' I insisted, raising my voice.

'This is your home. You live with me. You are thirty-two years old. I am thirty-eight years old. We've been married for...'

I waited as he took another drink, unable to continue.

Why can't he continue?

'I want to call my mother,' I said.

'Your mother?'

'Anna Greig Jacobs,' I stated.

'She's gone, darling. Remember?' he questioned.

Remember? Remember what?

'Gone? Where?'

I could feel the panic rising in me.

He didn't reply.

I watched as he drained the contents of his wine glass.

'I want a phone. I need to call her! I want to speak with her!'

Still, he would not look at me.

'NOW!' I shouted at him, banging my fist on the table and making my knife and fork jump off my plate.

I watched as the dogs, startled by my outburst, jumped up.

'She's gone,' he repeated quietly.

I was certain I picked up a hint of sadness in his voice.

Why? Because you can't remember? Remember what?

'You're lying to me! Let me speak to her!'

I looked up to find Mrs Taylor had materialised by the doors.

'Shall I take Mrs Langdon upstairs now?'

I watched as he turned to her and nodded with some reluctance.

'What? NO! Are you even listening to me?' I raged. 'I want to speak to my mother! She'll tell me exactly what's happening and why you've brought me here. I mean, does she even know I am here? DOES SHE?'

Neither one spoke. I looked at Mrs Taylor, but she remained perfectly erect with her hands folded in front of her, refusing to acknowledge me.

'I want to call her! Give me my phone!' I demanded, jumping up. 'I know I have one! Where have you hidden it?'

'Mobiles don't work here. There's no signal for miles around,' he explained. 'No one's mobile phone works here.'

'A landline? You must have a landline.'

He nodded.

'Mr Langdon?' Mrs Taylor questioned. 'Isn't it best I take Mrs Langdon upstairs? Perhaps this has been too much for her.'

'No! I want to talk to my mother!' I snapped.

He suddenly stood up and walked over to a table with a chair next to it by the French doors. He lifted a black cordless phone off its handset and looked over at me. 'Shall I call her number for you?'

'No! I don't trust you!'

I ran over and snatched the phone from his hand.

Mrs Taylor came forward but stopped as soon as he raised his hand.

'Fine! You can try to call her but...' He faltered, looked at Mrs Taylor and shook his head. 'She won't answer it. She's gone, my darling,' he repeated as he tried to touch my face.

I stepped back away from him. 'Don't!' I hissed. 'Don't touch me!'

I began slowly keying in my mother's landline. The number had never changed from when I was a child.

'Muscle memory,' I heard Mrs Taylor suggest to him.

I looked up to find her now hovering next to him, both of them watching me intently. Waiting to...

Waiting to do what to you?

I listened as the number tried to connect, warily watching them both.

'You have dialled an incorrect number,' an automated voice then stated. 'Please hang up and try again,' it advised.

'I don't understand,' I said, confused as the line was disconnected.

I saw him put his hand on Mrs Taylor's arm to stop her from taking the phone off me.

'Let her try again,' he suggested to her.

'Surely, I should just take Mrs Langdon to bed,' she stated.

He shook his head.

I could feel myself panicking as I redialled the number.

What aren't they telling you?

Again, the automated message clicked in again: 'You have dialled an incorrect number. Please hang up and try again.'

'Where's my mother? Where has she gone?' I frantically cried out.

My mother was the only person I could think of who could end all this craziness. She would take me away from here, back home with her.

'Darling, your mother has gone,' he gently repeated. 'Remember?'

'Gone? Gone where? What have you done to her?' I screamed at him as the phone fell from my hand, crashing to the floor.

'Try to remember,' he pleaded with me. 'Please?'

'I want to go home!' I sobbed, inching back from Mrs Taylor, who had surreptitiously edged closer to me.

Like a cornered animal, I stared at them, unsure of how to escape. I looked at the open doors leading out into the hallway.

Run! RUN!

I couldn't get through them, so I suddenly lunged to the side of him, trying to escape. But he was faster than me and grabbed me. He hugged me tight against his body, holding my head into his chest.

'Shh!' he murmured. 'It's all right. You're safe,' he reassured me as he restrained me.

'Get off me! LET ME GO!' I screamed, kicking and striking out at him as he held on to me, his height and weight easily overpowering me. 'GET YOUR HANDS OFF ME!' I yelled, twisting and kicking to get him to release me.

'Mrs Taylor, please, help,' he instructed as he twisted me around so my back was against his chest.

His powerful arms pinned me to his body as he held on to me.

'Shh... Darling, please... Calm down.'

'STOP! STOP! YOU'RE HURTING ME! HELP! HELP!' I screamed and hollered as loud as I could.

I didn't know if anyone else was in the castle, but my cries made no difference. No one came.

Then I felt my dress pulled up and my panties yanked to one side, exposing my buttock cheek.

I turned to see Mrs Taylor beside me.

'NO!' I howled, kicking out as hard as I could against him, but it was futile. I tried to sink my teeth into his arms so he would release me, but I couldn't get my head far enough down to reach his flesh.

'Shh... Darling, it's all going to be all right. I promise,' he whispered soothingly as though I were a child.

His voice was pleading as if he was trying to reassure himself that what he was doing was acceptable.

Déjà vu hit me hard. This had happened before.

Countless times...

I felt the familiar icy stab as the needle dug into my flesh.

'NO! WHAT ARE YOU DOING TO ME?' I screamed as she then pulled the needle out from the side of my exposed buttock cheek.

He didn't reply. Neither did Mrs Taylor.

I sobbed and yelled, threatening to call the police.

Or was that threat to call the police only in your head?

The world I had resurfaced in, started to melt away.

I felt him deftly scoop my collapsing body up. Secured in his arms, his lips brushed gently against my cheek as my head lolled to the side.

Terrified, I heard disembodied voices floating above me as my fluttering eyelids finally sealed shut.

'Did we do the right thing bringing her here?' I heard him ask.

Was that doubt in his voice? Or pain perhaps?

'What other choice is there? Maybe you should be more concerned with how Mrs Langdon reacts when she does remember what happened to her.'

Oh God... What happened to you before... Before you woke up to the reality that you can't remember anything of your life with him – your husband?

If he is who he says he is...

'Perhaps you should accept that your marriage is over.'

'And if I do, what becomes of her? Of my wife?'

'You live your life as if she never existed. You try to find happiness again. You have someone else to think about now...'

NO... NO. What are they suggesting? What are they going to do to you? And who else is in his life?

6

The door objected as it opened. I turned to witness a familiar tall, grey, slender figure quietly entering my room carrying a tray with my breakfast.

And medication.

'Ahh, Mrs Langdon, how are you feeling this morning?' she greeted, smiling at me.

Did I register a flicker of surprise when she saw me standing by the window? I couldn't say. Her face remained typically inscrutable.

I didn't answer her. Instead, I stared back across at the pebble-strewn beach beyond the rocks below my window. It remained deserted. If I had been hoping to see someone, I was bitterly disappointed. It seemed that Mrs Taylor hadn't lied when she said this place was isolated. However, I hadn't stepped outside – not yet. But that was my plan. To get outside and figure out where I was and how to escape.

You could be anywhere. You only have her word that you are on the west coast of Scotland, surrounded by acres of uninhabited terrain.

The seductive clap of waves against the rocks below compelled me to look down. I could feel the water luring me as if it were the enchanting song of the mythological Greek sirens, calling me to my death.

'Come, you must be cold standing there barefoot and in a sleeveless nightdress. Let's get you back into bed,' Mrs Taylor suggested, as if reading my dark thoughts.

Or perhaps she can also hear the three sirens below imploring you to join them.

Not that I could follow them; the black iron bars beyond the windows prevented me from falling to my fate.

Or is it that the bars are there to prevent you from escaping?

'Come along, Mrs Langdon, while your toast and scrambled eggs are still warm,' she stated, placing the tray down on the table.

She then came over and ushered me away from the window.

'I want to go outside. I want to walk on the beach with...' I hesitated. It felt odd saying his name. 'With my husband and the dogs. I've never been out there. I want to feel the sun on my skin and breathe in the ocean air. I want to go outside,' I requested.

'Of course. Why don't you have some breakfast first? But you have walked on the beach with your husband and the dogs. Remember?'

'I have?' I whispered, shocked. I tried to recall those moments. Nothing came to me. 'Are you sure?'

She nodded. 'You'll remember at some point. You always do.'

'And what if I don't?' I asked, scared.

What if you never remember and relive this loop of waking up to Mrs Taylor bringing you medication and breakfast again and again?

I could feel the icy terror of that nightmarish reality – my current reality – coursing through my veins. I only had her word that I would remember.

As if reading my mind, Mrs Taylor reassured me: 'It will come back to you. And when Mr Langdon returns from London, I am sure he'll walk with you again on the beach. And if you're feeling up to it, maybe even around the grounds. There are some beautiful walks beyond the castle grounds towards the mountains. Quite something to behold. I am sure the fresh air will do wonders for your recovery.'

But I didn't hear her.

All I could focus on was the fact that he was in London. That he had left me here in this remote place, alone with his housekeeper.

Why?

'He's in London?' I questioned. 'Why? What is he doing there? Why didn't he take me? He knows I want to return there. To go back home. To—'

'Mrs Langdon, come back to bed,' she said, cutting me off. 'Come, and I will pour you a cup of tea to help calm your nerves.'

I slowly breathed in, steadying myself, fighting the compulsion to scream at her. I knew that she and my husband were hiding something from me.

You tried to call her – your mother.

Remember?

But the line had been disconnected.

Oh God...

'Why is he in London?' I repeated, feeling the agitation build as the memories of Saturday night started to flood back.

Maybe he has gone to see your mother. Maybe. To tell her that—

I stopped myself. To tell her what? That he was holding me against my will in some isolated ancestral home where no one would ever find me.

And where no one can hear your screams...

My mind threw me back to last night when I had hollered and yelled as they held me down and—

I blocked out the thought as she gently guided me back to bed.

Silent, I watched as Mrs Taylor rearranged the pillows and then fluffed the duvet.

'Come along. In you get,' she said, turning round to me, smiling.

I did as she asked. She then pulled the duvet over my bare legs, but not before I noticed the recent addition of bruises from last night – Saturday night.

If it even was Saturday evening. You only have their word. Days mean nothing to you now.

But now I had some memories to hold on to, so I could somehow figure out a way to escape this nightmarish existence. Knowledge gave me power. I knew that every morning, Mrs Taylor would arrive and force me to take my medication, followed by a few mouthfuls of something that resembled toast with butter and some sloppy substance masquerading as eggs or porridge, but which was as tasteless as soggy cardboard, accompanied by tea as flavourless as lukewarm water. It was supposed to be Earl Grey. It wasn't. There was no subtle citrus flavour or smell from the crucial ingredient of bergamot essential oil, which gave the tea its distinctive taste and aroma.

It was all lies... All pretend. Why did they think you wouldn't notice?

I had no access to the outside world to confirm what they were telling me was true. I hadn't seen a mobile phone, tablet or computer. It was as if this place, Dunstrafne Castle, was trapped in the past.

As are you.

'Why is he in London?' I repeated.

But before Mrs Taylor had a chance to answer me, I caught sight of the whiteboard which represented my life now.

The prompts are because of your lack of memory. Remember? That's what she – Mrs Taylor – told you.

I looked at the number of days I had been held here.

Today was...

I stared. When did I write that? I had no memory.

Monday: Day 48.

What happened to Sunday? How could I have lost another day and night?

Last night was Saturday, so how could I have possibly jumped to Monday?

'How is it Monday?' I demanded, terrified as I turned to her. 'How? What happened to me?'

Then I remembered the intramuscular injection into my buttock cheek administered by Mrs Taylor while my husband restrained me. Whatever drug they had forcibly administered had rendered me unable to do anything other than sleep for an entire day and night. But I hadn't forgotten what had happened to me on Saturday evening. I remembered.

Something had changed.

Or is it, as Mrs Taylor has repeatedly assured you, that your memory is starting to come back? Maybe you will recall walking on the beach again. Maybe you'll even begin to remember him – your husband – and the real reason why he is keeping you here.

I could still remember waking up in Dunstrafne Castle on Thursday morning. That memory hadn't left me. That was the first day I became aware of my existence. And of theirs: the housekeeper and my husband.

Whether I had been here for forty-eight days was a moot point if I couldn't remember that time. I suspected that they were lying to me anyway in a bid to drive me insane. Considering the cocktail of drugs they were forcing me to take, it was no surprise that everything was foggy and I had struggled – until Thursday – to grasp on to any tangible memories from before...

What was your life even like before here?

Some semblance of events remained with me. It was like a gigantic jigsaw puzzle with tiny pieces floating together in a remote corner of my mind. I remembered losing the rest of Thursday after I went back to bed. It merged into Friday, which hadn't existed for me, and all of Saturday until the evening: days and time all lost to me after taking the medication forced by Mrs Taylor. Then came Saturday evening – I was lucid on Saturday evening. Why?

Perhaps you weren't so heavily medicated because your husband desired your company at dinner.

Maybe... It makes sense.

'Mrs Langdon? Did you hear me?'

Her voice cut through my thoughts. I shifted my gaze from the whiteboard to her concerned figure.

I shook my head.

'You were so exhausted from going downstairs to dinner on Saturday evening that you ended up sleeping straight through the following day and evening.'

'No...' I mumbled, shaking my head. 'That's not true... You... You injected me with something that made me pass out.'

She smiled at me. 'Not at all. I helped Mr Langdon carry you upstairs to your room. You were so exhausted you literally collapsed into bed. I had to change you out of your dress and into your night-clothes. Remember?'

'No...' I murmured. 'I... I...'

'Pop them in your mouth,' she instructed, handing me a small paper cup.

I took it from her and warily studied the contents. I didn't want to take them. I wanted to keep remembering. I had to if I was to escape from here.

I recalled the final snippets of conversation that I had heard before everything became hazy. The final words came back to me:

'You live your life as if she never existed. You try to find happiness again. You have someone else to think about now...'

It hit me then that perhaps the reason my husband was in London was because of someone else.

Oh God... He's seeing someone else...

'Mrs Langdon?'

I looked up at her waiting figure.

'Sorry,' I mumbled.

I stared at the yellow 5 mg tablet. The others were white. I counted them. Eight white tablets, one yellow.

They've increased. How? How is that possible?

Didn't I also take medication at night? I vaguely recalled Mrs Taylor coming to my room some evenings and settling me in bed before placing two blue tablets under my tongue. I presumed that since they immediately dissolved, they were fast-acting. I had asked her what they were for, and she had explained that they were lorazepam, a benzodiazepine, to help me sleep as I suffered from insomnia.

'Have you changed my medication?'

'No, Mrs Langdon. Why do you ask?'

'The yellow tablet. It's new. And there's two more than usual.'

'Your medication hasn't changed, Mrs Langdon. The yellow tablet is diazepam. You've always taken it.'

'I have?' I questioned. 'What is it for?'

'It is to help reduce your anxiety, Mrs Langdon,' she assured as she handed me a glass of water.

I stared at the tablet, not trusting her reasoning for giving it to me. I wasn't suffering from anxiety. I was here against my will with no access to the outside world. How did she expect me to act?

I was sure that diazepam was another word for Valium. I didn't know how I knew that, but I was sure they were the same drug.

So why is she giving you Valium?

But it wasn't only Valium they were forcing me to take, so it was no surprise that I could barely remember anything when I was being so heavily drugged. All the symptoms I was experiencing were surely the result of mixing Valium with other drugs: confusion, dizziness, drowsiness, difficulty waking up and loss of memory.

Mrs Taylor had reassured me my migraines caused these debilitating symptoms. That was why I was under the care of a neurologist. It was this Professor Walker, who I couldn't remember, who had allegedly prescribed these countless pills for my migraines and...

Breakdown? They said you had a breakdown...

But what if she is lying to you? What if they are drugging you to make you feel like this? The disorientation, confusion and the inability to wake up. To resurface back to reality.

It all came back to one question: why?

What don't they want you to remember?

My mind went into a tailspin, throwing me back to Saturday night. I couldn't forget those chilling words:

'Maybe you should be more concerned with how Mrs Langdon reacts when she does remember what happened to her.'

What did they mean? What was it that they wanted me to forget? And why?

'Come along, Mrs Langdon,' Mrs Taylor prompted gently. 'You've done this many times before.'

I nodded. She was right. I had done this many times.

Too many times.

I placed the paper cup on the duvet and slowly took out each pill, swallowing them back with the water Mrs Taylor had given me.

I left the diazepam until last. I then popped it in my mouth, slipping it under my tongue before taking a mouthful of water and pretending to swallow the tablet.

'Right, breakfast,' Mrs Taylor suggested, taking my glass and turning to collect the tray from the table.

I furtively spat the diazepam out into my hand and hid it in my palm while she had her back to me.

'Why is he in London?' I again asked.

'Mr Langdon left early yesterday morning. He had some business he needed to take care of, but he'll be back late this afternoon,' she explained. 'Perhaps earlier. He flew down from Glasgow and from what I believe is flying back early this afternoon from Heathrow.'

'Has he seen my neurologist? I still want to see this Professor Walker,' I stated.

She started to pour some tea and missed the delicate cup, spilling some scalding liquid into the saucer and onto the white linen cloth covering the tray.

'My book,' I called out, alarmed that it might get damaged.

'Your book is perfectly safe, Mrs Langdon,' she assured me. 'See?' she said, picking it up and moving it away from the tray and any threat of water damage.

'Thank you,' I said.

For some reason, I couldn't remember what the book was that was on the table, just that it meant a great deal to me. I was surprised that the sudden memory of its existence there on the table had come out of nowhere.

I watched her as she dabbed at the spillage with a napkin. I wondered whether my migraines affected my ability to remember. Maybe Mrs Taylor was correct. After all, why would I be under the care of a neurologist?

'Did my husband go to see my neurologist?' I continued, insistent that she answer me. I wanted to add my mother, but I was reticent after what had happened to me on Saturday evening.

She continued what she was doing.

'Mrs Taylor?'

She paused and looked over at me. 'I suspect Mr Langdon will tell you everything when he returns, Mrs Langdon. I am not privy to his affairs,' she said, shutting down the conversation.

But there was something in the tremor of her hand, which had caused her to spill the tea, that made me suspect she was lying to me.

And not for the first time.

Again, the chilling words I heard on Saturday night as the drug they had injected me with started to take effect came back to me.

'You live your life as if she never existed...'

I knew I had to get away before it was too late, and I ended up in a permanent drug-induced state – or worse. The medication had already increased, and despite Mrs Taylor claiming it was the same, I knew it wasn't. For I was starting to remember. And crucially, I was aware that no one was coming to save me.

For who knows you're here? Your neurologist? You've not spoken to them since you've been here – if ever.

And what about your mother? Why was her number not recognised? Did you misdial it? Perhaps... Perhaps that was the reason the automated voice said you had dialled an incorrect number.

I slowly breathed out. It made sense.

Yes, you must have made a mistake when keying in her number.

Twice? Had I misdialled it twice?

Perhaps your nerves and the medication had affected you.

I wanted to believe that was true. I wanted to believe it so badly. But I couldn't remember talking to my mother while I was here. I couldn't even recall the last time I had seen her. The only memories I could grasp were from years back when I was a child. My husband claimed I was thirty-two years old. Yet, I couldn't remember the two years I had been married to him, despite scratching and tearing at my mind, feeling as if I was going insane, trying to find some clue of this lost time.

And where was my mother? Why would she allow this to happen to me?

A chilling thought seared through me like an ice-hot blade.

What if something has happened to her and you can't remember?

I could feel the sinewy hold of fear as it gripped my throat.

'Mrs Langdon? Mrs Langdon? Can you hear me? Mrs Langdon?' prompted Mrs Taylor, her concerned voice bringing me back to the present. She was sitting on the edge of the bed next to me. 'Are you all right?'

I swallowed. Nodded.

'Let me get you some breakfast. That might make you feel better,' she suggested, standing up and walking back over to the table to retrieve my breakfast tray.

I noticed the silver plate cloche covering what was supposed to be scrambled eggs. The thought of eating the tasteless, congealed canary-yellow gloop made me feel nauseous.

I shook my head. 'I need the... the bathroom, first,' I managed to say.

She fixed her black, beady eyes on me.

I couldn't tell whether she was suspicious or not.

I waited.

She finally nodded. 'Do you need help?'

'No... No, I'm fine,' I mumbled, pulling the duvet back and swinging my legs out of bed.

I could feel her eyes burning into my back as I made my way to the door that led into the en suite. I closed the door behind me and headed to the sink, turning both taps on full. I then threw the tablet into the sink and watched as the torrid gush of water flushed it away. Shakily breathing out, I splashed my face.

What are you doing?

I grabbed a towel and patted my face.

You're reclaiming your life back. That's what you're doing.

There was an assertive knock on the door, followed by: 'Mrs Langdon?'

'Yes?' I weakly called out.

'You haven't been sick, have you?' she questioned, throwing the door open before I had a chance to answer.

'No,' I replied. 'I've been washing my hands and face. I'm coming now.'

She waited, holding the door open for me to leave.

* * *

I allowed Mrs Taylor to feed me mouthfuls of what she claimed were scrambled eggs. She was concerned I hadn't eaten anything on Saturday evening, and of course, I had slept all Sunday. I didn't argue with her that she had forcibly drugged me on Saturday evening, nor did I protest that the insipid yellow slop she was feeding me was tasteless. Instead, I complied and swallowed back the watery lumps without chewing. I then managed to drink a cup of lukewarm greyish-brown liquid, which Mrs Taylor claimed was Earl Grey tea. I wanted to be left alone, and the sooner I acquiesced with her insistence I eat, the sooner she would go.

After breakfast, I said I was tired and asked Mrs Taylor to close the curtains, which she did. I then heard the chair groaning by the table as she sat down to watch me.

How often does she watch you?

I then pretended to fall asleep, focusing on slowing my breathing down. I lost track of how much time had passed when the sound of a phone ringing downstairs brought me back. I heard the housekeeper suddenly stand up, signalled by the jangling of keys and other appendages on the silver Victorian-style decorative belt hook around her waist. She approached the bed and stood over me before the retreating click of her flat heels on the wooden floor and the door groaning behind her. I opened my eyes, relieved that she had finally left me alone.

I held my breath, not daring to move for fear that she was waiting outside, but I heard the faint continuous ring of a phone, followed by the hurried clicking of Mrs Taylor's Oxford shoes disappearing as she chased the call.

Now what?

I didn't move, worried that she would return.

More time slipped away until, certain she wasn't coming back, I climbed out of bed. I crept to the bedroom door expecting it to be locked. I ever so slowly turned the round brass handle and was surprised when I found it unlocked.

Why has she not locked you in?

I remembered she had left quickly to answer the phone. She must have been expecting an important call. Otherwise, she would have ordinarily taken the time to lock the door. I knew from experience that the door was always locked whenever I tried it. I couldn't get out, but they could get in.

My heart pounded like a trapped wild animal desperate to get out. I turned, unsure whether I dared to leave. My eyes caught sight of the whiteboard. I had been a prisoner in this room for forty-eight days. The acknowledgement was enough to spur me into action.

I turned, and seeing my white linen dress from Saturday evening hanging outside the wardrobe, I ran over to it, pulled it off its hanger and placed it on the bed. I hurriedly dragged my nightdress over my head. I noted the pair of white panties neatly left on top of the chest of drawers. I pulled them on, followed by the dress.

I looked around the room for shoes. There were none. I walked over and opened the wardrobe, and stared in disbelief. Two identical dresses to the one I was wearing were hanging inside. I checked the labels, all the same.

How odd?

But there were no shoes. Nor was there anything else inside.

I presumed my shoes were downstairs. Curious, I opened the chest of drawers, only to find they again contained two identical white nightdresses. I then pulled open the second drawer, which revealed numerous white panties. I pulled out the two lower drawers; one was empty, and the other contained a thick, oversized white Arran cardigan and an off-white cashmere throw.

It was strange. Surely, I had some different clothes. Let alone, items with colour. It struck me as peculiar that they lacked any individuality or unique style. They were simply functional. But the weather would be turning soon, so where were my heavier clothes, or outdoor wear?

But you haven't stepped foot outside, have you? Maybe that's the point. You don't need other clothes as they don't want or expect you to ever leave this place.

Or have you gone out but don't remember? Mrs Taylor said you had, so maybe you left your shoes downstairs.

My findings made me more determined to leave. I picked up my much-loved, leaf-eared book, a first edition published in 1938, from the table. I touched the fraying yellow cover and let my fingers trail over the title printed in bold red letters. Not that I could read the title as the words deceived me, blurring into one another. I tried to remember the name of the book, but it frustratingly eluded me. I placed it in the large left-side pocket of my dress for safekeeping. I suddenly remembered why I liked the dress, not because of its colour or style, but because of its functionality. Its cavernous pockets meant that I could carry the book everywhere with me. It was all I had from my previous life, and it felt more like a talisman than ever before.

My mother had given me the book, once gifted to her from her mother, when I had been bed-bound with some ailment in my early teens. It had journeyed with me through to adulthood and had miraculously survived to this point. Recently, I had attempted to read a sentence or two, but the words blended together, becoming indecipherable. I didn't want it left behind as it was my only possession from before here, tethering me to my past life and my mother.

I had no intention of coming back to this room and every intention of escaping.

I returned to the door and pulled it towards me, wincing as it creaked open.

Oh God!

I was alarmed to find one of the dogs lying in my path.

Henry...

I held my breath as he stared up at me with doleful eyes while his long red tail thudded enthusiastically on the floor.

'Shh...' I murmured as I crouched down to stroke him.

You remember Henry, too. You do... You remember. You remember him as a puppy and a young dog. And then? The memories are gone. Wiped out.

He covered me in slobber as he lovingly licked my cheek.

'I missed you as well,' I cooed, burying my face in his fur. 'Did James buy you for my birthday before we got married, eh?' I questioned as I now held his handsome head, staring into his soulful eyes.

I would have been surprised if he was older than three or four.

'Where's your brother hiding? Eh?' I questioned, straightening up.

I expectantly looked around for Jack, but he was nowhere to be seen.

'Shh!' I repeated as Henry suddenly jumped up at me, throwing me off balance before turning and bounding down the hall.

He stopped, looked back at me and waited for me to follow him.

Frozen, I stared at him, not knowing what to do.

I had a sense something was wrong. The brothers were typically inseparable. So why was Henry without Jack? I crept along the hallway, following him, pausing by the lavish staircase and peering down at the grand hallway below. I could hear Mrs Taylor's faint voice drifting from one of the rooms below. It sounded as if she was on the phone. I hesitated. The desire to wait and seize my moment to call the police and tell them I was here against my will was overwhelming. Then I turned and looked at Henry's sad eyes imploring me to come.

You can't ignore him... What if Jack is hurt?

Mrs Taylor didn't strike me as an animal person, and with my husband away, who else was here to look out for the boys?

As if picking up on my uncertainty, Henry gave out a whine.

'Quiet, Henry!' I urged, terrified that Mrs Taylor would come out to check the noise and find me skulking when I should be in bed.

I tiptoed across the first-floor landing after him. He vanished around a corner. It wasn't until I caught up with his shadow that I realised I wasn't allowed in this part of the castle.

Do you remember Mrs Taylor's warning as you came down to dinner on Saturday evening?

I paused at the memory of her hand supporting me as I walked past the west wing towards the stairs as she explained to me why I wasn't allowed to explore the west wing of the castle:

'Mr Langdon does not want you in that part of the castle. It's too dangerous, Mrs Langdon. Storm damage last winter has made it uninhabitable. His only instruction is that you do not go anywhere near the rooms there. Promise me you won't break his rule. Promise me!'

I had dutifully promised her as she guided me down the stairs, refusing to allow me any lingering glances in that direction. Now, here I was on the precipice of getting caught. After pretending to take the Valium tablet and faking falling asleep, I should have been trying to find a way to get out and find help, not putting myself at more risk.

Seriously? What are you doing? If she finds you here, then—

Too terrified to contemplate what she would do to me, I stopped myself.

'Henry?' I whispered. 'Where are you, boy?'

I heard a whine, low and faint.

I tiptoed along the hallway feeling as if I was trespassing. I avoided looking at the portraits hanging on the wall, not wanting to meet their accusatory gazes.

You don't belong here...

I looked past the portraits and up at the ceiling for water stains from the storm that had allegedly damaged the west wing. However, I couldn't see any such telltale signs.

Then I came to the end of the hallway and a large wooden door. Henry was lying outside, scratching and whining to get in.

'What's wrong? Is Jack in there?' I asked him as I approached.

Henry looked up expectantly, his gentle eyes meeting mine. I could hear his brother, Jack, whimpering on the other side.

'You're a clever boy, aren't you, Henry?' I praised, stroking his head.

I placed my hand on the ornate brass knob, twisted it, then pushed the door open. A gust of wind startled me, attempting to force me backwards, as well as a rather grateful and overly excited red fox Labrador who launched himself at me.

'Hey, Jack,' I said, laughing at his enthusiasm. 'Careful! You'll knock me over!'

I fussed over him for a few moments before standing up. It was then I saw the room for the first time. Shocked, I remained transfixed, unable to move. The large double windows were wide open and, presumably, the north Atlantic winds driving in off the ocean had slammed the door shut, closing Jack in. But it wasn't the dramatic, unadulterated ocean view and the encroaching storm on the darkening, bleak horizon that had me held captive, unable to turn and run.

Just go... Go, before Mrs Taylor finds you here. Run away from this place while you still can.

But I couldn't leave. Captivated, I stepped inside the forbidden room. All thoughts of fleeing left me as I stared and stared at her.

Who are you?

7

I jumped as the leaded windowpanes violently slammed shut.

Oh God...

The feeling that I wasn't welcome here overwhelmed me.

The wind suddenly shook the loose windows, threatening to force them open again and shatter them into tiny fragments. Without thinking, I ran over and secured them. I turned back for Henry and Jack, but – happy to be reunited – they had fled and left me alone. I dashed back to the open door to escape after the boys. But something stopped me.

Nervous, I dared to look back at her: the beautiful young woman in the portrait. Her long, wild spirals of blonde curls cascaded down her perfectly symmetrical face and past her bare shoulders. Her large brown beautiful eyes defiantly stared down at me. Her full lips were curved ever so slightly in a half-mocking smile, as if she knew some terrible secret about me.

She wore an off-the-shoulder emerald-green ball gown, the colour intensifying the richness of her seductive, dark eyes and the milkiness of her unblemished, youthful skin. Her cheeks and lips were flushed a deep red as if she had been running from somewhere or someone. I found myself coveting her curvaceous figure with her full breasts and hips, accentuated by the perfectly fitted gown. Jealousy coursed through me, vile and vengeful. I looked down at my simple white linen dress hiding my underweight, shapeless body covered in scars and bruises, hating her for making me feel so ugly and pathetic. Even though I didn't know what my face looked like, and I couldn't remember, I knew she was more breathtaking and exotic than I could ever be.

I enviously gazed at her luscious, thick, abundant spiral curls. Everything I lacked, she possessed as if she had absorbed my very essence. I felt her defiance, her boldness emanating out from the canvas. At that moment, I wished I could have her life as depicted in the portrait, one of passion and power, remembered in perfect, minute detail. And yet, here I stood, unsure of who I was and why I was here. I yearned to be her, yet feared her. For there was something about her that struck a chord deep inside me. That made me feel uneasy, threatened even. The glint in her eye spoke of a knowing – about me. It felt that she too was equally studying me.

Filled with a sense of unworthiness, I dropped my gaze to the canvas backdrop. I recognised Dunstrafne Castle with its sweeping centre staircase and columns. The antique weapons dating back to the Jacobites and centuries-old hunt trophies that decorated the walls in the background. It struck me that nothing had changed. I presumed the grand hall had remained untouched for centuries, holding on to its past glory. To one side of her stood the most majestic and tallest Nordmann fir Christmas tree I had ever seen, decorated with what I suspected were real candles. I gazed at the burnished orange and snake-eyed yellow naked flames as they teasingly twisted and turned, dancing upwards, whispering of promised times. All lost to me.

But it was her ethereal presence that my gaze compellingly returned to, holding me captive. She felt other-worldly, too precious to be earthbound. I could imagine the sudden hush at the Christmas ball as all eyes fell on her as she descended the castle's staircase in her extravagant emerald-green gown.

Who are you? And where are you now?

I imagined there would be a family cemetery in the grounds of the castle. I wondered whether she had been laid to rest there amongst the Dunstrafne Castle ancestors. For some inexplicable reason, I yearned to know her. I edged timidly forward, slowly into the room. I was an outsider. I didn't need Mrs Taylor's warning to keep me away from the west wing to know I shouldn't be here. I didn't belong.

You don't belong anywhere.

I dragged my eyes away from her spellbinding gaze and looked around what appeared to be the principal bedroom. It was an impressive size, easily accommodating the antique, hand-carved four-poster bed positioned directly opposite the large windows opening out on to the expansive view of the ocean.

Had this been her room?

The furnishings were immaculately preserved. I noted the many plumped-up pillows and scatter cushions covered in splendid gold-embossed material that adorned the high, sumptuous bed as well as the heavy, ornate gold-threaded curtains tied back, waiting to be released when the night came.

Does someone still sleep here, or is it preserved in perpetuity? If so, why?

I glanced around at the polished wooden floor and the blue and red antique Persian rug in the centre of the room. Two Queen Anne leather armchairs with red and gold embroidered scatter cushions waited on opposite sides of the striking beige and cream marble fireplace. I noted the kindling and coal in the cast-iron hearth in anticipation of the cooler evenings sweeping in from the north Atlantic. A bulging coal scuttle and neatly arranged logs in a basket lay to one side of the hearth in preparation.

For whom?

A sudden clatter startled me, making me gasp, adding to the paranoia I couldn't dispel that I wasn't supposed to be here. That my presence had disturbed something unseen – someone. I looked over at the writing bureau positioned in front of the windows rattling in discomfort at the mercy of the wind hell-bent on getting inside the room.

I could see that a photograph frame had crashed forward. But not by the force of the wind as I had closed the windows.

By her, perhaps.

I glanced nervously back up at her to witness her smiling down at me as if enjoying my discomfort.

You're being ridiculously hypervigilant. Why? There's no one here. Just you and the wind. No ghosts from the past to ward you off. The people you need to be fearful of are the living – your husband and his housekeeper.

I stepped towards the writing bureau, my hand delicately brushing the back of the oxblood Chesterfield captain's chair as I imagined someone sitting here, looking out at the ever-changing ocean as they contemplated what to write. I noted that the matching antique oxblood leather bureau insert was spotless, as were the objects adorning the desk. The countless silver picture frames still managed to gleam despite the bleak grey morning light.

I picked up the fallen frame and turned it over.

Oh God... How can it be?

Stunned, I stared at the black-and-white photograph in the frame. The young woman beaming back at me, glowing with evident joy, was the identical figure in the portrait. Her long spirals of blonde curls carelessly fell across her beautiful face, her delicate nose wrinkled as she laughed with abundance as a man held her from behind, whispering something in her ear. It was an intimate moment, serendipitously caught for posterity. I had assumed the woman in the portrait belonged to a time that had long since ceased to exist. And yet, here she was in this contemporary-looking photograph.

But something wasn't right. It took me a moment to understand that she was wearing a simple delicate wedding dress and that the man holding her, dressed in a Buchanan tartan kilt, was the groom.

But that man was also my husband – James Buchanan Langdon.

How? How is that even possible?

Horrified, I stared in disbelief at the image. It was my husband's face, albeit younger. Much younger.

And he was married to...

I turned and stared up at the portrait of his wife. Her secretive smile seemed to have widened as she gazed down upon me and my discovery.

How could you not know?

But I didn't know. I barely knew my own history.

You've been married for two years. Or so they told you.

How long was he married to her?

I turned back to the desk. I shakily placed the photo frame down and then studied the other images. Two more in black and white, two in colour and all of them together as a couple. There was no mistaking she was the same woman, or that the man with her was my husband. One of the black-and-white photographs, another wedding shot, was of their hands held together, showing off their Celtic love-knot patterned wedding rings.

What wedding ring was he wearing on Saturday evening? The same Celtic love knot? No. That can't be possible... Can it?

But I couldn't remember if it was a plain white-gold band or the same as the one in this photograph.

A pang of sadness overwhelmed me. I had no understanding why. Perhaps it was because I couldn't remember my wedding day.

Where are your wedding photographs?

It struck me as odd that I couldn't recall seeing any. Why weren't there wedding photographs of us on display in my bedroom or elsewhere? And yet, here were photographs of him on his wedding to another woman – one he had never mentioned to me.

Or has he, and you can't remember?

A wave of nausea hit me as I studied their smiling faces, so in love with one another, so happy. He had been even more handsome then, if that was possible, in his late twenties. His white-toothed smile matched hers. They looked perfect together, joyously beaming at the camera.

That's your husband... And he's with another woman. A woman you didn't know existed until now. And this is her room... Their room?

I felt faint as a cold sweat took hold. I wasn't sure if I was going to be sick. I stumbled, heading for what I hoped was the bathroom. I threw the door open and entered a luxurious en suite with an antique Victorian claw-foot bath on a raised platform in front of a large stained-glass window that opened out. It struck me that there were no bars outside this window nor on the windows in the adjoining bedroom.

Perhaps it's just your room with bars on the windows.

I blindly made my way to the sink and turned the tap on full and splashed cold water over my clammy skin. I held on to the sink with my head down, knees bent, breathing slowly in and out, trying to regulate my erratic heart rate. I didn't feel as if my body belonged to me. It felt so light as if it could possibly float away.

Stay focused... Don't let yourself go, whatever you do.

I closed my eyes against the dizziness that had taken me hostage. I remained like that for some time, trying to centre myself and process what was going on.

Process what you have found in there... Your husband was married to another woman... Before you.

I splashed my face again in an attempt to wake myself up from this nightmare.

But it made no difference. I was still in her bathroom, surrounded by her items. I had already caught sight of her countless exotic perfume bottles and the extravagant face creams and serums as if she was still here.

Is she?

Soaps and bath products also lay carelessly scattered about from when I assumed she had last used them.

When was that?

Why would all her toiletries be left behind? Why wouldn't she have taken them with her? And, crucially, why were some of them abandoned in such disarray as if she had been in a hurry? Perhaps she had been in a desperate dash to leave here. To get out and as far away as possible.

My eyes fell upon a delicately engraved gold-cased lipstick left behind on the grey and white marble counter. I shakily picked it up and opened the lid, twisting the contents upwards. I stared with a morbid fascination at the intense deep-red colour.

I couldn't imagine ever having the confidence to wear something so bold, so powerful. But the woman I had discovered here in the west wing was that and more. I realised that red must have been her go-to lipstick as she was wearing this provocative colour in the portrait and all the photographs on her writing desk.

And you? Who are you in comparison to her? You're no one. A ghost haunting this castle, seeking your lost identity, your lost past. You've resorted to obsessively searching through someone else's life, their personal effects, and for what? To torment yourself?

You're not supposed to be in here. Remember?

You need to get out of here! Do you understand? GET OUT!

Mrs Taylor came to mind. I imagined that she would be checking on me soon. I didn't have long before she would know I had escaped. I slowly exhaled. It didn't matter if he had been married to another woman before me. Or that she looked too beautiful to have ever existed in the real world. I needed to get out while I still could. Without thinking, I put the lipstick in the other empty side pocket of my dress.

Why have you done that? Put it back! It doesn't belong to you.

But for some reason, I wanted to hold on to it precisely because it didn't belong to me – it was hers. I splashed my face again before reaching for a soft hand towel and dabbing at my wet skin. I then lifted my head, and froze. It felt as if someone was standing behind me.

I spun around. It took me a moment to comprehend the enormous antique mirror that dominated the wall behind me from the floor to the ceiling. Stunned, I gazed at the ghostly reflection looking back at me through the tarnished, oxidised, centuries-old glass.

Oh God... Is that you? No...

Who are you?

I didn't recognise myself. Paradoxically, I didn't know what I had looked like before... Before now. But this haunted, hollowed-out figure reflected at me through a hazy surface was unrecognisable.

What happened to you? What have they done to you?

I stepped forward, closer to the figure that was supposed to be me.

I felt my stomach lurch. I could feel the remnants of my tasteless breakfast threatening to resurface. I swallowed down the bile at the back of my throat as tears began to slip down my cheeks.

The contrast between the image looking back at me and the woman in the portrait over the fireplace couldn't have been more different. I pictured her held in my husband's arms in the photographs on her desk as he proudly showed her off for all to see.

And you? How could he be married to you? How? After being married to her?

It didn't make any sense.

Look at you! LOOK AT YOURSELF!

But I couldn't bring myself to acknowledge that the figure reflected was me. Not yet. I was the antithesis of the woman in the portrait, the stunning bride in my husband's arms.

Is this the reason why you aren't allowed any access to mirrors? To prevent you from seeing yourself. From witnessing what you have become.

I broke away from the tormented, questioning gaze. Finally, I raised my head and met my intense deep-brown eyes in the mirror.

I gasped, a barely audible sound, as I dared myself to continue staring back at my reflection. With a trembling hand, seeing it for the first time, I tentatively touched my lips to make sure it was me I was looking at.

I turned my head from one side to the other as I stared at myself. My dark brown hair was aggressively cropped, cut in a messy pixie style. It made me look much younger than my years, accentuated by my androgynous body. My high cheekbones were so pronounced that I looked ill. I dropped my hand to my collarbone, jutting through my pale skin.

What have they done to you?

I was so underweight that the bones protruded through my taut flesh as if in desperation to escape from my starving body. I delicately ran my hand over my visible collarbone and down my flattened chest to my prominent ribcage.

Oh God...

I was aware that if I continued losing weight now, I had such little fat stores left, my body would begin consuming muscle to convert to energy, placing me at risk of organ failure.

How have you become so emaciated? And why would they let you waste away like this, isolated in some ancestral castle in west Scotland? Your husband and his housekeeper.

I somehow knew that without food and water, the body could survive for approximately a week. However, with water and no food, a person could possibly survive for as long as two to three months.

How long have you been here?

I could feel the knot of terror in the back of my throat as I let out a strangled sob.

Forty-eight days...

Is that why they have you locked away from prying eyes? So they can slowly starve you to death.

How long could I possibly survive on food that lacked any taste, making it virtually impossible to eat? It made me want to gag when Mrs Taylor pleaded for me to open my mouth so she could feed me what I refused to eat. I couldn't recall her bringing me any other food that tasted remotely palatable. However, I remembered the bloodied fillet steak, asparagus and delicate new potatoes my husband had devoured, washed down with a light red Pinot Noir on Saturday evening. I had had no appetite and discreetly fed what I could to the dogs, not wanting to offend him.

Why didn't you just eat it?

But I knew why. For some reason I had lost my appetite. Perhaps because what I had been given was so tasteless that it didn't remotely resemble food. I had appeased Mrs Taylor this morning when I had dutifully allowed her to feed me the scrambled eggs. And on Thursday morning when she fed me toast cut up into soldiers dunked into a soft-boiled egg. But the other mornings? The other evenings? What had I eaten over the course of those other forty-three days?

The food she brings you tastes of nothing. Smells of nothing. She's doing it intentionally to slowly starve you.

Why?

Because she doesn't want you here, that's why. She told him to try to find happiness again... To forget about you. And he already has, hasn't he? He went to London without you, leaving you in her vindictive hands. Didn't she say that he already had someone else to think about now?

Is that who he is visiting in London?

Suddenly I heard a door creak shut.

I jumped. I stared at my startled reflection, not knowing what to do.

Is it her?

I froze and waited. Shame scorched through me, followed by terror. I felt like a common thief snooping around someone else's possessions. The west wing was explicitly out of bounds. I knew I wasn't supposed to be here. So why did I stay? Why didn't I turn and run?

I was too late. I was about to be caught.

8

Creeping over to the bathroom door, I finally braved it and peeked out after waiting for what felt like an eternity. I had remained perfectly still, holding my breath, straining to hear someone in the other room. But no further noise had followed the door closing.

I had expected Mrs Taylor – or the woman in the portrait – to find me hiding in the bathroom. But no one had come in.

I needed to get out.

Now! Before someone catches you in here. For surely Mrs Taylor will be looking for you.

I peered round, looking for a sign that someone else was there. But the room was empty.

Or is it?

My eyes warily glanced up at her.

Her smile seemed wider, her lips fuller, the lipstick redder than when I had last looked. She was bolder, brighter, even more beautiful than before. I automatically touched the nape of my bare neck, reaching for my crude, cropped hair, feeling even more worthless. For now, I knew what I looked like. I had seen myself in her mirror. I was the obverse of her beauty and vivaciousness. I was grey, drained of all life, all vibrancy, physically fading away until it wouldn't only be my mind that I had lost, it would be my body.

I looked across the room and found that the door to the bedroom was now closed. I presumed since no one else was here, the wind had slammed it in a fit of pique that I still hadn't left. But the windows were closed. Had I imagined hearing the door creaking shut?

Worse still, had I closed the door behind me when I stepped into the room? I couldn't be sure. But I was certain about one thing: I didn't belong here in my husband's first wife's bedroom.

I let out a gasp of surprise when I saw myself again reflected in another mirror. It was also a large, antique, floor-to-ceiling, gold-framed mirror leaning on the same wall as the door leading out of the bedroom.

How could you have not seen this mirror?

But I knew why. The portrait had pulled me in, making everything else in the room fade into insignificance.

I glanced furtively around to see what else I had missed. The imposing four-poster bed caught my attention. I imagined the newly-weds' naked bodies intertwined, protected from the jealous winds and raging roar of the north Atlantic Ocean, buried underneath the heavy throws and sumptuous duvet in a world exclusive to them. Jagged jealousy consumed me as I thought of her Rubenesque body wrapped in his muscular physique as they lay under the four-poster canopy together. Again, it struck me that my husband didn't share my bed. Not that I wanted him within such intimate proximity, but it was odd that I couldn't remember when we had spent the night as husband and wife.

Why?

I wondered what it was that had attracted him to me. Not my physical appearance, for I could never compete with her – his other bride. Perhaps it was my mind, my intellect, that had captured him.

But what now that it was fading away? What was left for him to admire, to love about me?

I then noticed another door on the other side of the bed. Unable to resist, I found myself moving, as if sleepwalking, towards it. All thoughts of Mrs Taylor pushed to the dark recesses of my mind. Reaching it, I twisted the handle, pushing it open. I fumbled around in the blackness for a light switch and, finding it, flicked it on. I gasped as light suddenly illuminated what was a surprisingly spacious walk-in closet. Individually lit white shelves, open-plan wardrobe units and wide drawers lined the walls on one side. On the other was what resembled an art installation of intricately arranged women's shoes and handbags. A large, floor-to-ceiling fitted LED-lit mirror dominated the wall directly ahead, and a contemporary cream leather chaise longue lay to the side.

This is hers. It all belongs to the woman in the portrait and the photographs.

It was a beautifully, softly lit space designed to not only store but exhibit her clothes, shoes and bags on elegant, custom-made stands. I wasn't surprised that she had such exceptional and expensive taste. However, I was confused as to why it was still here. I tried to ignore the disquiet that I felt. It was as if it had been left in situ until the woman in the portrait returned.

Returned from where?

I curled my toes under, deep into the plush cream woollen thick-pile carpet, enjoying the luxurious sensation. It was a stark and pleasant contrast to the waxed wooden and stone floors throughout the rest of the castle. My fingers enviously brushed her countless evening dresses carefully hanging up. I spotted the green ball gown she was wearing in the portrait. I couldn't resist lifting the hanger from its secure holding and placing the dress against me. I gazed into the mirrored wall opposite, turning and twisting, imagining myself descending the castle's central staircase as if I were her.

Then I caught sight of myself.

What are you thinking? You'll never be her... Never.

Realising how ridiculous it looked against me, I let it fall from my body before hastily hanging the ball gown back with the other dresses. I allowed my covetous eyes to drift over the extravagant clothes, resisting the compulsion to try something on. However, I knew nothing would come close to fitting my shapeless body. I opened one of the soft-closing drawers, staring at the precisely arranged lace and silk lingerie. I let my fingers trail over the delicate material of the matching full-cupped bras and panties, desiring a body befitting of such underwear.

I walked over to the shoes and boots, gazing upon the array of artwork. I picked up one of a pair of breathtaking shoes off their stand, recognising them as Christian Louboutins by the signature shiny red soles at the bottom of the stiletto heels.

I stared down at my bare feet, tempted to try them on as they looked like a close fit. Before I had a chance to try them on, I came to my senses.

Why are you pillaging some other woman's wardrobe? You haven't got time to daydream. You need to get out!

I carefully placed the shoe back next to its partner and longingly cast my eyes around what was a treasure trove before walking out. I flicked the light switch off and pulled the door to behind me. It was then that I noticed the large antique walnut wardrobe on the same wall as the walk-in closet door. Curious, I pulled the objecting doors open. Inside was a gentleman's wardrobe compartment on one side and drawers on the other. It was empty, bar coat hangers, mothballs and something hanging wrapped in a protective bag. I unzipped it, wishing I hadn't. I immediately recognised the Buchanan tartan kilt from the wedding photograph on the writing desk. It belonged to my husband.

Where are the rest of his clothes and other accessories?

I yanked open the drawers and other small compartments. All barren.

I knew he was in London, but surely he wouldn't have taken all his clothes with him. Unless he wasn't planning on returning? Or maybe he didn't use this room any more. Perhaps it was left as a shrine to her. His first wife.

I closed the doors of the wardrobe.

What are you doing poking around...? You need to go!

I closed the wardrobe and headed to the door and reached for the doorknob. I twisted it to release the catch, simultaneously pulling it towards me. It didn't move.

What the...?

I tried again, forcing the door to open. It was jammed.

No... It's locked.

How? How could it possibly be locked? Then it hit me.

Someone has locked you in.

Who? And why?

Or is it that the heavy door is simply stuck and you're not strong enough now to pull it free?

My weak, fading body came to mind.

Perhaps...

I started to gulp in short, shallow breaths of air as I tried again and again to release it. But it was stuck. I could feel the panic rising, threatening to subsume me. I wanted to get out of this room and as far away from this place as possible. I had wasted enough time and was worried that it wouldn't be long before Mrs Taylor checked on me.

What are you doing here? You should have left when you let Jack out. Now you're running out of time. What then?

Panicking, I pulled at the door, but still, it wouldn't budge. I turned around and searched the expansive, luxurious principal bedroom for the culprit, but no one was here – apart from her. I looked up at the portrait of my husband's first wife as she watched me.

I couldn't dispel the feeling that she didn't want me to leave. Not yet. For some reason, I had a sense that she hadn't finished with me. That there was something she still wanted me to find.

I shook off the thought. It was crazy.

You really are starting to lose your mind.

I was about to bang and scream on the door to alert Mrs Taylor to my situation when I suddenly questioned whether a key for the door was kept in the heavy Victorian mahogany writing bureau by the window. If there was a key here, it seemed the obvious place to keep one.

If it is indeed locked and not jammed...

I ran over to the bureau and started pulling out the drawers and rummaging around. I made myself take a deep breath and slow down. If there was a key hidden in one of the drawers, I would miss it in this frenzied state.

I searched the top drawer closest to me, rummaging through writing paper, envelopes, pens and other paraphernalia. There was nothing of interest which caught my eye. I opened the drawer below and again poked around, hoping to feel the hint of cold metal against my fingers. Nothing. I noted the letters, invoices and other papers. Curious, I pulled them out. Some were dated as recently as two years ago, when I had married James Buchanan Langdon.

I stared at the letter in my hand. It was addressed to a Lady Isabella Langdon of Dunstrafne Castle.

'Isabella Langdon,' I murmured as I turned to the portrait. 'So, that's who you are.'

I held her mesmerising gaze, conceding that she fitted the Italian name Isabella.

The Italian word '*bella*', meaning 'beautiful', embedded in the name perfectly suited her, as she was the epitome of beauty. I wondered whether she went by Bella, an abbreviation of Isabella, or if she preferred her full name.

What would my husband have called her, I wondered. Isabella, Bella? It struck me that he called me 'darling'. Had he also called her 'darling' or some other term of endearment? Something particular to her, befitting of her, and not just a generic word of affection.

What is your name? Who were you before you became Mrs Langdon?

I let out a strangled sob as the question goaded me. I couldn't remember. I couldn't remember my own name.

How? How is that possible?

The whiteboard... Was your name on the whiteboard?

But all I could recall were two harsh black words: Mrs Langdon. Nothing else.

I tore viciously at my mind, ripping apart any memories I could find. But there was nothing there. I had forgotten who I was before becoming James Buchanan Langdon's wife. But he already had someone else before me, another wife.

Again, I could feel the toxic spread of envy seeping into my veins. It was odd. I didn't want or desire this man – my husband – as I couldn't remember ever loving him, yet, paradoxically, I felt the ravages of jealousy knowing the depths of his love for her, Isabella Langdon. I could see it, feel it, caught in his adoring eyes in perpetuity in the photographs on the writing bureau. He was obsessed with her, captivated by her. So why would he let her go? Or had she run from him?

What happened to Isabella Langdon? And why does your husband keep her bedroom and belongings as if she still occupies this castle? Or as if he expects her to walk back in at any moment?

And what is it she wants you to uncover? What? Why won't they just unlock the door and let you go? Or at least let you find the key to the door so you can let yourself out?

I needed to find the door key, if there was one here, and then get out and forget this godforsaken mausoleum that my husband kept in honour of her – his other wife. Irritated, I shoved the letters back in the drawer and slammed it shut.

I pulled out the final drawer on that side of the desk. I was surprised to discover countless photograph clippings from what I assumed was some local paper near Dunstrafne Castle in Argyll. I scoured the paper extracts for a date but failed to find any. I picked up other clippings from some country magazine. Again, the dates were missing. I came across photographs of their Highland wedding set in the grounds of the castle. Surprised, I leafed through the adoring clippings of the bride and groom with a bagpiper standing on ceremony in the background. There were even photograph clippings in various rooms inside the castle. Again, I couldn't find any reference to a date.

What about your wedding day?

But I couldn't remember it. I had a feeling it would have been a low-key affair with just the two of us, without a professional photographer or guests. I didn't have the captivating beauty of Isabella Langdon worth parading to all and sundry.

Perhaps that's why there are no photos of the two of you on your wedding day.

Again, I was struck with jealousy as I stared at them so happily together, oblivious to what the future held for them. I stared at her symmetrical face, so perfect, so rare. She was truly beautiful and mesmerising. What happened for it all to have fallen apart? For James Buchanan Langdon to have left her for me?

Or did she leave him? Is that what happened? And if so, where is she now?

I turned and looked up at her portrait above the marble mantelpiece. But she gave me a half-knowing smile, keeping whatever secrets she held to herself.

'What are you hiding?' I mumbled.

I looked back down at the clippings. It was disconcerting staring at my husband's public social life with another woman. But she wasn't just 'another woman', she was his first wife. The one before me whom I knew nothing about. It was evident that they had both loved being at the centre of local affairs. There were newspaper articles about the official opening of the castle gardens to the public throughout the summer months. I noted the large hunting parties, photographed with the castle behind them, ready to embark on a day of shooting. There were even a couple of post-hunting celebratory shots of Isabella and James, standing proudly with their unloaded shotguns, holding seven or so wild red grouse between them, flushed out, I imagined, by a line of beaters and hunting dogs, flying up and over into the waiting line of their guns. In all the photographs, a middle-aged manservant, whom I assumed was my husband's gillie, stood in attendance to his laird. I stared at this man, wondering where he was now.

I flicked through more country-style magazine clippings on Laird James Buchanan Langdon and his new wife, and again, I spotted his gillie in the background waiting on him. The glossy pictures were of them riding together. I stared at Isabella Langdon confidently sitting astride a headstrong chestnut horse which gave the impression it was chomping at the bit to take off. She looked exquisite in her gleaming leather riding boots, beige jodhpurs, tweed jacket and black riding hat, seemingly unperturbed by her horse's marish impatience. The sickening reality hit me that she was everything I wasn't. Not only was she beautiful, she was accom-

plished in ways I never would or could be. It was a life I didn't relate
to. Nor did I recognise the confident, athletic man in the
photographs, riding alongside her, with a whip resting across his
thigh on an equally restless black horse. The man who would later
become my husband.

I expected that there would be stables located somewhere on
the property. I hadn't seen or heard anyone else in the castle or on
the grounds, which led me to believe that, aside from Mrs Taylor,
no one else worked here, including stable hands. But where was
the middle-aged gillie pictured in the photographs, standing dutifully behind my husband, or even an estate manager who worked
the 5,000-acre estate? But if they were here, wouldn't I have seen
them and vice versa? Again, it added to my suspicion that my
husband and his housekeeper didn't want anyone to know I
existed.

Or is he embarrassed of you? Ashamed of what you have become?

I thought of the other wife. I suspected that Isabella would have
been a competent rider and perhaps eventer and, as such, would
have owned horses while residing here. Again, I felt a wave of
nausea in the pit of my stomach at how suited she had been to
country living, unlike me.

It was transparent that Isabella Langdon and my husband
shared the same passions, evidenced by the newspaper and magazine articles about them and their active country lifestyle.

*What do you have in common with him? Laird James Buchanan
Langdon?*

He had a life here with her before me at Dunstrafne Castle. But
this wasn't our home. Our home was in London. This place
belonged to his past life with his first love, Isabella Langdon. In
contrast, I ached for the noise and excitement of the city where
people were everywhere, at any time of the day or night, unlike
here, where all I had for company were the ghosts of centuries

gone. The stillness and the silence offered me no solace, just the discomfort of barely existing, waiting for it all to end.

I imagined it must have pained my husband to come back with the memories of his life here with his other wife.

Is that why there are aching gaps on the walls in the hallways and dining hall where paintings once hung? Were they of Isabella Langdon, removed because they were a reminder of what he had lost?

But why bring you here?

It made no sense. Unless, as Mrs Taylor had said, it was to recuperate.

Or is he hiding you away? Why return to London and leave you here? In a place you abhor with only his housekeeper for company.

I noticed that the wind had retreated as if something had threatened it away. I shivered, feeling a sense of disquiet descend at the sudden stillness. Something felt wrong.

Come on! You need to find that key!

I pulled out the narrow middle drawer and fumbled around. I was about to close the drawer when I caught a glimpse of what looked like a small notebook wedged at the back. I fumbled around until I eventually yanked it free. I studied the intricate water-coloured wildflowers that decorated the handmade cover. 'Isabella Langdon' was delicately written across the middle. The writing was beautiful, with sweeping, delicate curves. I thought of my crude, individual block childlike letters on the whiteboard.

Oh God...

Something escaped from between the pages. I watched what looked like a black-and-white photograph float to the floor. I let go of the book, dropping it on the desk, and bent down to pick up whatever had fallen out. I held the small picture in my right hand as my left hand fluttered like a trapped butterfly, not knowing where to settle. Finally, perhaps instinctively, it came to rest on my queasy stomach.

Oh God...

She was pregnant. His other wife was pregnant...

I felt as if I was going to be violently sick as I held the private clinic's ten-week grainy ultrasound picture of Isabella Langdon's baby. The scan date was over two years back, shortly before our marriage.

I dragged my eyes up from what I was holding and looked at the portrait above the fireplace.

Is this what she wanted you to find?

I held her knowing gaze, searching her face for answers.

What happened to her and her baby?

9

I held the black-and-white image, struggling to make sense of it. I had no idea how much time had passed as, mesmerised, I gazed at the tiny head, body and developing limbs.

How can you know nothing of your husband's past before you married him? How is that even possible?

I now understood why he didn't want me in the west wing for fear of finding this room inexplicably filled with his other wife's clothes, toiletries and...

I faltered as I looked at the ultrasound picture in my hand.

Why would she leave this behind?

I raised my head again to meet her stare.

Where is Isabella Langdon? What happened to her? And what happened to her baby?

I then remembered the book with her name elegantly written across the front. Could that be her diary? And if so, maybe the answers were in there?

I reached for the book, opening it. I was right in my assumption: it was a diary. I could feel my body trembling as I processed the date of the first entry: two years ago. How was that possible?

You have been married to him for two years. Does that mean he was still with her when he was with you?

Terrified, I forced myself to read the opening words:

I'm losing him. I think he's seeing another woman... Someone connected to the ALD Life Charity in London that he's on the board of! And I don't know what to do. After seven years of marriage, he's cheating on me! How could he? I saw the text messages she sent him flash on his phone screen while he was in the shower, proposing catching the Eurostar for two nights in Paris after the ALD Life meeting next week. They were explicit enough for me to know that this wasn't the first time – or the last. How could he do that to me? We have everything here. The perfect life. What more could he want!

I stared open-mouthed at those opening lines. The ink had smudged, suggesting she had been crying when she wrote it. The entry continued on, but the words were swirling in and out of focus. I blinked a couple of times, then rubbed my eyes when that failed, but still, I couldn't read the following sentences. Not that I needed to. The opening line was damning enough.

Why did you read it? What gave you the right to intrude upon another woman's inner thoughts?

But I had looked into the abyss and was horrified when I saw my own dark reflection staring back at me.

Guilt grabbed me by the throat and held me tight.

Are you the other woman? Oh God...

Did you work at that charity? Are you responsible for destroying her marriage?

I couldn't remember. Maybe I was her – the other woman. Had I worked at this charity? Was that how I had met him, her husband? My husband now.

I had no memory of our wedding day, let alone what had brought us together. But here I was, holding his other wife's memories, her life with him, in my hands.

But what had gone wrong between them and with their idyllic life here at Dunstrafne Castle, with a baby on the way, for it to have ended? For him to have had an affair – with me.

My mind went into a tailspin, throwing me back to the ultrasound picture of her ten-week-old baby. She was pregnant. His first wife had been pregnant when he married me.

What did you do? Are you responsible for her misery?

I tried to swallow. Couldn't. I wished I had never found the diary, let alone read the first page. I breathed out, slowly and deliberately, to stop myself going down a dangerous rabbit hole.

Maybe you didn't know about her. About his first wife.

Of course you didn't know. You've only just discovered that she exists.

I thought of my husband, James Buchanan Langdon.

What did HE do? Oh God... What did he do to her?

I flicked through the pages, shocked that only the opening pages had entries. It suddenly abruptly stopped after three days. I scoured every page, but she hadn't written anything else. It was odd.

Three days? Why? Why did she stop?

Then a chilling thought occurred to me. I stopped myself from going there. I didn't want to think that my husband was capable of... But what did I really know about him?

Nothing... All you know is what Mrs Taylor, his housekeeper, has told you and what is written on the whiteboard.

I questioned whether he knew about his first wife's diary. I suspected, perhaps not, as it was at the back of the drawer. And if he did, wouldn't he have destroyed it?

You need to read it.

I can't! I can't read it!

I tried again, but the words refused to stay together, and instead floated off, disjointed in different directions. No matter how hard I willed them, I couldn't fuse them back into some semblance of sense. I wiped at the tears, angry with myself for being so weak.

You're pathetic! You can if you force yourself. You can read those words and find out. Then you'll know what became of her.

READ THEM, YOU COWARD!

But I was too fearful that her fate would become mine. I knew something had happened to her. That somehow, my husband had made her disappear and replaced her with me. And now?

Now he's trying to make you disappear. Just like your predecessor.

I tried to stop the thoughts assailing me. But *she* wouldn't go away. It was as if Isabella Langdon was in my head. I looked up at the portrait and at her with her secretive, all-knowing smile. But I knew she was right. Our husband had silenced her. I didn't know how, but I knew why.

To replace her with you.

And she wanted me to find out what had happened to her. After all, didn't I owe her that, since I had taken her place, and she had suffered the consequences like one of Henry VIII's wives? And now I was next. I was being replaced.

I held the evidence that something had happened to her in my hand: the few ink-blotted pages in her diary and her ultrasound photo. If she had left him, why would it still be here in Dunstrafne Castle? Unless they had separated and she had continued living here while he relocated to London. But where was she now? And why were her possessions still here?

I exhaled shakily, trying to centre myself, not wanting to panic and spiral into free fall. I needed to stay present and not lose myself. I tried to think of somewhere safe to keep me calm. A happy place where I felt protected. There was only one place that could elicit all those feelings of security and well-being. I had felt it first when I visualised the charming Victorian end property in a private lane overlooking a quiet country-style road. Opposite, on the other side of the road, a stone wall with clumps of overgrown vegetation and a thicket of impenetrable trees hiding the glory of Hampstead Heath. I somehow knew, sensed, that this was my home – our house together – in Hampstead with the high-brick-walled, private Victorian rear garden filled with climbing and procumbent roses in all radiant colours. These were the wild roses and the rambling, large garden that I had fallen in love with when we first viewed the property. The rear garden had sold me, and so had the property's proximity to the Heath. I could see *my* home in my mind's eye like some 1960s children's View-Master creating the illusion of three-dimensional scenes of small Kodachrome photographs of my past life.

But I could also feel it: the safety, the reassurance, the peace and, ultimately, the freedom. I belonged there, not here. Now I remembered it, just as Mrs Taylor had promised, I yearned to be back there, able to traverse both worlds with the intimate village feel that Hampstead offered and the vibrant, bustling city life that my husband had isolated me from, believing I needed the tranquillity of his remote ancestral home, so far removed from the bohemian atmosphere I yearned for. To be surrounded by creative types and the rich cultural history of Hampstead and to wander once again around the Freud Museum and the Keats House museum and attend eclectic, exciting performances at the Hampstead Theatre. It was all a far cry from shooting parties, riding and other country pursuits in which my husband and his first wife had so readily and enthusiastically participated.

This remote location in Argyll on some cliff surrounded by 5,000 acres of private land on the west coast of Scotland wasn't my home and never would be. It belonged to Isabella Langdon. The leafy, aspirational, arty place that was Hampstead was my haven. Situated within the borough of Camden, north London, it was perfect in its range of parks and gardens, and in particular, my favourite haunt, Hampstead

Heath, with its ponds, expansive woodland and panoramic views of the city. One of my ideal places to visit was the English Heritage Kenwood House. It was situated on the edge of Hampstead Heath, surrounded by beautiful landscaped gardens and 112 acres of divine parkland. The interior rooms of Kenwood were equally breathtaking, filled with a sought-after art collection with the likes of Rembrandt, Vermeer, Gainsborough, Constable and Turner. I had spent many days wandering the rooms and halls of Kenwood, admiring the paintings and exquisite furnishings. And equally, as many days traversing the gardens of the grand house. Hampstead had everything one could desire, from open-water swimming in the three ponds, more akin to small lakes, surrounded by trees, to the festivals held there, including the Hampstead Summer Festival. Hampstead Jazz Club was one of my treasured hang-outs, which hosted the EFG London Jazz Festival.

An overwhelming feeling of melancholy overcame me as I longed to be back there in our four-bedroom end Victorian property with no intrusive live-in housekeeper watching my every move and forcing me to swallow pills, stripping me of my memory – of my very identity. I wanted to return to my former life, one of freedom and enjoying the thriving and dynamic arts and music scene in Hampstead.

I felt the stinging sensation of burgeoning tears as my body ached for old, familiar comforts while my terrified mind wailed at me to find a way back before it was too late and I became trapped in this place forever with her – Isabella Langdon.

Come on! You need to leave here.

I nodded, unsure whether that was her voice or mine.

I took out my book from the large side pocket of my dress. I placed the baby scan photo in the front of the book for safekeeping and returned it to my pocket.

Why? Why are you keeping it?

I ignored the chastising inner voice. I didn't know why. I just felt compelled to keep it – for now. I could always return it later.

And the diary?

I stared at it, wondering if I should take it. I looked back up at the portrait. There was something about her – Isabella Langdon – that seemed to be imploring me to find out what had happened to her.

Is the secret in those few pages?

Without questioning it, I ripped out the few written pages from the diary and carefully wedged them into my dog-eared old book, so if Mrs Taylor searched my room, which I knew she did, she wouldn't find them. I knew what would happen if I took it to my room: it wouldn't be long before she uncovered it, no matter how well I hid it.

She wouldn't suspect that I would have something hidden within the pages of the book I carried about with me. Nor did I want my husband to realise I had discovered it if he knew of its existence. So, I pushed the diary with the ripped-out pages and the beautifully hand-painted cover to the back of the drawer where I had found it. I didn't feel guilty about defiling it or taking something so personal and intimate as the documented thoughts of another woman. But this wasn't just some other woman; she was my husband's other wife. And something had happened to her. I knew it. Felt it. Every inch of my body screamed that he had done something terrible to her, just as he planned to with me.

Just as he is doing to you now! Holding you here against your will. Drugging you every morning and night with a cocktail of unknown drugs and injecting you intramuscularly with God knows what sedative to silence you. To make you sleep and forget.

Forget what? What is he trying to make you forget?

I hadn't forgotten those words spoken by my husband's housekeeper after he had held me down on the floor and she had injected me with a tranquilliser.

'Are we doing the right thing keeping her here?'

'What other choice is there? Maybe you should be more concerned with how Mrs Langdon reacts when she does remember what happened to her.'

I could recall that moment, but I couldn't remember what had led me to this godforsaken place or the forty-three days I had spent here before waking up on Thursday: Day 44. Now it was Monday: Day 48. Where had I been before then? Hospital, perhaps, if I had a breakdown. But then, I was allegedly under the care of a neurologist for my migraines: Professor Alex Walker.

Why can't you remember what happened to you? And why is your husband so fearful of you finding out?

I slammed the middle drawer shut, angry at my failing mind. I was also frustrated that I hadn't found the door key and remained trapped inside this room. I could feel the anxiety building at being imminently caught here by Mrs Taylor.

The sudden impact of my violent outburst dislodged a small, wooden, intricately hand-carved box, making it fall off the desk. I watched as it bounced on the floor, the lid opening, spilling its contents. A gold-plated vintage cigarette lighter landed heavily next to the box. But the small, shining object that bounced, then rolled off, took me by surprise. Fascinated, I watched as a gold ring escaped across the Persian rug, finally coming to rest in the centre of the floor. I scrambled after it, crouching down to pick it up. It was a wedding ring. I straightened up and spun around to the windows, holding it to the light.

Ohh... No... It can't be...

I turned it this way and that. I was sure I recognised the unique Celtic love-knot pattern encircling the white-gold band. I felt a knot twist and tighten in my stomach as I realised I had seen it before. I walked back to the writing desk and the silver-framed photographs on display. In particular, the evocative black-and-white one of my husband and his new first wife with their hands together showing off what I suspected were custom-made wedding rings. I brought the ring down and held it next to the photograph.

I heard myself gasp. I was holding the smaller and more delicate of the two wedding rings showcased in the photo.

This is her wedding ring.

Again, I deferred to the dominating portrait above the marble fireplace seeking answers from the owner of this piece of jewellery. But she gave none. Not even a hint of what had happened to her and why her wedding ring was hidden away in a box on her writing desk.

I placed it on the tip of my index finger, delicately feeling inside the band. There was an inscription and what felt like a date. I slipped it off my finger and held the ring close to my face, praying I could read the words. Squinting, I managed to make out a name, '*Isabella*', intricately inscribed on the inside, intertwined with '*James*' and the date of their wedding day. It correlated with the diary entry, substantiating they married nine years ago.

Why would she take her wedding ring off and leave it behind?

I found myself placing the ring over my third finger on my left hand. But as I suspected, it was a couple of sizes too large for me. I held my hand in front of me as I appraised the ring. It was beautiful.

A stab of guilt coursed through me that I was standing here admiring her wedding ring. Worse, wearing it.

I looked back to her portrait.

Where is Isabella Langdon, and why is her wedding ring here?

She gave me a knowing smile, as if she was playing with me.

I turned my back to her, bent down and retrieved the small wooden box and the gold-plated lighter. I turned the Cartier gold-plated lighter over, studying the sunray etched design. Then, I noted the inscription.

To my beloved wife, Isabella. Truly yours, J x

I wondered whether she smoked cigarettes or if the Cartier lighter was simply a statement piece. I could imagine her smoking, sultry and mysterious. It was as if I could feel the lighter burning the palm of my hand as jealousy coursed through me.

Why are you jealous of her? She's not a threat to you.

The sudden thought triggered a disquieting feeling.

If she's not a threat, that would mean that she's—

I stopped myself. Perhaps, I was being ridiculous.

I slipped the lighter in my pocket, next to her lipstick.

Should I try to read the final entry of her diary? I didn't want to, but knew I had no choice.

I pulled the captain's chair out and sat down at the desk. I took the book that my mother had given to me as a teenager from my pocket and removed the sparse diary pages. With trembling fingers, I carefully turned the few pages over, quickly reaching the final one. It was dated three days on from the opening entry.

I told James I was pregnant. I was so excited when I surprised him with the ultrasound scan picture, but instead of being happy, he was angry, claiming I shouldn't have made a unilateral deci-sion. That he had explained to me his reservations about having children. He then made an excuse about an urgent business call, promising to talk about it this evening, and left.

What choice did I have? I knew he would never commit to a child. I thought the news would outweigh his fears. But maybe it's an excuse. Maybe this is about this woman from the ALD Life Charity he's been seeing.

I mean, 'it' is our baby! I feel sick – not morning sickness sick.
But an uneasy, bad feeling about tonight. I didn't want him to talk
me out of the pregnancy. What if he doesn't want me any more?
What if he wants a new life with her? What happens to me?

It ended there. The last words she wrote before she...

She what? Disappeared?

Shocked, I let the paper fall from my hand. I could feel Isabella Langdon's beautiful face beaming at me from the silver photograph frame next to me, oblivious.

Are you the woman who her husband was seeing when he was in London?

And what had happened that evening, two years back?

I swallowed, feeling tears burning my eyes as my mind threw me back to the conversation I had overheard between my husband and his housekeeper:

'Perhaps you should accept that your marriage is over.'

'And if I do, what becomes of her? Of my wife?'

'You live your life as if she never existed...'

Is that what happened to you, Isabella?

He remarried – me – and lived his life as if she never existed. But what now? Would what happened to her happen to me? The desperate fear crippling me was athazagoraphobia – the anxiety of being forgotten or replaced. It had already happened to his first wife – Isabella Langdon. I was already fading into oblivion, forgotten about and forgetting about my past life. Would he make me disappear as well?

You already know that answer.

What are you waiting for? You need to get away.

But how? The door is locked... You're trapped in here.

10

I scrabbled for the few sheets of paper with her final thoughts and carefully wedged them in my book, next to the ultrasound photo, replacing it in my pocket. I hid her wedding ring in my other pocket, next to her lipstick and the cigarette lighter. I now needed to go. To leave here – *her* – and find help. *To find a way back home.*

Yet, the inexplicable pull of this room held me there, mesmerised by the expansive freedom beyond the lead-paned windows and the ancient castle walls. The ocean was as grey and churned up as my thoughts. The tense sky, equally unsettled, reflected itself in the dark waters beneath.

You need to leave. Otherwise, you'll be dragged down, never to resurface.

I looked at the rattling windows as the wind picked up again outside as if protesting at my plans to abandon this place. Or was it because I had taken her things? But without her possessions, no one would believe me that the other wife existed.

You need to go... Stop procrastinating. GO!

How? Without a key, how do you get out?

The thought awoke me. Gasping, as if for air, frantic, I stared at the desk, hoping beyond hope I would see the door key hidden amongst the silver-framed photographs, glass paperweights and papers scattered on the desk. It was then I noticed, for the first time, the vintage 1920s black and bronze candlestick phone. Had it always been there? I couldn't remember. Tentatively, I picked up the receiver with a trembling hand, heart pounding at the prospect it was just an ornament. I held my breath as I listened, relieved at hearing the crackling of white noise in the antiquated earpiece.

Thank God. There's a connection... Your mind isn't playing tricks on you.

My mouth was dry, and my breathing erratic as I dialled my mother's landline. I remembered that she still lived in the house I grew up in, which was also a Victorian property in Hampstead near the Heath.

Were you close to her?

Yes... Yes, I think so.

But the memories were now eluding me. It felt as if a fog had infiltrated my mind, preventing me from seeing my past. The clarity I had in what felt like moments ago dissipated into wisps of whitish, ethereal mist.

What is wrong with you? Why can't you remember? WHY?

I swallowed down the anger and frustration, resisting the temptation to scream and swipe everything off the writing desk, railing at the unfairness of it all. To go to the objecting, infuriating windows, throw them wide apart and arise like some mythical burning phoenix unleashing fire on the raging elements outside.

Then, amidst all the fury and fear, I could hear the whisper of something tangible penetrating this remote land. I waited, not daring to breathe as the line clicked and hummed as it reached out to her.

Please connect... Please! Oh God, please!

But it cut to an automated message informing me I had dialled an incorrect number.

NO! Where is she? Where has she gone?

Terrified, I hung up. I had no idea what had happened to my mother. I tried again, hoping that I had misdialled. The line sang its hissing, mournful song before switching to the same cold, automated message informing me I had dialled an incorrect number. I hung up again, not knowing what to do. I sat perfectly still waiting for some memory or knowledge to form to explain to me where my mother had gone. Nothing came apart from hot and salty tears spilling from the corners of my eyes as I sat bewildered and terrified. I needed her more than ever, and yet I couldn't reach her. She was lost to me not only in memories, but in the real world.

Again, I waited for something to come to me. To tell me what to do next. How to get out of this room. I let out an audible gasp when the obvious struck me.

Call the police. YES!

I dialled 999 and waited as the line crackled as it tried to reach out for help.

Please work... Please...

'What's your emergency?' questioned a distant voice.

'I need the police,' I cried.

'And what's your emergency?' repeated the call handler.

'I... I need the police. I'm being held against my will.'

'You're being held against your will?' they questioned.

'Yes... Please, help me. They're drugging me and... And I don't know how long I've been imprisoned here.'

'First, can you tell me your name?'

I then heard the door handle turning. Someone was trying to get in. I spun around to see the brass handle twisting backwards and forwards.

Oh God... It's her.

'I've got to go. Someone's coming. Please?' I hissed. 'Please send the police to Dunstrafne Castle. Did you get that? Dunstrafne Castle!'

Without waiting for a response, I rammed the receiver in place and jumped up from the captain's chair and away from the phone. I darted behind the writing desk towards the windows. Then I saw something glinting on the floor at the side of the desk.

What the...?

I didn't have time to think about how it had ended up there. I bent down, grabbed the brass door key and held it to my chest like some religious icon, attempting to ward off an evil presence as I backed my body against the wide stone windowsill, terrified of whom it was trying to get in. Not that I was ordinarily superstitious. At least, not that I could recall. But I was scared and fear made me desperate.

Then the door did the impossible. It swung wide open.

How? It was locked. Or maybe it had been jammed, and you didn't have the strength to pull it open? Could you have got out all this time?

I stared in horror.

'Mrs Langdon?'

I curled my fingers around the brass key and deftly dropped my hand, sliding it into my pocket, to hide it from Mrs Taylor.

Her black eyes burned into me as her tall, thin grey figure seemed to fill the doorway. I noted her raven-black and silver-flecked hair, typically scraped back into a tight, no-nonsense bun. But her face was different. It was significantly paler than usual, as if in shock.

Is it because you found this room and its contents? Proof of your husband's other wife?

She had forbidden me from entering the west wing. Now here I stood, in Dunstrafne Castle's principal bedroom which – *had* – belonged to Isabella Langdon.

Terrified, I turned and looked out of the windows to the gardens below. A thirty-foot drop to my death – my only escape.

It took her a moment to find her voice.

'What are you doing in here, Mrs Langdon? Remember, I told you Mr Langdon's explicit instructions, that no one is allowed here.'

'I... I...' I struggled to find an explanation of what I was doing.

'You had me worried when I found that you weren't in your room. Didn't you hear me calling for you? I've been searching the castle for you for over ten minutes. The last place I expected to find you was here. Not after I explained to you the west wing is forbidden for your own safety.'

I wondered how long I had been here – the other wife's room. How much time had passed while she had been on the telephone before discovering me missing? It felt much, much longer than ten minutes. It was as if time had stopped, like the grandfather clock in the grand hallway downstairs.

'Please come away from there, Mrs Langdon. Let's get you back to your own room so you can rest. You look exhausted. Why don't I make you some camomile tea to help settle you?' she suggested as she started walking over to me.

But I wasn't listening. All I could hear was the explosive crash of the waves below. I turned, and looked out as if for the first time at the breathtaking view.

It was sublime.

I imagined the wind as it roughly caressed my bare skin. I closed my eyes, breathing in the power of the ocean as she raged at my torment. Again, I could hear the sirens calling from the waves for me to be free with them. I felt alive, as if for the first time.

This could be your escape...

I tried to open the windows.

'Mrs Langdon! Please, don't open those windows.'

I ignored her in my struggle to release the latches.

'Mrs Langdon, no! Step away from the windows! NO!'

Succeeding in freeing them, I threw the windows wide apart, my hands finding security on the ledge outside as I leaned rapturously into the gust of air. The wild wind drove around me, seeking its way into the room, making the heavy, long curtains billow out, surrounding me.

'Mrs Langdon! PLEASE! STOP!' she shouted.

Her panic snapped me back. I opened my eyes, surprised to be greeted with the view of the expansive lawned area below stretching to the small stone wall with the cast-iron gate leading to the stone steps that twisted and turned downwards to the forbidden shore. Not that I could see the beach – strewn with pebbles and rough, ragged rocks – from here, but I knew it awaited me. As did the small white sailing boat moored there.

How do you know that?

I tried to retrieve the elusive memory, but it was so fleeting that all it left was a sense of knowing. A feeling. I could see the ornate cast-iron gate and old, worn steps carved in stone that descended down and down to the beach and ocean in my mind's eye as if I had just walked down there. The wildflowers that sparkled like hidden gems in the wild grass and the smell of the intoxicating salty air as the sea spray kissed my skin. I could hear the herring gulls screeching at one another as they dived into the water. It left me filled with a longing to join them. To open the gate and run down until I reached the water's edge.

I turned and glanced at the portrait behind me of the first Mrs Langdon.

Did she manage to escape? Did she sail away in the little white boat?

Or did he make her disappear just as he's trying to make you fade until all that's left are the brittle bones and scant flesh of the person you were before him?

I spun back to the view of the outside world. I felt giddy as the air whistled through me, as if I no longer existed. I could feel my body yearning for me to let go.

'MRS LANGDON!'

I gasped as Mrs Taylor suddenly grabbed my waist and dragged me backwards away from the lure of the open windows and the beckoning ledge.

'Mrs Langdon! What were you thinking?' she cried, gasping in exertion. 'Oh, my goodness!'

Did I hear a tremor of fear in her voice? Had I scared her? It felt odd, as she was the one who scared me.

My hand caught a vase of freshly cut flowers on the writing bureau as I stumbled backwards in shock.

You nearly fell thirty feet to your death... What were you thinking?

I couldn't tell whether Mrs Taylor had spoken those words or if they were only in my head.

I let Mrs Taylor guide me out from behind the desk as water gushed from the fallen vase across the oxblood leather insert of the writing bureau and down its drawers.

Is she trembling, or is it you?

'Are you all right, Mrs Langdon?' she questioned, unable to hide the tremor in her voice.

'Yes,' I mumbled.

She waited a moment, studying me as if uncertain that I was all right.

'Wait there a moment while I close these windows,' she instructed.

I watched as she hurriedly secured the windows against the wailing gulls first before reaching down and picking up the vase of flowers.

'Why are there fresh flowers in here?' I questioned, finding their presence odd.

'Mr Langdon, I presume,' she answered. 'Stay there while I refill the vase.'

Whatever tremor of fear had slipped into her voice was now gone.

I remained silent.

Not that she noticed.

I watched as she hurried to the door leading to the bathroom.

I heard a gush of water from the tap as she refilled the vase.

'Right, I'll wipe up this water on the floor and then I'll help you back to your room,' she said as she walked back over to the writing bureau carrying the flowers and a hand towel.

I watched as she mopped up the spilt water before placing the vase down.

'What made you come in here?' she asked, looking up at me.

'Jack was locked in here. I came to let him out and then...' I faltered.

Then what?

'The dogs were with me downstairs,' she replied.

'They were up here first, and then they ran away when...' My voice trailed off.

When what? What happened in here?

'Did you touch anything?' she asked, looking around the room for a sign of my unwelcome presence here.

I saw her eyes rest on the antique mirror leaning against the wall by the door. I was unsure whether the sight of the mirror troubled her.

Is she anxious in case you smashed it or because you might have seen your reflection?

I couldn't tell.

She sighed as she turned back to me. 'Let's leave, shall we?'

At that moment, I knew Mrs Taylor would never let me out of

her sight. Nor would she ever forget not to lock me in my bedroom again. I now knew I would never be free of this place.

The police... You called the police. Remember?

Questioning whether I had imagined it, I glanced at the desk. The 1920s candlestick telephone was still where I last recalled it to be. It was real.

Mrs Taylor followed my gaze.

'Did you call someone?' she suddenly questioned.

'My mother,' I replied. 'But I must be misremembering her number as it keeps telling me I've dialled it incorrectly.'

Mrs Taylor nodded, then smiled. 'It will come back to you. It always does.'

You called the police after your mother. Remember?

Or did you imagine making the call? Did you really speak to someone on the outside? And if you did, when will help be arriving? If at all...

11

I was acutely aware that my punishment for transgressing would be to lose my ability to leave my own sparse white bedroom. Locked in, I would be over-medicated and reduced to an incapacitated state where I would lose all sense of time. I would end up aimlessly wandering the annals of my mind, unsure of what was real or imagined.

I felt Mrs Taylor take hold of my arm.

'No!' I cried out, pulling away from her touch.

'Please, Mrs Langdon, I'm just trying to support you,' she explained.

I shook my head, not trusting that she wouldn't hurt me.

'See,' she said, gently placing her hand on my arm. 'I'm only here to help you. Let's leave, shall we? I think we've both had enough excitement for one day.'

'Wait!' I insisted, resisting her. 'The woman in the photographs and the portrait, who is she?'

I watched as Mrs Taylor, perhaps caught off guard by my question, looked over at the large oil painting above the fireplace. She then turned back to me. Whatever she was thinking was lost to me. I couldn't read her expression or the emotion in her black eyes.

But something in that moment as she held my gaze scared me.

What is it? You can't read her face. So, why are you scared?

'I think it's best you ask Mr Langdon,' she suggested.

'Was he married before?' I asked.

She stared at me as if contemplating whether to answer before replying: 'Why do you ask such a thing?'

'Because... I... I...' I shook my head.

'He has only ever been married to you, Mrs Langdon.'

So, if that is true, why do you have all the opening pages of the first Mrs Langdon's diary in your pocket with the ultrasound picture, cigarette lighter and her wedding ring?

'But the woman in the wedding photographs? Mr Langdon has his arms around her. They're both showing off their wedding rings. And she's the same woman in the painting over there!' I insisted, twisting my head to see the portrait.

'Mrs Langdon, please come along,' she said. 'You're overtired.'

'You're hurting me!' I objected as I tried to tear my arm free from her hold.

'I'm being as gentle as possible,' she answered. 'Please, let's just go back to your room.'

'NO! Not until you tell me about her!' I yelled, gesturing with my free arm at the portrait.

'There's nothing to tell,' she replied. 'Now let's leave. Please? You are not supposed to be in here.'

'Isabella Langdon,' I threw at her. 'That's her name! The woman Mr Langdon was married to—'

She cut me off: 'How do you know that name?'

Was she surprised or angry? I couldn't tell.

'I... I just do,' I replied, not wanting to admit that I had rifled through her writing desk and personal effects, discovering her diary in the process.

'I think it's best if you direct that question to Mr Langdon when he returns.'

'Where is he?'

'Remember I told you he flew to London yesterday?'

I vaguely remembered her telling me. 'He's back today though?'

She smiled at me. 'Yes. Yes, you remembered that I said he would be back later this afternoon. Let's go back to your room, shall we? As I said, Mr Langdon will be back later and he'll be able to tell you everything you want to know.'

Everything? Does that include his other wife?

I allowed Mrs Taylor to guide me out of the room. I waited as she closed the door and then locked it with what I assumed was a master key. She then led me through the maze-like corridors of the west wing. I gazed at the portraits as I passed, looking for her – Isabella Langdon. But there was no trace of her amongst my husband's ancestors.

On the way back to my room in the east wing, we passed the impressive centre stone staircase that was painted for posterity as the background of the portrait of Isabella Langdon hanging in her bedroom.

I pulled away from Mrs Taylor, heading for the staircase.

'Mrs Langdon? Where are you going?'

'I just want to look at the paintings in the main hall downstairs.'

I was looking for her: the first wife, Isabella Langdon. I wanted to see whether there were any other portraits of her or if I was right in my suspicion that if there had been, my husband – *her husband* – had them removed, evidenced by the gaping spaces on the walls.

'There'll be plenty of time this evening to admire the paintings.'

'There will be? How?' I questioned.

'Mr Langdon has requested your company this evening. He has

some news he wants to share. So, perhaps a lie-down before you see him will do you some good. As I mentioned, you've had quite a lot of excitement already,' she said, delicately taking me by the arm again.

I didn't have the strength to object. She was right, I was tired.

But a chill coursed through me when I saw my room up ahead. Panic started to build at the fear she was going to lock me inside and that I would never be allowed out again.

Did she lie to you about going downstairs this evening? Was it all a ruse to get you back to your room?

Upon reaching the door, Mrs Taylor pushed it open. I hesitated, not wanting to step into the bare white room, the antithesis of what was once Isabella Langdon's luxurious surroundings. This room was perhaps a fifth of the size of the principal bedroom in the west wing, lacking any of the comforts or decadent trappings. Nor were there any of my personal effects. No photographs, paintings or diaries. Nothing that told me who I was or why I was here. It was as if my identity was stripped bare, and I awoke to find myself placed inside this white box for safekeeping.

Safekeeping from whom?

I stared at the white room and what it represented. It was blank, like my memory. Was that intentional? I thought of the other wife's bedroom. All her belongings were still there as if awaiting her return.

Where are your personal effects? Do you even have any? And why does your husband not share your bed with you if he is your husband?

Then it hit me. Did he sit in their room in the west wing in one of the Queen Anne high-back chairs by the fire roaring in the dark, waiting for her to return, knowing the glow of the fire would lure her back with her deathly cold flesh?

It struck me then that I was cold. I touched my arms. The skin was warm. Not that I sensed it. Was I too dead?

'I'm cold. Is it cold?' I asked.

'I'm sorry?' Mrs Taylor replied as she stepped inside ahead of me.

'I'm cold,' I repeated, standing still.

She turned back to me and nodded. 'Let's get you inside your bedroom and I'll help you put your cardigan on.'

'Where are my shoes?' I asked, remembering I couldn't find any in my room.

'We keep them downstairs. You don't like them in your bedroom.'

'I don't?'

'No, Mrs Langdon. You like everything to be sterile and clean. Remember? You get upset if anything is placed in there. And for some reason only known to you, you prefer to walk around inside barefoot.'

I numbly shook my head. No, I didn't remember. She could tell me anything and claim it was true and that I simply couldn't recall it. I felt as if she was gaslighting me, slowly trying to send me mad.

'Is that why I have nothing in my room? No paintings or photographs?'

She nodded. 'Yes. You find it too confusing. The white calms you, remember?'

'And my clothes. I have no clothes?' I questioned.

'You have clothes, Mrs Langdon. You're wearing clothes, aren't you?'

'Yes, but...' I shook my head. I thought of all of Isabella Langdon's beautiful clothes waiting for her return in her walk-in closet. 'My clothes are—'

'Exactly what you requested. You refuse point-blank to wear anything other than the white summer dress you have on. That's why there are duplicate dresses in your wardrobe. The same with your nightdress. You won't wear any other style or colour.'

'I... I don't remember refusing to wear anything else,' I disagreed, not trusting what she was telling me. It made no sense. Why would I insist on wearing the same colour and style of clothing? It was as if she and my husband wanted me stripped of any individuality.

'If you're no longer content with your clothes, you can have a word with Mr Langdon. I am confident he will do what he can to make sure you're comfortable while you're here.'

'How long am I here for?'

'Oh, I don't know. That is up to your neurologist, Professor Walker, and Mr Langdon.'

I had forgotten about my neurologist.

If they exist.

'When can I talk to this Professor Walker?' I heard myself asking.

'I believe that Mr Langdon arranged a telephone consultation for you while he was away.'

'He did?'

She nodded.

'I'm cold,' I found myself repeating as I stared at the room awaiting my return.

'You're no doubt feeling cold because you're tired from your exertions. Mr Langdon will accuse me of not properly taking care of you while he's been away,' she said, smiling at me. 'Let's get you settled back in bed and then I'll make you that camomile tea.'

'Can I have a hot-water bottle?' I suggested.

'I'm afraid not,' Mrs Taylor replied.

'Why?'

'Because you burned yourself when I gave you a hot-water bottle the last time you complained of being cold.'

'I did? How?' I asked, surprised.

'You took the screw top off and—' She stopped herself. 'That is of no concern now. It's a warm, humid August day, Mrs Langdon. I think we'll be having thunder and lightning later if this continues,' she noted. 'But as for you being cold, bed with a hot cup of camomile tea, followed by a nap will do wonders to restore you.'

'Where does he sleep? My husband? Was that his room that I was in?' I questioned.

I watched her face, studying it for some recognition that what I suspected was true, but her expression was inscrutable as ever. It was as if she wore a mask and no matter what I threw at her, her reaction was always the same – blank.

She shook her head. 'Where Mr Langdon sleeps is none of my business. I am only interested in following his instructions and keeping you out of the west wing because of the storm damage.'

'That's a lie to keep me out of her room. I didn't see any storm damage,' I retaliated.

'I can assure you that there is storm damage in the west wing. Not in the master bedroom, but in a couple of the other rooms.'

I shook my head, not believing a word of what she had said.

'I don't trust you!' I fired back. 'You're lying to me!'

'I am trying my best to keep you safe. Now come along. Please come into your room,' she suggested.

'Safe from who?' I demanded, resisting entering my room.

'From yourself, Mrs Langdon.'

'That's not true. You're lying!' I cried out again.

'Please calm down, Mrs Langdon,' she said.

'I am calm!' I yelled. 'I just want to get out from here. Why won't you just let me go?'

'You're staying here to recuperate. Remember? This is all for your own good. You can leave once you are feeling better.'

'But I want to leave now!' I said, feeling the tears threatening to fall.

'You're exhausted,' she explained. 'Mr Langdon will be back

later. Why don't you lie down for a few hours? Then, when he returns, you can discuss how you are feeling with him.'

I found myself nodding. I was exhausted. And so cold.

I noted her hand on the silver chatelaine attached to the belt around her narrow waist, waiting to use the same key she had used to lock Isabella Langdon's room. I assumed it had to be the master key giving her access to all the rooms in the castle.

The doorbell suddenly chimed: loud and intrusive, echoing throughout the grand hall below.

Mrs Taylor didn't react.

It rang out a second time.

She looked expectantly at me without any acknowledgement that someone was at the main door. But I noted her cheeks begin to colour.

I didn't move.

Forceful banging from below followed.

The police? You called the police... Remember?

'Mrs Langdon, please come into your room.'

For the first time I could remember since meeting her, Dunstrafne Castle's housekeeper looked flustered. I was certain there was an atypical flush to her high-boned cheeks.

'Please?'

'No,' I answered as the banging downstairs intensified.

'Why not just come in and lie down,' she reasoned.

'Because I know you plan to lock me in here with that key in your hand.'

I watched as she glanced down, as if unaware she was now holding it.

'Mrs Langdon, you're tired. Please, come into your room and I will help you get into bed.'

I realised we were at an impasse. It was evident she wasn't going to leave until I had done as she asked.

'Please don't lock me in,' I said, my eyes on the key she still held.

Then the banging suddenly abated, followed by the sound of the heavy main door swinging open.

Footsteps entered below, ricocheting off the main stone-flagged floor and walls in the hallway as multiple voices carried up.

People were here.

The police?

I stared at her. But she didn't react. I could still hear other muted voices, barely discernible now, but they were all the same. It was as if they were being led somewhere.

Can she hear them? Or is she gaslighting you? Trying to make you think you are hearing voices? That you're going insane?

'Why do you lock me in?' I challenged her.

'For your own safety,' she replied.

'Why? What would I do?'

'You might hurt yourself, Mrs Langdon,' she explained.

I shook my head, not believing her. I turned to the bars on the window. 'And the metal bars? Is that why I can't open the window?'

She hesitated for a moment before answering: 'Yes. Remember we have had this conversation before? The bars are there for your own protection. There are some terrible gales here and with the rocks below, it's safer that the bars are there to prevent any further accidents.'

'Accidents...' I murmured. That didn't ring true. 'I tried to escape? Isn't that the truth?'

'No. You tried to take your life, Mrs Langdon,' she replied quietly.

I gasped. 'No! You keep lying to me! Why do you say such heinous things? You're trying to convince me that I am going mad. But I'm not! I would never try to end my life.'

'You're unwell. Remember? We discuss this every morning. It is there on your whiteboard. Look over there,' she suggested.

I did as directed. I glanced over at the jumbled-up black words. My life. But I couldn't make sense of it.

'The whiteboard, Mrs Langdon. All the answers are on the whiteboard. Now why don't you lie down? You look a little pale.'

I nodded. I felt light-headed as if I was going to pass out. I stumbled across the threshold and over to the bed as Mrs Taylor pulled the duvet back for me.

'Shall I help you out of your dress and into a nightdress?'

I shook my head. 'No... No... I'll lie down with it on.'

I didn't want Mrs Taylor to find the other wife's cigarette lighter, red lipstick and the key to her bedroom in the pockets of my dress. Mrs Taylor hadn't noticed my pockets – distracted, I suspected, by the activity downstairs.

I noted again, as she turned her head in the direction of the stairs, her cheeks flushed an even deeper red now.

I climbed into bed while she wasn't looking and quickly pulled the duvet over myself so she didn't get a chance to notice anything bulging in my pockets.

'Your book?' she said, now looking at me.

'My book?' I questioned.

'Yes. It's in your pocket. I imagine it will be uncomfortable.'

I fumbled around and retrieved it. I pulled it out from under the duvet and handed it to her, terrified she would inspect the pages. But she didn't. Without realising it contained Isabella Langdon's diary entries and the ultrasound scan photo, she placed it carefully on the table by the window.

Relieved, I closed my eyes.

'Mrs Langdon?'

I opened them to see her standing over me holding a paper cup and a small glass of water.

How? The paper cup and water, where have they come from?

'No... Not now. Later.'

'Is your head hurting?'

'Yes,' I muttered as I closed my eyes against the strain of the light. I was beginning to feel disorientated again. 'How do you know my head is hurting?'

'You've turned terribly pale, Mrs Langdon. Take this, it will help with the pain and enable you to sleep.'

'Is it safe?' I sceptically questioned.

'Of course. These are two painkillers. Naproxen. One five-hundred and one two-hundred-and-twenty-five-milligram tablet.'

'Didn't I have that this morning?' I sceptically questioned.

'No. Hopefully, this will prevent it from getting any worse.'

'Who prescribed it for me?'

'Professor Walker, Mrs Langdon,' she answered. 'Remember you have asked me this before?'

'And how do you know what to give me and the quantity? How do I know that you won't overdose me?' I demanded.

'Professor Walker gave me careful instructions, Mrs Langdon,' she assured me.

'And why does my husband not administer my medication? Why does he leave it to you?'

His housekeeper...

'Because Mr Langdon trusts me to look after you.'

But you don't trust him. So how can you trust her?

I thought of *The Yellow Wallpaper*, a short story by the late nineteenth-century American writer Charlotte Perkins Gilman. The protagonist's words surprised me by flooding my mind as her plight became mine:

> If a physician of high standing, and one's own husband, assures friends and relatives that there is really nothing the matter with one but temporary nervous depression – a slight hysterical tendency – what is one to do?...

So I take phosphates or phosphites – whichever it is, and tonics, and journeys, and air, and exercise, and am absolutely forbidden to 'work' until I am well again.

How can you recall that passage and yet... and yet you can't remember your life or even yesterday?

'Mrs Langdon? Please?'

She sounded harried. Desperate, I imagined, to get downstairs and see who was there.

I leaned up on my elbows and tipped the contents of the paper cup into my mouth. Mrs Taylor handed me the glass of water and watched me swallow the two tablets.

'Open your mouth, please.'

I did as she asked, acutely aware she didn't trust me after this morning. I assumed she suspected I had somehow managed to avoid taking the diazepam, or Valium, as it was known. Otherwise, how could she explain why I had failed to sleep the morning away as usual?

'Lift your tongue for me.'

I acquiesced, too tired to protest.

'Good. Now rest. I'll be back soon with some sandwiches and camomile tea. We need to build your strength back up. And you'll be hungry after your adventure this morning.'

I lay back down and closed my eyes.

I heard her heels clicking and her keys and other appendages jangling as she hurried out of the room. The door closed, followed by the swift turning of a key.

She's locked you in!

I waited until I heard her footsteps retreating before leaping up. I ran to the bathroom, leaned over the sink and forced my fingers down the back of my throat to bring the medication back up.

In as much as she didn't trust me, I didn't trust her. I had no idea what she had just administered. I made myself gag as I bent over the running tap. Finally, reassured that I had brought both tablets up, I swilled water around in my mouth and spat out the dregs. I watched as the remnants of the tablets disappeared down the drain.

I now needed to hide the items I had taken from Isabella Langdon's room. It was the evidence I needed that proved something had happened to her. That she existed before my husband married me. I knew I would get out of here, and when I did, I would tell the world what he had done. That he had made her disappear, just as he was trying to make me fade into oblivion until there was nothing of me left.

Then I remembered the other voices downstairs. The reason why Mrs Taylor had rushed.

The police. You called the police... Remember?

12

I lay for an eternity staring at the ceiling, which felt as if it was falling onto me, as I repeatedly reminded myself again and again:

The police. You called the police. Remember?

The police... You called the police...

I tried to hold on to the thoughts, but they were too ethereal to grasp: translucent, formless shapes, disappearing from the recesses of my mind, then fleetingly returning to taunt and tease me. It physically hurt to try to hold them, to form something out of nothing. And if I wasn't vigilant, they would vanish forever, and I would be left with a sense of loss, not knowing what it was or who had left me.

The clicking of heels forewarned me of her arrival, followed by the release of a lock and the handle turning. The door gently creaked open.

I pushed myself upright, leaning back against the headboard and turning to face her.

'You promised you wouldn't lock the door!' I childishly accused, unable to hide my agitation.

I had been banging and pounding on the door, followed by cries for help, but no one had come. I had then turned to the window, hoping to see someone and attract their attention by pounding on the glass. I knew people were here. I had heard their voices in the main hall below. But what hope I had dissipated when I looked out at the desolate rocks and pebble-strewn beach beyond. The ocean, inky black in parts, caught my attention as the wind baited it, stirring up the seabed so its waves crashed in fury on the rocks and cliff face below. The dangerously darkening skies were moving ever closer and lower, the approaching air filled with menace.

Mrs Taylor was right, it looked as if a storm might be heading this way.

In the end, I had lain down and waited it out. My headache had miraculously abated despite throwing up the naproxen earlier. I had feared that refusing to allow my body to absorb the medication would lead to a migraine.

'And you promised me you wouldn't go into the west wing,' she replied quietly. 'I only locked the door because I was worried about your safety. Remember you opened the windows in the master bedroom of the west wing? If I hadn't grabbed hold of you, you might have...' She faltered as she looked at me as if unsure of whether to say it. 'You might have fallen,' she concluded.

I looked at her. She was as dispassionate as usual. There was no trace of anger, annoyance or even irritation in her. Her face was blank, her watchful eyes as soulless as ever.

I realised at that moment that I meant nothing to her. I was on the way out, for hadn't she advised my husband to move on? To forget about me and find happiness elsewhere. Her words came back to me:

'You live your life as if she never existed. You try to find happiness again. You have someone else to think about now...'

Who? WHO? Who was that someone else?

'Mrs Langdon? Mrs Langdon? Please focus.'

I stared at her. She wasn't carrying a tray as I expected. Nor had she entered the room. Instead, she was expectantly holding the door open.

'I said, tea and sandwiches have been prepared for you downstairs in the drawing room.'

'The drawing room? Why?' I questioned, confused.

This had never happened before. Or had it?

'Mr Langdon suggested it would be good for you to join him for some afternoon tea.'

'My husband is downstairs?'

'Yes. He caught an earlier flight than expected and traffic was light on the drive back from Glasgow Airport.'

'Who...' I faltered as I tried to remember.

But Mrs Taylor's presence had broken that tenuous thread, which I had held on to so hard, desperate to keep those thoughts from evaporating.

You heard voices. Remember? Yes... Yes, voices. Someone else is here. Who?

'Who else is there?' I asked.

'Mr Langdon is waiting for you,' she said, ignoring my question. 'Hurry now.'

I stood up. I felt for my book in my pocket, but it wasn't there.

'My book?' I asked her. 'You've taken my book. Why?' I demanded as panic turned swiftly to anger.

She looked around the room.

'Your book is on the table where I left it,' she answered, directing my attention to the table and chair in the corner of the room.

I ran over and snatched it, holding it to my chest.

'My mother...' I began as some form of explanation for my irrational behaviour.

But it wasn't that. It was something else. A message hidden deep within the pages of the tatty, dog-eared paperback. Turning my back on Mrs Taylor, I opened the book, searching for what I couldn't remember.

I released a low gasp of surprise. I had forgotten about her – the first wife.

'Isabella...' I muttered to myself as I fingered the few torn diary pages.

I hadn't imagined her. She was real.

'Mrs Langdon? Please, Mr Langdon is waiting for you downstairs.'

'Yes. Yes, of course,' I replied, replacing the book on the table, resisting the urge to keep hold of it.

I was worried that, if I did, Mrs Taylor or my husband might see the diary pages. A page might accidentally fall out, and then they would know I had taken it from his first wife's diary. What little there was of it. It made more sense to leave it in full view on the table until I returned.

Her other items floated back to me.

Her lipstick. The cigarette lighter, her wedding ring and the door key to her bedroom. Where did you hide them?

I glanced at my bed.

I had pushed them under my mattress to the centre of the bed so that when Mrs Taylor changed my bedding, she wouldn't detect them. Every morning, she methodically tucked in the bed sheets, feeling along the edges for any contraband. I had watched enough times to understand what she was doing: the same when she plumped my pillows and lifted my duvet to shake it on the pretext of airing it. I knew she was checking my room for items that didn't belong to me or something that could help me escape.

'As I said, Mr Langdon is waiting,' Mrs Taylor repeated, smiling as she walked across to me. She took me carefully by the arm and gently led me out of the room.

I wondered whether she was fearful of adding to the bruises and scratches on my arms and legs now that I was beginning to remember things, and that was the reason behind her sudden concern when touching me.

She hurt you... Remember? Your bruises. Those cuts... She did that to you.

Mrs Taylor guided me down the stone steps, holding on to my arm as if fearful I would fall.

Or make a run for it.

I attempted to pull away from Mrs Taylor, but she somehow held on to me. 'Careful, Mrs Langdon. These stone steps are dangerous,' she warned.

When we finally reached the main entrance hallway with the columns, I looked back at the majestic, sweeping central staircase, imagining Isabella Langdon gliding down in her exquisite emerald-green ball gown to a hushed audience, all in awe of her.

My eyes then swept across the portraits, tapestries and archaic Celtic weapons adorning the castle's main hall's walls. There was no sign of her – the other wife.

Did you imagine her? Maybe...

Then I remembered her bedroom with her beautiful portrait above the impressive marble fireplace in the west wing and the lead-paned windows opening on to the expansive rolling gardens and the ocean. I thought of her and those few precious pages of the diary she had started. The entries blotted with tears, smudging the elegant writing that had so abruptly ended. And the fragile ten-week-old ultrasound picture. What happened to you, Isabella Langdon?

Are you in some way responsible for her disappearance?

'Please, come along, Mrs Langdon,' the housekeeper urged gently, breaking Isabella Langdon's spell over me.

'No,' I mumbled, standing still. 'I want to look at the portraits.'

'Later. I promise,' she assured me. 'First, let's join Mr Langdon. He's looking forward to seeing you.'

'He is?' I questioned, surprised.

'Of course he is,' she replied. 'Are you feeling all right, Mrs Langdon?'

'No,' I answered, feeling more agitated and out of sorts than usual.

I wondered whether it was because I had spat out the Valium this morning, along with whatever other medication I had thrown up earlier. Perhaps I had become accustomed to being drugged.

I allowed Mrs Taylor to continue holding my arm despite having safely descended the stairs, past the walls lined with hunt trophies and other such past glories as I sought some reassurance that my husband hadn't wiped all trace of Isabella Langdon from the main castle. But there was no evidence that she had ever existed. Aside from the shrine that was her bedroom in the west wing. The area that was strictly forbidden – to me.

I assumed we were heading in the direction of the drawing room, trusting the housekeeper to lead me there. Her step had quickened, as if avoiding the rooms leading off from the main hall-way. I looked longingly at the heavy, solid double oak doors as we passed them.

Your way out...

I held my breath as the memory of what lay beyond them flooded my mind. I could see the carefully tended grounds and the long, snaking, gravelled driveway leading far away from the castle and the ocean. I recalled the high, impenetrable centuries-old walls defensively surrounding the property and the decorative wrought-iron gates with the regal stone stags mounted on the gate columns forever guarding the premises against outsiders. I remembered the tall gates remained locked at all times, keeping not only unwelcome visitors out, but me in.

How will you get through the estate gates once you get out of the castle?

I frowned at the troublesome thought. It was as if I had tried to escape once before and had encountered the gates barring my way and the stone walls too high and treacherous to climb over. The only other access out was by the ocean. But the little white sailing boat moored by the beach was gone. I had run down there once before to the boat, climbing down the winding ancient stone steps at the bottom of the garden where the cliff ended in a sheer drop.

Why was it gone?

How do you know it even existed in the first instance?

I couldn't trust the memory. Perhaps it was just a dream.

I could hear deep voices coming from the room directly ahead, interrupting my thoughts. An explosion of laughter followed, relaxed and carefree from behind the closed door.

'Who is here?' I hissed, turning to Mrs Taylor. 'I don't want to see anyone.'

'It's only Mr Langdon and—' Her quiet voice was cut off as the door facing us swung open, releasing a sudden blast of warmth.

It took me by surprise.

My husband followed. When he saw me, his face broke into a broad smile.

I looked behind him, not at the strangers but at the forbidden room. It was his room. I was never allowed in there. When he wasn't in London, he would spend his days ignoring me, pretending I didn't exist, hiding himself and his conscience away in there as if he couldn't bear to look at me.

How I coveted the beautiful hardbacks – their rich, deep-coloured spines standing to attention, waiting for inspection – that filled the polished bookcases which lined the walls in there. I wanted to venture in and run my fingers delicately over the books, choosing one at random to flick through, then another. But it was his library. It was where he would retreat to sit alone with the dogs in the evening. Sometimes, I would hear him on the phone; his voice would be low and meditative.

But to whom? The future Mrs Langdon perhaps...

I wondered what else he kept hidden away in there from prying eyes – my eyes.

A portrait of her? His other wife, Isabella Langdon. Does he keep photographs of her on his desk so he can stare at her beauty and compare her to you and all that he has lost?

Is that why he won't let you go in there?

'There you are, darling,' he greeted, still smiling. 'I was just explaining,' he said, looking over his shoulder at the two men following him out of the library, 'that migraines have plagued you recently, and you were lying down. You still look a little peaky to me. But at least Mrs Taylor was able to rouse you and help you down the stairs.'

Baffled, I looked at him, but his comment was directed to Mrs Taylor.

His smile had slipped.

Does he know what she does to you? Does he?

But I had a feeling that he knew perfectly well how she treated me.

I couldn't tell whether he was concerned or not as, when he turned back to me, he smiled again. 'Perhaps some early afternoon tea and a walk along the beach will do you the world of good, eh? The boys would love your company for their afternoon walk.'

'Where are they? The boys?' I asked, trying to remember their names again.

Henry? And... And Jack. Yes, the boys. Your boys.

A sudden rush of happiness filled me at the thought of the two red fox Labrador brothers.

'In the library, lying by the fire. You know you can't move them when there's a fire burning. There's a decided nip to the air, so I decided to light it as I need to do some admin work later.'

'In August?' I questioned, taken aback. 'Why would you do that? Fires are for winter. Not summer. It is summer, isn't it? Or are you trying to gaslight me again? Make me think it's winter. You're trying to mess with my head again. Aren't you?'

He looked at me, then turned briefly to his companions as if confirming something they had discussed prior to meeting me.

He's patronising you! He's insinuating that you are ill. You're not ill... He is making you ill. He and his housekeeper are drugging you. Remember?

'Don't do that! Don't speak about me!' I hissed at him.

He turned back to me and smiled. 'As I said, there's an unseasonal chill to the air. Remember how damp it gets here in the summer months with all the rain? A fire in the library stops the books getting damaged.'

'No... No, I don't remember...' I mumbled.

'My wife has trouble remembering sometimes. These... These migraines of hers are a terrible affliction and can make her confused,' he explained, turning to his guests.

Why was he acting as if he was ashamed of me? Embarrassed by me.

Maybe he is...

I thought of my aggressively short, androgynous dark hair and my emaciated, child-like body wasting away under my long, floating white dress. Perhaps I wasn't what he desired in a wife. Then there was his other wife – the beautiful, desirable Isabella Langdon.

Did she even exist or is she a figment of your imagination?

I could feel the panic rising as the world I had somehow managed to hold on to was disappearing – fast.

I turned to Mrs Taylor, confused. 'When I said I was cold, you said it was August and hot. You even looked out of the window and suggested a storm was coming because it was so hot.'

Mrs Taylor nodded. 'Yes, it is August, Mrs Langdon. The end of August. And I do believe a storm is coming as the weather is oppressive.'

But I noted the way she looked at my husband and the two men standing behind him as if implying I was losing my grip on reality.

Are you? How could you have lost a month? Is that even possible?

I distractedly pinched at my arm as I tried to make sense of what was happening here – to me.

You have lost more than a month. You have lost forty-eight days of your life here... forty-eight days as a prisoner.

Oh God... What is happening to you?

But I understood exactly what was happening. They were gaslighting me. Trying to make me think I was going insane to justify locking me up here.

But how can you lose days, weeks, months and have no recollection of that time passing?

But I knew how. I was being drugged to forget. Everything was starting to become clearer now I was resisting the medication. My husband and his housekeeper were slowly but surely eradicating every fragment of my mind until, eventually, I wouldn't exist any more.

Just like her – his other wife. The one you aren't supposed to find out about.

* * *

I shivered. My body felt cold. Again. It was as if the coldness was radiating from my very core.

Are you dead? Like her? Like the other wife?

I pushed the irrational thought away. I had no evidence that she was dead. All I had were some tear-stained torn pages from a diary.

And the ten-week-old ultrasound scan photo...

I shivered again as ice-cold guilt ebbed through my veins.

'Am I dead?' I heard myself ask.

I looked down at the stone floor, feeling the chill of a draught slipping seamlessly around my feet and ankles. Maybe my husband was right, and there was a nip to the air despite it being late August. I realised I was still barefoot and wearing a simple linen summer dress. It was no surprise I couldn't get warm. I wouldn't be shocked if Mrs Taylor hid my shoes and other clothes to make me think I was losing my grip on reality. For surely, I possessed more than those few identical white linen summer dresses. I was also certain she jumbled up the days on the whiteboard, making them disappear along with weeks and months. That, combined with a toxic combination of mind-blurring drugs, would pull anyone to the edge of madness.

'Darling? Why would you say that?' my husband asked.

I watched as he looked to Mrs Taylor when I failed to answer him.

'News?' I mumbled as I remembered Mrs Taylor telling me he had news he wanted to share when he returned from London. 'What news do you have to tell me?'

That one word – news – elicited a sense of dread in me. I was acutely aware I had no sense of agency, no control over my life. I had no news, as I had no voice. Whatever words I spoke were discredited. My husband had complete power over my body and my mind. I was no longer an autonomous being. I drifted, pulled one way and another, from one day to a week, without any control of my destiny or my journey.

'Later, darling,' he said, smiling.

I stared at him. Why was he smiling?

To convince you or them – the two men with him – that he is the loving husband?

But I didn't trust his smile. It felt disingenuous. I realised his words weren't for my benefit, they were to impress his companions. I looked at them scrutinising us – my husband and me.

Why are they here?

I heard him clear his throat as he turned to his companions behind him. 'This is my wife, as you know, Mrs Langdon. Of course, you've met Mrs Taylor, who looks after her,' he introduced, nodding at his housekeeper.

He then looked back at me.

Did he look anxious? I couldn't tell.

'Darling, this is Officer Ross and his colleague, Officer Ritchie.'

The two men stepped out of his shadow, standing on either side of him. They were of equal height and stature to him, tall, muscle-bound and intimidating. I watched as he looked to either one as if to make sure they believed his act.

I felt Mrs Taylor's presence so close to me, I could feel the tension radiating from her skin.

'Mrs Langdon,' Officer Ross, the taller and more senior of the two men, said. 'Your husband told us that you're still having some issues regarding your health.'

Still?

'What? What have they told you? What has he told you?' I asked, trying to keep my voice level.

I waited as Officer Ross shifted his attention to my husband as if unsure of how to respond. He then looked back at me. 'That you're still not well.'

Still? What does he mean by that?

'You're real police officers?' I sceptically questioned, despite their powerful physiques, enforced by their police hats, bulky black uniforms and hi-vis vests with their police radios attached.

'Yes, Mrs Langdon. Officer Ritchie and I are with the Argyll and West Dunbartonshire division. We've been here—'

I cut him off. 'I rang for you!'

'Yes. That's why we're here, to follow up on your call,' he assured me.

I looked from him to his younger colleague, who couldn't bring himself to look at me.

Why? Why can't he look at you?

What did your husband and his housekeeper tell him about you? What terrible misinformation did they seduce him with?

'Why didn't you talk to me first?' I demanded, my voice louder than I intended. 'Aren't you meant to take nine-nine-nine calls seriously?'

'Of course. That is why we are here. But you weren't up to seeing us when we first arrived. So Mr Langdon updated us with—'

'I was locked in my bedroom!' I exclaimed.

'As I was about to say,' Officer Ross continued, 'Mr Langdon explained to us that he visited your neurologist when he was in London, and he's booked an appointment for you to return to London for another evaluation.'

I turned to him – my husband.

'Is that true?' Could this be the news he was going to share with me?

He nodded. 'Yes.'

'When?' I demanded, trying to still my agitation.

Whispers of freedom filled my mind. Hope... I had hope... A word so fragile, once lost to me. I had the elusive promise of getting out of here. To be able to talk to a doctor about what was wrong with me – if anything. And to discuss the drugs my husband and his housekeeper insisted I take, allegedly prescribed by this neurologist. But was this Professor Alex Walker really my clinician? Did they even exist, or was it all fabrication? A means of duping me into taking whatever mind-numbing drugs they were administering.

You haven't talked to a Professor Alex Walker. So, how do you know they even exist?

'Well, I have to call Alex in the next day or so. I said I would discuss this with you first before finalising returning to London—' my husband began.

'I can go back to London and...' I said, cutting him off, unable to contain my excitement. I then faltered, not quite certain of what would happen next. But at least I would be away from this hellish place and her – Mrs Taylor.

Hope soared through me again, promising an end to all this confusion and profound misery. I would be back home. A place I knew, remembered, where I felt secure and safe. And my mother...

Where is she?

I suppressed the doubts. There had to be a logical explanation why I couldn't reach her. There could be something wrong with her phone line, or perhaps I had misremembered a digit. I knew, felt it deep inside me, that she would be there waiting for me to return.

'If that's what you want,' he said.

'You know it's what I want!' I fired back. 'When? Now? I want to leave now!'

'No, darling. I need to make some arrangements. It's not that straightforward. But I promise you, if that's what you want, we'll return to London. And you can meet with your neurologist, and we can decide what happens from there.'

As I stared at him, the hope that I was leaving this place dissipated. I couldn't find any assurance on his face or in his deep dark brown eyes that he was telling the truth. It was as if he were saying this to appease the police. It was all lies. Once the police officers left me with him and his housekeeper, I knew I was going nowhere. If they called by again to check up on me, and I had disappeared, he would remind them of this conversation. That I wanted to return to London and he had obliged my wishes. They wouldn't think to investigate my disappearance, trusting his word. Not mine, of course, as I was certain he had made me out to be irrational and unreliable. Not that he would have mentioned the cocktail of drugs he and his housekeeper forced me to take. Consequently, I existed in a half-conscious state, in a shadowy, unnavigable world, neither living nor dead, just existing, clinging from one terrifying moment to the next, not knowing what was real or not.

'Right, now that's settled and everything seems fine, we'll be leaving,' Officer Ross concluded.

'NO!' I cried out, panicking, fearing recrimination for calling them out here. 'You can't leave me here with them. I'm not safe. They're trying to kill me!'

'Darling? Seriously? Did you hear anything of what I have just said?'

I looked at him. His hurt tone may have sounded convincing, but his expression was blank. Gone was the smile and any discernible hint of emotion. Again, he was acting the role of a loving husband for the police. How could they believe his act? Was it his title as laird of Dunstrafne Castle, and his ownership of 5,000 acres of land and who knew what else in these parts? Did his power extend to the local police?

For why would they believe him and not you? Why?

'Why don't we let these good officers go and do some actual policing? I think we've wasted enough of their invaluable time. Don't you agree? And we can discuss arrangements for returning to London later.'

'No!' I fired back. 'Don't make out that you care about me! It's all lies! LIES!'

Frantic, I turned to the officers. I didn't want my husband dismissing them with the assurance everything was fine, that his wife was simply unhinged. He had apologised for wasting police time on my behalf. But there was an actual crime happening here right in front of them. However, I could see from their disinterested expressions and body language that they didn't see it. Or perhaps, didn't want to see it.

'Didn't you hear me banging on the door and screaming for you?' I challenged them, my voice again rising higher than I wished. 'And whatever they've said to you is a lie. There's nothing wrong with me,' I insisted, blurting my words out fast and furious, terrified that I wouldn't get this opportunity again.

If they leave you here, then your husband and his housekeeper will never let you leave that room. Not until you're finally—

I stopped the terrifying thought.

I didn't understand why the police couldn't see something was very wrong here. Surely, they were trained for such situations. It was evident I was being kept here against my will. I had said as much to them. So why weren't they listening to me?

I could feel my flushed cheeks burning, my body flicking from freezing to an uncontrollable raging furnace. I wiped my sweating palms on my dress as I tried to ignore my accelerated heart rate. But I had every right to be fearful. This was my chance to get out. To escape from this place. To be free of my husband and his house-keeper before what happened to his first wife became my fate.

I needed to keep things simple and not get erratic or confused. Crucially, I needed to appear controlled. Otherwise, the police would leave me here with them. I could already tell that the younger officer, Ritchie, had formed some speculative opinion about me. Instead of looking at me, trying to appraise the situation, he distracted himself with the surrounding walls adorned with past triumphs and ancestors long buried. It was evident he believed whatever spurious tales my husband and his housekeeper had told him and his colleague.

I looked directly at him. Realising I was staring at him, he caught my eye, then immediately dropped his gaze as if to inspect his immaculate black boots.

'Why don't you look at me?' I questioned. 'WHY?'

His older colleague gave a short cough.

I shifted my challenging gaze to the senior police officer, who appeared to be in his mid-forties.

'I rang nine-nine-nine for help, so why have you spent this time talking to...' I faltered, not wanting to say the word 'husband'. 'Them! Why didn't you come upstairs and let me out? Isn't that what you're supposed to do?'

'Mrs Langdon,' he began, squaring his shoulders as he spoke, as if anticipating trouble, 'we requested to see you when we arrived; your husband said you were asleep. But he did send Mrs Taylor to wake you and bring you down so we could talk to you.'

'I wasn't!' I argued. 'I was awake! He was lying to you! And she lied to me!' I said, turning on Mrs Taylor. 'She didn't tell me you were here. She said that I was to come downstairs for afternoon tea. Not that the police were here. If you hadn't come out of the library when you did, you would have missed me. How is that policing? How is that safeguarding me?' I raged at him.

'Mrs Langdon, please calm—'

'NO!' I yelled. 'I won't calm down. I want to get out of here. NOW!'

I stepped back as my husband and the two officers made advances to surround me.

'Keep away from me!' I hissed. 'Don't touch me!' I warned Mrs Taylor without looking at her.

I was watching the two officers, feeling whatever chance I had of escape disappearing. It was evident that they didn't believe me.

Officer Ross turned to my husband. 'What do you want us to do?'

'I want you to help me! ME! I am the victim! Why are you asking him what he wants you to do? I called you! Ask me what I want! Not him! ME!'

Officer Ross looked back at me. 'I know you did, Mrs Langdon. And we came to make sure you're safe. Just as we have done the three other times you have called the police out to Dunstrafne Castle.'

'What?' I spluttered. 'No! NO! I only called the police this morning. I... I...' My voice broke off as I scratched and tore at my memory for some truth to his statement. But there was nothing there.

How could you have called them when you have been kept drugged and locked up? How? It isn't possible...

13

'You're lying to me,' I whispered as I stared at Officer Ross's intimidating figure. 'Why are you lying to me? You're meant to protect me.'

I felt as if I was losing my mind. I was frantically trying to think of a way to convince him that my life was in jeopardy.

It was evident that my husband knew how to handle the police and deflect any suspicion that something might actually be wrong.

'If I have called the police here so many times, doesn't that suggest to you that something is very wrong? That I am in danger and desperate to get away from...' I furtively glanced at my husband and his housekeeper. 'Them!'

Officer Ross nodded. 'I understand this is a challenging time for you, Mrs Langdon.'

Challenging?

I stared at him, struggling to understand why he wasn't taking me seriously.

'But, I'm afraid there is nothing else we can do if your husband doesn't see the need to have you...' He paused, as if deliberating his choice of words. 'To escalate the situation and have you removed for your own safety and that of others.'

'What? Me a threat to them? I'm the one who is in—'

My husband abruptly cut in: 'I can assure you that my wife is no threat to Mrs Taylor or myself. As I explained earlier, my wife is under the medical care of Professor Walker who agreed, albeit reluctantly, to her recuperation here at Dunstrafne Castle. But I concede that perhaps we need to re-evaluate the best course of action, which isn't, can I add, moving her somewhere strange at this time. It would be hugely detrimental to her ongoing recovery. By all means, ask Mrs Taylor for her opinion on the matter. She has spent the past two years with my wife and understands her needs better than anyone.'

Two years? You've only been here for forty-eight days... Or so Mrs Taylor claimed. So how can his housekeeper have known you for two years?

Confused, I shook my head. 'No... I haven't been here for two years,' I interjected.

'No... No you haven't, darling,' he replied, smiling at me.

Why is he patronising you? And lying to you... to the police?

He ran his hand through his thick, curly black hair, suggesting he was uneasy. Not that I could tell from his expression.

He turned his attention back to his housekeeper. 'You agree that it would be detrimental to Mrs Langdon's recovery to have her...' He paused, unable to continue. Instead, he lowered his head.

His performance was very convincing. I looked at the two officers, who seemed persuaded that leaving me here under his care was in my best interest.

No... God, no... You need to tell them about... About whom?

Voiceless, I watched on, unable to remember whom I needed to tell the police about. But I found their presence too overwhelming, my husband too distracting, making it difficult for me to think.

'I concur with Mr Langdon. Professor Walker, her neurologist, has been appraised of the ongoing situation with Mrs Langdon, and she will be returning to London. As Mr Langdon stated when you first arrived, it has become more and more evident to me that Mrs Langdon isn't coping as well as we would have hoped. And dare I say it,' Mrs Taylor said, looking at my husband for affirmation, 'I feel that things are starting to escalate exponentially. Whether Professor Walker needs to review her medication, I can't say, but the current situation isn't sustainable.'

I stared on in horror, not believing what I was hearing – or seeing.

The two officers seemed to be convinced by their act.

'I'm sorry, Mr Langdon,' she added as my husband raised his head to meet her eyes. 'I think it needed to be said.'

He didn't reply.

I looked up at him, startled that he could let her talk about me in this way. He dropped his gaze from mine, unable to look at me.

I realised that Mrs Taylor finding me in the west wing this morning had made my situation here untenable. Had my discovery of Isabella Langdon's room expedited my demise? I knew something terrible had happened to her. Whether they realised that I knew was immaterial, as I doubted they would take a risk where I was concerned. If he had murdered his first wife, how far would he go to silence me? Again, the conversation I had overheard on Saturday evening came to mind, in particular the housekeeper's advice regarding my husband accepting that his marriage was over:

'And if I do, what becomes of her? Of my wife?'

'You live your life as if she never existed...'

The housekeeper's words hit me like poisonous darts. I could feel her venom coursing through my veins.

'I... I... need to sit down,' I said, suddenly feeling light-headed.

Mrs Taylor quickly put her arm around my waist to support me.

'Perhaps let Mrs Langdon rest on the sofa in the library for a moment. As soon as you gentlemen leave, we'll carry Mrs Langdon back to bed. I'm afraid it's all been too much for her.'

'I'm not sure it's such a good idea to bring Mrs Langdon into the library. Let me carry her upstairs to her bedroom now,' my husband suggested.

'No!' I protested weakly. 'Please, not my room. Please? The library. Let me sit for a minute...'

I watched as the two police officers waited for my husband's response.

'Of course, darling,' he conceded.

But I could hear the reluctance in his voice. I knew he didn't want me in his library and that he had lied to the police when he had said I could spend the afternoon in there with him. It was all lies. He had no intention of spending the afternoon with me languishing on the sofa with our dogs while he worked. I would be locked in my room, perhaps forced to take some sedative while, between them, they decided my fate for transgressing. Surely, Mrs Taylor had told him that I hadn't slept this morning and instead had disobeyed her and gone into the west wing where I entered their bedroom – my husband's and his first wife's.

He stepped back, out of the way, as Mrs Taylor supported me into the library.

She guided me over to the tan Chesterfield leather four-seater sofa. I lay down and watched as she took a cream-coloured mohair throw and gently laid it across me.

'Thank you,' I mumbled, as I gazed at the open fire, fascinated as it hissed and spat at my intrusion.

'Shall I get you some water and maybe something sweet to bring your blood sugar levels back up?' Mrs Taylor asked.

'Please,' I answered.

Then I remembered it was all an act for the police.

'Lie there and rest. I'll be back shortly.'

I didn't follow her figure as she passed between my husband and the two officers. Instead, I smiled weakly at Henry and Jack, who lazily whacked their tails on the rug as they lay outstretched in front of the hearth, too comfortable to make more of a welcome.

My eyes drifted to above the grey and white marble fireplace. There was an obvious spot where a large painting would have hung. The wallpaper around the space had been bleached by the sunlight, whereas the area protected by what had once hung there was much truer to its original colour.

Shocked, I turned to the doorway to see him – my husband – watching me, his eyes narrowed. Waiting. He was waiting for a reaction from me.

'Where is she?' I asked him.

I wanted him to say it. To admit to it in front of the two police officers.

He didn't answer me.

'Please? Tell me. What have you done with her? Tell me! I know you've hidden all her portraits!' I cried out. 'The painting that was on the wall above the fireplace, where is it? Where have you hidden it?' I demanded.

'Darling, no one has hidden anything. That painting has been taken away to be restored. It will be back soon enough,' he answered, smiling. 'It's good that you remembered there was a painting there.'

'No... you've hidden it, just like you've hidden her. Where is she?'

'Where is who, darling?' he asked.

'Her! What have you done to her?' I accused.

He shook his head. 'I have no idea who you're talking about. I do agree with Mrs Taylor. I think your nerves are overwrought. This whole experience has been too much for you,' he concluded, turning his attention back to the two officers.

Something passed between my husband and the older police officer.

His authoritative voice dispelled any suspicion I might have sown with my desperate words. I knew my tone verged on the edge of hysteria. I could hear myself, and my frenzied words seemed delusional – even to me.

His answer was calm, controlled and unmistakably paternalistic: the antithesis of my state, endorsing the belief that my words were worthless.

'I think it's self-evident that my wife is being suitably cared for,' he stated to the officers. 'As I said earlier, I apologise for wasting your time. Now is there anything else you would like to know before you leave?'

I knew he wanted to get them off the premises before I said something to make them question the situation further rather than taking it at face value. For I knew my appearance bore no authority, and I understood my voice and words lacked subtlety and cognisance, instead portraying me as emotional and erratic. My mind cruelly threw up *Studies on Hysteria* by Sigmund Freud and Josef Breuer, published in 1895. I found myself questioning whether my husband had suggested to the attending police officers that I was suffering from this nineteenth-century malaise or malady.

'Can I suggest that perhaps you restrict Mrs Langdon's use of the phone? Obviously, we have to attend when it's a nine-nine-nine call, but we haven't got the resources to keep coming out when it's a non-emergency situation.'

I watched on, not believing that he – *they* – were acting as if I didn't exist.

'Of course, and you have my guarantee that this won't happen again,' my husband assured them. 'I will be disconnecting all the phones aside from this one here in the library, and I'll be keeping this door locked from now on.'

'That sounds like a good idea,' agreed Officer Ross. 'Perhaps keep a better eye on her.'

My husband laughed abruptly. 'Yes, easier said than done.'

'I'm sure,' Officer Ross sympathised.

I stared at them in disbelief. I was right here listening to their conversation about me.

'You have to forgive me for the state of the grounds and castle. Discharging most of the staff seemed a good idea at the time,' my husband explained, looking at the French doors leading out to the grounds, again running his hand through his hair as if agitated. 'I didn't want anyone here to distract or confuse her. But...' He faltered, shook his head.

I thought of his gillie whom I had seen in the countless photographs, standing in the background behind his laird – my husband.

Where is his gillie now? And does he even know about you? Or what happened to his other wife in the photographs?

It crossed my mind that he had discharged most of his staff, including his loyal manservant, because he was ashamed of me, embarrassed to admit that I was his wife. Was I the woman he had an affair with in London? The one he brought back to Dunstrafne Castle to replace his first wife – the beautiful, elegant Isabella Langdon.

My husband turned and briefly looked back at me as if reading my mind.

The younger officer followed his gaze. He caught my eye and quickly turned away.

'Is she going to be all right?' asked Officer Ritchie of my husband.

'Yes, she'll be fine. She won't remember any of this, anyway,' my husband confided. 'And she'll be gone in a few days.'

'You say, you're taking her to London, back to...' Officer Ross faltered.

'Hampstead Heath. We have our property there and her mother's house, of course. Perhaps it would have been better to have stayed in London when I had her discharged from hospital after what happened. It's just, I thought she would love it here. That the fresh air, mountains and the ocean would help with her recuperation. But I couldn't have been more wrong. Hindsight and all that?'

'Yes, I read the report. A colleague of mine attended the scene,' Officer Ross sympathised.

'Shh!' hushed my husband.

I could hear the annoyance in his voice.

'I'm sorry, I didn't realise that she didn't know.'

'She doesn't remember,' my husband explained. 'Better that way,' he suggested.

Panic ensnared me.

What don't you remember? And why is it better you don't remember? Better for whom?

But I did remember. I remembered the night they had drugged me when I fed Henry and Jack pieces of the fillet steak that I couldn't bring myself to eat. The same night they had injected me with a sedative that stole a day from me. How many days, weeks had I passed here in a drug-induced stupor?

I also remembered my husband questioning that same evening, in a moment of clarity, whether he was doing the right thing by keeping me here at Dunstrafne Castle. It was Mrs Taylor his housekeeper's response that had chilled me, and since I had heard those words, the cold had stayed with me, refusing to let the warmth in again.

'*What other choice is there? Maybe you should be more concerned with how Mrs Langdon reacts when she does remember what happened to her.'*

I stared at the aching space on the chimney breast above the mantelpiece.

Why can't you remember what happened to you?

I used the heel of my hand to swipe at the tears slipping down my cheeks.

'Please? Please don't leave me, here. I'm scared...'

The older officer looked back at me. 'Mrs Langdon? Did you say something?'

'Take me with you...' I mumbled. 'He'll kill me... Just like he killed her. His other wife. The one in the painting,' I said, raising my hand and pointing at the blank, screaming space above the marble mantelpiece.

'Darling? Really?' I heard him question.

'You did! You know you did! Tell them! Tell them what you did to her! You killed her! He killed his wife. Ask him. ASK HIM!' I yelled at them.

I waited, expecting the two officers to do something. Anything. Instead, they turned away from me, as if they hadn't heard me. Or didn't want to hear me.

'Get away!' I screamed at my husband as he approached. 'NO! Don't touch me!' I yelled at him as knelt down in front of me.

'Darling, shh...' he said, his voice low and deceptively soothing. 'You'll scare the boys. Jack and Henry. Look,' he suggested. 'Look at the boys. Why don't you stroke them? That will help calm you—'

'You're lying to them,' I spat, cutting him off. 'Pretending that you love me and you don't. I know you don't and I know what you plan to do to me. You're going to kill me, aren't you? Is that what you did to her? The other wife? Did you kill her? DID YOU?'

I watched as he recoiled from my words. He then sighed. 'Darling, I don't have another wife. There's only you. I should never have brought you here. I should have listened to Alex,' he said, standing up.

Exhausted, I collapsed back against the couch. More hot tears slipped down my face at the realisation it was all pointless. He would never admit what he had done to his other wife. I closed my eyes, unable to look at him any longer or at them – the two police officers damning me to my death.

'Yes, you lie back and close your eyes. It's no surprise you're exhausted, my darling,' he said.

I felt him bend over and kiss my forehead. His lips felt cold on my skin as they lingered there, in an attempt to convince the officers that I was in safe hands.

But that couldn't have been further from the truth. His hands and the hands of his housekeeper were responsible for the bruises and cuts covering my body.

Why haven't the police seen that? Why?

'My wife's overtired,' I heard Laird James Buchanan Langdon explain as he walked back over to the police officers. 'She's not used to seeing people. It distresses her, which is why she's...' He faltered, shot me a glance, then turned back to them. 'After what happened, well, it makes her more emotionally unstable. Let me see you out,' he insisted, seemingly eager to put some distance between them and me.

In case they realise there is more going on here than they understand.

'Shouldn't we wait until Mrs Taylor returns? Shouldn't someone stay with Mrs Langdon?' Officer Ritchie asked.

'No,' I heard my husband say as he guided them out of the library. 'She'll be fine. She can't go anywhere. All the doors leading out to the grounds are permanently locked.'

'Locked?' repeated the younger officer. Either his colleague or my husband must have shot him a look as he added, 'Of course, I should have realised. For her own protection.'

'After the last time, I have no choice but to keep the doors locked. She managed to get out on to the grounds, but I was too late to stop her.'

Stop you? Stop you from what?

'She managed to outrun me across the lawn to the steps that lead down to the rocks. And before I had chance to reach her, she...' His voice cracked and broke off.

I wished I could see his face to tell whether he was lying.

And you what? What was it you were supposed to have done? Tried to escape? Wasn't that obvious? Doesn't that alert the police to the fact that they're keeping you here against your will?

There was an inexplicable feeling buried so deep within the very bones of my body, and in the darkest recesses of my mind, that my husband had done something terrible to me.

What did he do to you? Is that why he drugs you, to prevent you from ever remembering?

Then I recalled that Freud proposed that when the patient failed to confront the memory of trauma because it was too much for them to bear, the detrimental consequences could result in the trauma being 'converted' into physical symptoms. Why couldn't I remember what had happened to me?

Could your memory loss be a symptom of some unspoken, forgotten trauma?

Something he did to you?

I realised at that moment that my life was in danger: that I wasn't catastrophising my situation. How far would he go to stop me from remembering?

Would he do to me what he had done to his other wife and make me disappear? I realised he had already forewarned the police that I would be gone in a few days.

Your disappearance is a certainty. The question is, how long do you have left?

14

I opened my eyes and looked over at the library doorway. No one was there. I listened for hushed, secretive voices. But they had disappeared.

The police officers had left me to my fate.

Oh God... How? How could they leave you here?

But my husband and his housekeeper had persuaded the police that I was safe. He would be assuring them at this moment, as they climbed into their police car, that I wouldn't be bothering them again. And, of course, I wouldn't because he was going to make sure that I had no means of calling anyone – ever.

You broke his rules and entered the west wing discovering that he had another wife. And then you rang the police... What do you think he will do to you now?

He'll kill you...

I could feel the panic suffocating me. I didn't know what to do. If the police didn't believe me, what chance did I have? What could I do?

You need to get out! NOW!

It was the only answer. I had no idea what my husband and Mrs

Taylor would do to me. What punishment awaited me for ringing the police and telling them my truth – that my life was in jeopardy. That my husband had killed his other wife. But, instead of taking me to safety, they had abandoned me in this ancestral castle flanked on one side by the north Atlantic Ocean and on the other by 5,000 acres of forests and mountains.

If you do get out, where will you go? You'll either drown in the ocean or die of hypothermia on this ancient Buchanan land. There's no one for miles upon miles. Remember?

So, where will you run? And who will help you now? Who will believe you if the police don't?

Then a dark thought paralysed me.

Whoever finds you will only bring you back here to him – your husband. You have no rights, no autonomy. What more empirical evidence do you need? The police came, and they did nothing. They left you – with him.

I felt a swarm of hornets explode in my stomach, buzzing and darting in all directions trying to escape. I gasped out as they stung me, vicious and spiteful.

I closed my eyes against the pain, shallowly breathing in and out.

Isn't it better to take the medication? Rather than be aware of this excruciating existence.

I suddenly desired to lose all concept of days, months and years. To disappear in the cracks between the polished wooden floorboards, falling down and down into unconscious oblivion. In that moment, I wished I had a handful of Valium pills that I could swallow back to drown out the stinging hornets hurtling in panic inside me, desperate to find a way out.

But there's no escape...

My husband had convinced the police that I was perfectly safe here. That whatever was happening was all in my head. My words were empty to them and fell around me like scorched ash. My world had imploded and I had no understanding of how to navigate it, nor how to survive it. For I was certain that I didn't have long left to figure out my escape. My husband had already foretold my disappearance, as had Mrs Taylor. They had, together, convinced the police that I was a liability to myself and that they would be taking care of me – of the problem. That I would be leaving Dunstrafne Castle to return to some neurologist in London that I had never seen or heard of before until recently.

But I knew it was all a lie. There was no neurologist. No clinic in London.

You are going to die here! Just like her – the other wife. You need to go! Now while you have the opportunity... Run!

I pulled the mohair throw off my legs and stood up. I felt dizzy from the sudden movement. All my body wanted to do was betray me by lying back down and drifting off to sleep in front of the fire, never to awaken. The temptation tormented me, cajoling and pleading with me. I wished to be at peace for once and all and free of the chaos and terror that resided within me. And, crucially, to be rid of the people who elicited that fear within me. Again, the welcoming thought of taking a handful of Valium pills returned to me to silence everything: the colours, the noise, the confusion that led to the fear that relentlessly held me in its ice-cold grip.

I felt something warm and wet and looked down to see Henry nuzzling my hand.

'Hey, boy,' I whispered, bending down to kiss his head. 'At least you believe me, don't you? You know that what they're doing to me is wrong. The question is, how do I get away from them? Eh?'

He licked my face and then jumped up on the sofa, seeking out the heat from where I had lain down.

'You keep it warm for me,' I said as I caressed him under the chin.

He whined at me, expecting me to lie down with him. A memory, elusive and delicate, told me that Henry would lie with me on that sofa while I idled my hours away in the foreign, exotic lands hidden in the bound pages adorning the bookcases.

Was it real, or have you imagined it, longingly wishing it to be so?

'I know... I know... But, I can't stay with you, Henry. I need to go. You've got Jack with you,' I reassured him.

I crouched down and stroked Jack, whose tail thudded in delight at my touch.

I leaned over and kissed him on the head as I murmured: 'Look after your brother, Henry, for me. Promise?' I gave him a final hug before straightening up, swiping at the tears that were now freely falling.

I couldn't silence the desperate feeling that I might never see them again.

I forced myself to step away. I needed to leave and I knew I couldn't take them with me.

Turning, the beautiful, custom-made wooden polished book-cases that lined the oak-panelled walls took my breath away as if I were seeing them for the first time. Wooden ladders were attached to one of the bookcases to allow access to the higher shelves. I walked across the expansive antique rug to the bookcase that filled the wall opposite, and stared in wonder at the spines facing me, letting my fingers trail over them. If only I had time to stay and explore the worlds hidden beneath their pages, but I knew that either my husband or Mrs Taylor would return soon.

I headed over to my husband's desk. It was covered in paper-work and files. I questioned whether there was anything in those papers about me. Curious, I picked up a file. But I realised I was wasting time. I needed to go while I still could. I dropped it, and as I did so, I mumbled, 'Isabella...'

She does exist... You didn't imagine her. You're not losing your mind...

There was a photograph of my husband and his first wife on his desk next to the phone. It was a striking black-and-white intimate headshot of them kissing one another. I gazed at it, struck by the intensity of the lovers' feelings for one another.

For some reason it elicited a twisted knot of jealousy. I wanted to be her, the woman that my husband held so passionately, his large, protective hands cupping her blushing cheeks as he pulled her into him, kissing her full red lips.

But I wasn't her and never would be. I resisted the urge to hurl the antique silver frame with the offensive photograph into the crackling fire to silence her cackling voice in my head – Isabella Langdon's voice. It felt like she was goading me for not being as beautiful or as articulate as her.

I suspected Officers Ross and Ritchie would have taken her seriously. They would never have dismissed her fears as those of a hysterical woman who, according to her husband, was mentally fragile.

Unlike you, Isabella Langdon had a voice. She had presence. She had possession of her mind. She was everything you are not. And yet, he still made her disappear.

I placed the photo frame face down, unable to look at her – at them.

I didn't understand how she could cause me so much pain, but she did.

I looked at the black cordless phone in the handset. It was why I had walked over to the desk. I contemplated calling for help but accepted it was futile. The police would never respond to another 999 call from me. My husband had made certain of that.

I glanced over at the double French doors leading out to the lawn. I then recalled that he had reassured the police that all the external doors were locked. But I could see the key in the lock.

You need to get out. RUN!

I ran over to the doors and turned the key. It clicked, releasing the lock.

Why would he have left the key there?

Then I remembered that he hadn't expected me to be in the library. That Mrs Taylor and the police's presence had forced his hand. Otherwise, I wouldn't have been allowed in here, his sanctuary. The key would still be in the lock because the boys were with him, and he must have let them out to relieve themselves while talking to the police. He would never have thought to slip the key in his pocket for safekeeping, as it would never have crossed his mind that I would enter the library. Or be left unattended in here.

I released the doors and breathed in the salty, cool air as it swept over my skin from the north Atlantic Ocean. The intensity of the noise of the waves crashing and tumbling against the unseen rocks took me by surprise. I hesitated, unsure of what I should do next.

You run! That's what you do! You run for your life!

I let out an audible gasp of shock at the thought as it brought me to my senses.

I stepped outside, luxuriating in the feel of freedom under the soles of my bare feet. I turned and fastened the doors closed behind me so the dogs didn't follow.

Now run! RUN!

I ran, sprinting towards the call of the ocean and the promise of escape. I instinctively knew there was an old wrought-iron gate at the bottom of the expansive lawn and garden, hidden from view by hardy bushes, wild roses and gnarled trees, twisted and bent like hunched-over ancient men, guarding the way.

RUN!

The thought coursed through my veins, hot and as desperate as my panting breath. I had barely moved for I didn't know how long, and my body struggled to keep up with my mind. But I continued, pushing through the burning in my lungs and the white explosion of pain in my side.

Then I felt the ground meet me as I lost my footing and tumbled forward. I lay sprawled out for a moment, unsure of what had happened, my face lying against the cool, damp grass as my blood roared in my ears and my mind screamed at my limbs to move, to get up and run. It screeched at me to head for the rusted gate and the centuries-old, worn stone steps carved out by my husband's Celtic ancestors.

But I couldn't move. My eyes caught sight of the oppressive mountains and the dense forests beyond the walled grounds.

Should you run for the trees?

I stared at the high stone wall. It was impossible. I wouldn't be able to climb it. Nor did I have time to follow the boundary around the estate, hoping for a gap in the stonework. And then, where would I go once I was beyond this prison? The forests and mountains would soon turn on me, their offer of liberation becoming my death sentence.

But I knew I would rather be free to decide my fate at the mercy of nature.

My only choice was to get up and head for the steps leading down to the beach. But I knew what would happen if I followed my instinct to find the old gate with the stones and the sheer cliff drop. I knew because it had happened before. My memory was like a palimpsest: a piece of rewritten vellum parchment with the original text still imperceptibly there underneath. I could feel the text, the bumps and grooves of old words, and past, forgotten times. It came to me in flashes, barely visible, playing back at me like bleached-out photograph stills with superimposed images over the original content.

Then it hit me, one terrifying moment, followed by another, as I lay there, breathless and in shock. When I had run from him – my husband – before, he had chased me along this lawned area towards the bushes and trees. Then beyond them to the gate, which I had forced open, and the stone steps I had run down, faster and faster, until I had reached the treacherous rocks below. I had leapt from one to another, sidestepping the predatory lapping water, not feeling any pain as the rocks cut into the soles of my feet.

With nowhere else to go, I had been cornered on a rock. I had heard him screaming at me, raging at my escape. Mrs Taylor was shouting my name from the top of the perilous stone steps when she saw me below, stranded with no place to run.

Did she think you were going to jump? Or was she warning you?

But before I knew what was happening, I had felt him behind me, grabbing hold of me, before pushing me, releasing my body into the cold, anticipating water. It had filled my nostrils, ears and my mouth as I gasped in shock and horror. The world had faded into grey as my body submerged beneath the white, frothing waves that snatched me under, tumbling and flaying as they claimed me as theirs, taking me back out with them.

How did you get out? How did you survive?

I didn't know. All I knew was that he had tried to drown me.

Kill you... He tried to kill you. You can't swim. Remember? He knew you couldn't swim...

I recalled his conversation with the police officers. I now understood what he had been referring to. But he had lied to them, implying I had tried to kill myself:

'After the last time, I have no choice but to keep the doors locked... She managed to outrun me across the lawn to the steps that lead down to the rocks. And before I had chance to reach her, she...'

But he had reached me...

And he pushed me.

Is this what you have forgotten?

15

Gasping for air, as if still submerged under the waves, I somehow pulled myself up from the ground. I could hear the housekeeper's frantic cries.

She knows you're missing!

'Mrs Langdon? MRS LANGDON?'

Stumbling forward, I continued. But instead of running for the gate and steps that led down the cliff face, I veered off around the castle, unsure of where I was going. But I expected my husband and Mrs Taylor would search the rocks and beach below, suspecting I would escape down there just as I had once before.

Panting, I ran on, hearing frantic shouts behind me. Flattening my body up against the castle wall, I peeked out to see the figure of my husband sprinting across the lawn in the direction of the gate leading down to the rocks and pebble-strewn beach, followed by Mrs Taylor.

I had no clue of where to go. All I knew was that I had to hide. Perhaps if I eluded them for long enough, they would assume I had leapt to my freedom from the treacherous rocks. I ran on, ignoring the gravel cutting into the soles of my feet. I reached one door, tried it, but it was locked. I ventured on, hoping that I would find refuge somewhere else.

The wind carried their frenzied shouts, assuring me I was getting further and further away from them. My mind was in free fall, spinning one way, then another, screaming at me that I should get as far away from the castle as possible. It screeched at me about the irony of seeking sanctuary in the very place that had imprisoned me for so long.

How long? How long have you been held captive here?

Is it only forty-eight days? Or is it months? Years even? He said his housekeeper had been looking after you for two years to the police...

You need to get as far away from here as physically possible.

I couldn't exit the locked gates or climb the boundary wall securing the estate's grounds. Nor was there a boat moored down by the beach. Not any more. I didn't know how I knew it was gone. I just had an imperceptible feeling. I suspected that my husband feared I would attempt to use it to escape. Or had he moved it to somewhere safe because of an impending storm? Or a past storm, perhaps. For I somehow understood that this isolated place, exposed to the elements, was subject to raging tempests.

I abruptly stopped running and stared at the decrepit house of glass ahead of me.

Do you recognise it?

It was as if it was calling out to me.

I headed towards what, in its heyday, would have been an imposing Victorian conservatory. I imagined it had once been a splendid addition to the fourteenth-century castle. But its glory was in the past. It was now overgrown with ivy and other such rampant, clinging vegetation, suggesting it had been abandoned and left to ruin for some time. The once-white paintwork, now an aged, curdled cream colour, had flaked off, exposing centuries-old, sun-bleached, blistered wood. Panes of glass had cracked under the constant beating from the driving gales off the Atlantic Ocean. Some were missing, letting the torrential rain inside, suggesting it had been ravaged by a recent storm.

A sudden melancholy came over me as I stared at the ruins. Whoever had once lovingly replaced the shattered glass panes, gouged out the rotting wood and repaired it, stripped and reapplied fresh paint, no longer existed. That person would have repaired the storm damage before it wrecked further havoc inside and returned the conservatory to its former glory.

Who was that person?

I couldn't recall. I reached out to the elusive memory, trying to scratch beneath the palimpsest of the surface for the hidden truth. But I couldn't quite uncover it.

I walked over to the double glass-paned doors and tried them, expecting them to be locked. I was surprised when they opened, creaking as they did so. I hesitated for a moment, unsure. I expected to be overwhelmed with the smell of decay and death as I took in the wilted potted plants and trees that had shrivelled up and died over time. But whatever had rotted, lingering in the air, was long gone. I was surprised that so many others had survived, fortunate to be in reach of the rain that fell through the missing panes in the glass roof and drove through the cracked glass walls.

Or had someone tended to them? Perhaps... But whom?

I took in the expansive space, surprised by the countless sheets of paper covered in drawings that lay everywhere as if a tornado had found its way in, whipping the artwork up and then scattering it about. I stared around me, questioning what had happened. Could a recent storm have broken through the panes of glass or blown the doors open, causing this disarray?

When was that storm? Thursday?

I remembered awakening that morning on Day 44, or so the whiteboard said. I had looked out upon a grey, bleak world of driving rain, winds and furious waves pounding the jagged rocks below my new prison.

It took me a moment to come back to the present and see beyond the potted plants and trees to the countless canvases and wooden paint-easel stands stacked carefully against the furthest, driest wall where the rain couldn't reach, leading me to assume it had once doubled as an art studio. I looked up at the pitched glass ceiling and the mute grey light streaming through. It would have been perfect as an artist's workroom.

I then saw a door against the back wall leading into the main castle. I stepped inside the conservatory, closing the double doors behind me. I assumed my husband and his housekeeper would eventually search the parameters of the castle grounds once they realised I hadn't sought refuge down on the beach. They would reach the same conclusion as me and try the conservatory, finding, as I had, the doors unlocked.

I crossed the path of shrivelled leaves disintegrating beneath my bare feet, sidestepping the shards of glass from the broken panes to reach the door. It struck me that I wasn't the first person to walk inside here recently. Someone had dragged the many canvases and wooden easels out of reach of the ruinous rain.

Your husband?

I tried the door to inside the castle, twisted and turned it, but it wouldn't move. I recalled my husband assuring the police officers I couldn't escape as he had locked all the doors leading outside. And, ironically, now I couldn't get inside after defying the odds and finding a way out.

Oh God... What now? There's nowhere left to run...

I could feel my chest tightening as panic engulfed me like flames, suffocating me.

Blinding me.

I didn't know where I could go to elude them. I knew, between them, they would hunt me down, until finally they had me cornered like some animal.

I tugged at the door one last time. There was no question that it was locked.

I gasped for air, trying but failing to expand my lungs. Terror had me in its sinewy grip. My body had fallen prey to fight or flight. But I could do neither and, instead, was paralysed by the knowledge it was over.

I dug my hands in my pockets, searching for my beloved book to comfort me. I knew from experience that touching it would soothe my tumultuous mind and body and silence the voices screaming at me to do something.

Anything! Don't just stand there. RUN!

But I couldn't run. The realisation that I didn't have it on me froze me to the spot. I had left my book in the bedroom.

Oh God... Why? Why would you do that? You always have it with you.

I suddenly knew why I hadn't brought it.

Her. My husband's first wife's torn-out diary pages and the ultrasound scan photo were hidden within the pages of my book. I had left it in my room for fear I would lose all that was left of her. The evidence that she had existed before my time here would be gone – forever.

I could feel the tears wanting to fall. But the voices in my head taunted at me for my pathetic indulgence.

RUN! You need to run!

I stepped back from the locked door, accepting my fate. I needed to leave here. It didn't matter where, I just needed to put as much distance between me and my captors.

Then I saw her. Isabella Langdon staring straight at me next to the locked door.

Oh God...

I stumbled backwards.

It took me a moment to understand that she wasn't real. But the image was so lifelike, so realistic, that my brain had to play catch-up.

It was a portrait of her which had been dragged to safety from the devastation that had swept in here, not her ghost haunting me. Following me everywhere. Her eyes observing me, waiting for me to remember.

Remember what?

I stared at her.

Remember what?

I trembled; a cold chill caressed my skin as I heard her whisper to me.

Remember what your husband – her husband – wants so desperately for you to forget.

I spun around, expecting to see someone hiding in between the tall remnants of plants and trees – her – but I was very much alone.

I turned back and noticed another oil painting. Another portrait of her – the other wife. It too was stacked against the wall, away from the ravages of the storm damage. A large potted cheese plant sought refuge next to it. The large green leaves hanging down, over the canvas – over her – as if she were hiding.

Who from?

You...

I broke her spell and turned away to look around me. I imagined it would have been idyllic here, once filled with exotic life and promise as leaves and vines intertwined. I noted the long wooden tables covered in paints and brushes still soaking in turpentine with potted plants interspersed between them. There was what looked similar to a wooden filing cabinet with large drawers, which I imagined stored further art paraphernalia such as bottles of linseed oil and turpentine, charcoals, pencils and tubes of paints. I scrutinised the conservatory expecting to see someone skulking in between the tall plants and trees – her – but I was still very much alone.

There was an old white Belfast sink with a drainer. I walked over to it, noting that someone had left a cup in the sink. The dregs left in the bottom had long since solidified, the black mass seemingly moulded to the porcelain. I picked the delicate white cup up. There were still traces of red lipstick around the rim.

I recognised the colour: the lipstick. The cup must have belonged to her – Isabella Langdon. She had left it here. It was suddenly scalding hot against my fingers as if filled with boiling black coffee. It slipped through my hand, falling into the bone-dry sink. Helpless, I watched as it shattered into tiny pieces.

Oh God... What have you done?

I panicked as I looked around, expecting someone to see my folly. But no one was there, apart from her – Isabella Langdon. The stunning, contemporary painting of her, partially obscured by the cheese plant, seemed to taunt me. That knot of jealousy returned, twisting ever tighter in my stomach as I questioned whether my husband had painted this portrait of her.

Had he?

The knot tightened at the realisation he had never painted me and that there were no portraits of me or photographs of us together. Instead, he kept a black-and-white image of his other wife on his desk. So when he shut himself off, it was to sit and stare at her, at what he had lost.

I looked back at the portrait of his other wife by the door, taunting me with her brazen, boundless beauty. Her high cheek-bones, the dark, luxurious eyelashes that framed her deep, sensuous brown eyes. Her thick spirals of blonde curls fell across her young face, down her shoulders, proudly showing off her sun-kissed, olive-coloured flesh.

I could feel the bile of hatred rising in my throat for what I lacked, bitterly combined with a covetous desire for all she possessed as I longed to be her.

Sickened, I turned away, noticing the velvet Victorian chaise longue. Had she lain on it to pose for him? Then I noticed something behind it, something hidden rested against a large potted tree. I forced myself to step slowly, avoiding any shards of glass lying on the ground, towards the large grey blanket covering what I presumed was an unfinished canvas. Why was it hidden?

Don't look... Don't! DON'T!

I snatched the blanket off and staggered back.

Why did you look?

It was a large gold-framed mirror. I choked back a strangled sob as I stared in horror at the figure looking back at me. It took me a moment to recognise myself from the reflection I had seen in the antique mirror in her bedroom.

It's no surprise Officer Ritchie couldn't stop staring at you.

Look at you. LOOK AT YOU!

But I couldn't look at myself and acknowledge what had become of me. I hated my reflection as much as I hated her image. Driven by disgust and jealousy, I ran over to the nearest wooden table and picked up a plant pot and hurled it at the mirror.

I breathed out, relieved as the glass shattered, distorting my reflection. I then scrambled on the floor for a large piece of broken glass. I turned and saw her – Isabella Langdon – laughing at me from the canvas, dragged to safety against the wall by... by whom?

Your husband... Of course, your husband wanted to save her portrait. To keep her beauty preserved for perpetuity.

Before I knew what I was doing, I ran at her and began slashing at her evocative, sublime beauty until all that was left were unrecognisable shards of cloth. Exhausted, I reached for the blanket that had covered the mirror and sought refuge in an antique rattan Emmanuelle peacock chair obscured by plants and low-hanging ivy and Virginia creeper vines. I collapsed on the worn seat. I pulled my knees up, covered my trembling body with the blanket and watched the conservatory doors, waiting. I looked down at my hand, still holding the jagged piece of shattered mirror.

It's over...

No more running.

16

Startled, my eyes shot open. I realised I must have drifted off. I thought I had heard something. The click of a lock turning. Or had I been dreaming of the promise of emancipation?

The light had dissipated to a shadowy gunmetal grey, all colour and warmth gone. I struggled to remember where I had fallen asleep. Then I saw her ghostly face watching me from one of the many canvases – the other wife.

A memory came back, vengeful and seductive.

Is she sad you destroyed her portrait?

A pang of guilt ebbed through me at the thought I had slashed the painting in a frenzied attack.

What else did you destroy in your jealous rage?

I looked across at the antique gold-framed mirror, the oxidised glass shattered and lying treacherously across the floor.

Why did you break it?

But I knew why. I remembered the lifeless figure reflected in the mirror, a spectre not of this world. I knew I had no choice but to destroy it. I couldn't bear to look upon myself any longer. Not when

I had been reminded so cruelly by the paintings and drawings of my husband's first wife that I could never be her.

I heard a low groan. Then silence. I looked up to see the door between the conservatory and the castle interior was open. Light bled through from the castle hallway, accentuating the lurking shadows surrounding me, empowered by the approaching night.

A few moments or so later: 'Mrs Langdon?'

The voice was delicate, nervous even.

I turned my head and found the housekeeper standing in the open doorway, light streaming from the hallway behind her.

'We've been looking all over for you,' she said.

I was surprised that her tone was of concerned relief, not annoyance.

However, her expression was as inscrutable as ever, and her long grey clothes and tightly scraped black and silver-flecked hair twisted in a knot behind her head, accentuating her skeletal features, remained unchanged.

But there was something different about her. Her voice?

Fear? There was a sliver of fear beneath the relief.

Why? Have the police returned? Did they suspect that all wasn't as it seemed?

I stared at her, and waited.

'Mrs Langdon?' she repeated, her voice barely above a whisper.

I didn't answer her. I was too tired to talk.

'What have you done? Oh… Mrs Langdon…'

I expected her to be staring at the shattered mirror and the shredded canvas. But instead, she didn't take her eyes off me.

I watched as she moved back out into the hallway, then disappeared.

'Mr Langdon?'

Silence.

'Mr Langdon?' I heard her repeat. 'MR LANGDON?' This time with more urgency. 'Come quick. I've found her. She's inside. In the conservatory.'

Fearing leaving me alone for so long, she returned sooner than I anticipated. Her face was flushed; I expected she had jogged back from the library after calling out to my husband from the French doors. They had been my escape route out on to the grounds, where I assumed he was still searching for me.

'How do you feel, Mrs Langdon?' she asked as she now stepped into the room, her black Oxford shoes scrunching the debris of the past beneath her feet as she approached.

I didn't answer her.

'I think it might be best if you come with me and I'll help get you into bed,' she said as she neared me. 'I'm sure you could do with something hot to drink and eat to warm you up.'

I realised I was still holding the piece of broken glass. I could feel my fingers tightly wrapped around it.

Why? What do you plan to do?

I didn't know any more.

My eyelids now felt too heavy to keep open. I struggled but failed to stop them from closing. Today's exertions had exhausted me. Or were those days? Had one day merged into multiple days, perhaps? I had no idea as I had little concept of time. The whiteboard functioned as my hippocampus, a pragmatic means of storing my long-term memories, offering me a trail of events and timelines. However, it was a questionable version that I didn't trust. I was acutely aware that something was blocking my brain's pathways from firing correctly. I suspected the drugs Mrs Taylor forcibly gave me were preventing these neuron transmitters from connecting. By destroying this connection between my short- and long-term memory, I was reliant on my husband and his housekeeper for crucial details lost to me about my past – my life – which ultimately meant they could tell me whatever narrative benefited them.

Why?

Because he – your husband – doesn't want you to remember...

I gasped as the oppressive feeling of being held down under water engulfed me again. Terror restrained me as I was held captive by the emotion triggered by the memory of my husband pushing me off the rock face and into the turbulent and treacherous north Atlantic waters.

How can you remember this event and nothing else?

For some inexplicable reason, I knew the answer. I didn't know how or why. I just did. Perhaps someone explained this to me once or repeatedly. However, I understood that the traumatic event of my husband pushing me into the waiting waves triggered a powerful emotion, and emotions played a crucial role in storing memory and recall. The stronger the emotions connected to the memory, the easier the recollection of that event.

'Mrs Langdon?'

I forced my eyes open. Mrs Taylor was bending over me.

'Let me see your—'

Before she could finish, she was cut off.

'Oh my God, darling! Have you been hiding here all this time? Do you know how worried I've been?'

I turned to see the tall figure of my husband blocking the light from the hallway, his face cast in gloomy shadow.

I watched as Mrs Taylor turned to him. She shook her head.

I couldn't tell whether he reacted or not, his expression hidden.

'What? What's wrong?' he questioned.

I heard a tremor in his voice that I didn't recognise.

Then he looked around, as if for the first time. Then at me.

'What have you done?' he murmured as he took in the devastation. 'Why? Why would you do that?'

I looked across at the portrait I had savagely cut up, unable to have her taunt me with her beauty any more. Then, the mirror I had smashed. Shattering the distorted image of myself, the one I struggled to reconcile with.

I tried to speak, but my mouth was too parched to form any words.

I turned away, unable to bear him staring at me in that way.

'Stay!' he ordered the dogs who had faithfully followed him.

I watched as he entered the conservatory. Pieces of the broken mirror crunched under his walking boots as he strode towards us. I noticed he was wearing his navy Barbour jacket and assumed I had been right and he had still been searching the grounds when Mrs Taylor found me.

'Are you hurt?' he asked me. 'Your feet? Have you cut your feet on the pieces of mirror? Christ! It's everywhere!'

I shook my head, surprised at the concern in his voice.

'Let me see,' he said. 'Please?'

'No,' I muttered.

He bent down beside me. 'Let me see,' he again said.

I shook my head again. 'Go away.'

'No. You need to let me see what you've done to yourself,' he insisted.

There was fear in his voice.

Fear of what?

That you now know about her? About his other wife?

'No,' I mumbled, turning away from him.

I found myself twisting my head back around to look at him.

All those canvases and sketches that he had kept locked in here. The majority were contemporary portraits of people I didn't know or care to know, exceptional pieces befitting of a gallery. All that interested me were the portraits of her.

'Did you paint her?' I mumbled.

'Paint who?' he questioned, distracted.

'Her,' I repeated.

He shot Mrs Taylor a look, before turning back to me.

She remained silent. Her hands crossed in front of her as she waited.

'Darling, let me see what's in your hand.'

I knew his gentler tone was simply a ploy.

'Get away from me,' I hissed, clutching it even tighter. 'I know what you did to me.'

'Darling, please?'

'Don't! I remember!'

'Remember?' he questioned.

I could hear the tremor of anticipation.

Of acknowledgement?

'You tried to kill me,' I stated.

He didn't reply.

I tried to hold on to the blanket with one hand. But it was futile. He managed to pull it away.

'Oh God... What have you done to yourself?' he mumbled.

He took hold of my arm with my clenched hand and held it upright.

'Darling, please? Let go!'

I held on to the thick shard of broken mirror sealed in my palm as his other hand tried to prise my fingers from around it.

'Let it go! You're bleeding! Please?'

I stared in shock at the blood trailing down my bare arm.

So much blood...

'I'll get some medical supplies,' Mrs Taylor suggested.

He nodded at her. Then turned back to me.

'Why, darling? Why would you hurt yourself?' he asked me.

I looked at him as he finally succeeded in pulling my fingers apart to release the piece of mirror. It fell to the floor, shattering and splattering blood as it did so.

'God,' he murmured. 'Why did you do this to yourself?'

'You did this to me,' I answered as I looked him straight in the eye.

He stepped back from me as if I had struck him. But he still held on to my arm, keeping it elevated.

I thought of her, his first wife.

'Why do you keep the paintings and the sketches of her? Why? Where is she? WHERE?'

'Darling, stop this! Please?' he begged. 'I can't... I can't...' He faltered as he caught sight of the ripped portrait leaning against the wall by the open door.

I realised in that moment he hadn't noticed what I had done to her.

'No...' he murmured as he stared at what I had done. 'Oh God, Isabella... Isabella...'

I gasped.

He had spoken her name.

She does exist... She's not a figment of your imagination or some cruel drug-induced hallucination.

I was surprised to see tears filling his eyes.

Why?

Because you have destroyed her portrait? Or is it guilt because he killed her? Just as he is trying to kill you.

'Why?' he whispered. 'Why, when I managed to save them?'

I tried to free my arm from his tightening grip, but he still held on to it.

I stared at him, hoping to find something. But his expression was as dispassionate as his voice. There was no emotion.

A chill snaked its way down my spine, forcing me to tremble in response.

He was devoid of any feelings for me. Not even hatred.

It was a terrifying realisation.

He doesn't care whether you live. Or die...

'Do you wish I'd died? That I hadn't survived?' I whispered at him.

He looked at me as if struggling to register the words.

The truth.

'When you tried to kill me?' I accused. 'For I remember what you did to me.'

I watched his Adam's apple quiver as he tried to swallow back whatever guilt was choking him.

He shook his head.

'Admit that you wished you'd killed me!' I goaded.

'No! God, no! What's wrong with you? Why can't you be more like—'

'Who? HER?' I screamed, leaning into his face.

Startled, he blinked and jerked his head back from me as if I were a rabid dog.

'I'm not HER! Don't you understand that?' I hissed. 'I never will be her.'

'No,' he murmured. 'You'll never be her. You'll never be Isabella. She died that night—'

'The night you killed her!' I spat. 'You killed your wife!'

Silent, he stared at me.

When he finally spoke, his voice was lifeless.

'No... It wasn't like that,' he whispered.

I stared at him. 'And you tried to kill me. You pushed me off the rocks so I would drown,' I accused. 'I REMEMBER!'

He stared at me for a moment. 'Darling? Why? Why do you say these things? I tried to stop you jumping in. Don't you remember? But I wasn't worried as I knew you were a proficient open-water swimmer. But for some reason, you didn't swim. You let yourself go under—'

'NO!' I yelled at him. 'Stop changing the narrative! I can't swim! You knew that and pushed me and would have watched me drown if it wasn't for Mrs Taylor. You only pulled me out because Mrs Taylor saw me in the water. Otherwise, you would have left me there to die. So why don't you admit it? ADMIT IT!'

'Maybe, I should have left you to die!' he threw back at me. 'Is that what you want me to admit?'

'Mr Langdon!' admonished Mrs Taylor.

How long she had been standing there, I couldn't say.

'I... I'm sorry. I just...' He shook his head. 'I... I can't keep doing this... She's destroyed it all. All of her paintings.'

'I know. This must be really difficult for you being in the conservatory where she used to paint,' she sympathised. 'But you need to not react. Remember, Mrs Langdon doesn't understand what she's saying.'

Her words took me by surprise. These sketches and portraits were Isabella Langdon's. She was the artist, not my husband. She had painted herself, which explained the large mirror.

Mrs Taylor walked over. 'Let me take a look,' she suggested quietly.

I noticed the medical aid bag she had brought with her.

I looked up at my hand and was shocked to see the blood.

So much blood.

I felt light-headed at the sight.

'Mr Langdon?' questioned Mrs Taylor when my husband didn't release my arm or move to allow her to treat me. 'Shall I take a look at Mrs Langdon's hand and—'

'No. Let's just get her upstairs. I'll bathe the cuts and seal them with wound closure strips.'

'Don't you want me to do it? Or to at least take a proper look at her injuries?'

I looked up at her. Her face was in shadow, but the surprise in her voice betrayed her.

'This will be my wife's last night here. I'd rather spend what little time is left alone with her.'

'Aren't you going to wait—'

He cut her off. 'For what? The inevitable? Look at what she's done, for God's sake! Look around you. Look at her! It's finished. I'm done trying!'

It's finished?

'Weren't you the one who said I needed to move on? Well, after this' – he gestured at the havoc I had wrecked in the conservatory and then at the jagged piece of mirror he had forced from my hand – 'I can't... Not any more.'

Oh God... What does that mean?

'Perhaps you're just exhausted, Mr Langdon. It's been a taxing day, and you've also flown back from London to Glasgow Airport and then driven here. Maybe you should relax, and I'll see to Mrs Langdon for you.'

'No.'

'But—' Mrs Taylor began.

'No.'

I watched as she folded her hands in front of her. She then nodded at him. 'Very well, Mr Langdon.'

'Why don't you pack up Mrs Langdon's clothes and toiletries? I intend for every trace of her to be gone from here by the morning.'

'Are you sure? I mean—'

'I have never been more sure in my life,' he affirmed. 'You were right. I need to start over.'

'No!' I struggled when he bent down, attempting to lift me up. 'NO!' I screamed at him, resisting his touch.

I had heard his words. I knew what they meant.

'At least let me dress Mrs Langdon's wounds before you carry her upstairs, otherwise you'll get covered in blood,' Mrs Taylor suggested.

'I already have her blood on my hands,' he muttered.

But for some reason he acquiesced and gently laid my arm down on the blanket and stepped back.

I turned my head, unable to look as Mrs Taylor knelt down and began wiping the blood.

'Do you want me to seal the wounds as best I can with butterfly stitches?' she asked my husband.

He didn't reply so she rummaged around in the first aid medical bag for the stitches.

I looked up at his distracted figure. He dragged a hand through his hair as if contemplating what to do – *with me.*

'I don't know what she's capable of doing next. I mean, she rang the police, for God's sake! You were supposed to be watching her and yet, she got out of her room and went into the west wing and—' He stopped himself. Shook his head. 'Do you know how dangerous that could have been? She doesn't know about... about what happened. If she found out... Then...' He faltered.

'I know. And I am sorry, Mr Langdon. I don't have an explanation as to why she didn't stay asleep this morning. She took her medication as normal.'

Their faces floated above me. All I could think about was what my husband had meant when he said:

'*This will be my wife's last night here...*'

What did he mean?

Terror scorched through me as my mind hurled at me the next question:

And why instruct his housekeeper to pack up what few belongings you have?

Where was I going?

Then it struck me:

You're joining the other wife, Isabella Langdon. Whatever happened to her is about to happen to you.

His fatal words rang in my ears:

'*I intend for every trace of her to be gone from here by the morning.*'

17

_____

I didn't resist him when he bent down and picked me up. What little fight I had left was gone.

Mrs Taylor walked behind him as he made his way upstairs.

'No, please? I... I don't want to go back to my bedroom,' I whispered, terrified.

I couldn't silence the fear that I would never leave – alive.

Those words. His words...

'I intend for every trace of her to be gone from here by the morning.'

'Please?' I begged.

He ignored my pleas.

'Why don't you let me sit with Mrs Langdon tonight?' suggested Mrs Taylor.

'No. I have to do this. Mrs Langdon's my responsibility. I made the decision to...' He faltered and shook his head. 'I need to see it through. I owe her that much,' he finally added.

'I assume you're returning to London in the morning?'

'Yes, as early as possible. I want to get back to—' He stopped, as if aware I was listening.

Whatever it was that he left unsaid, it was evident that Mrs Taylor understood him.

Who is he going back to? Could that be why he is always returning to London?

Then I remembered Mrs Taylor's words from Saturday evening:

'You live your life as if she never existed. You try to find happiness again. You have someone else to think about now…'

I tried to swallow. Couldn't. Terror held me captive.

He has someone else…

'I've spent too long trying to make this work. It's time to accept the situation for what it is,' he continued.

Oh God… What does he plan to do with you?

'You have removed everything from her room?' he asked.

'Yes. However, I have left out her nightdress.'

'Thank you.'

When did she do that?

Then I recalled that she left me briefly with him after she had bandaged my hands. Not that he had talked to me. Nor could he bring himself to look at me. He had simply guarded me until she returned to tell him my room was ready. I heard him say it was better that I didn't understand what was happening to me.

But you do understand… You understand all too well.

'As of tomorrow, I want Mrs Langdon's room locked up. No one is to ever enter it. Understand?'

'Yes, Mr Langdon.'

'No…' I mumbled.

You can't fall asleep! No… Please…

But I could feel myself drifting down and down into the blackness, not knowing if I would ever come back up again.

Are you drowning? Are you? Or has he drugged you with those blue dissolvable tablets? Did he put one on your tongue to make you sleep? To make you forget everything? Again.

I felt a warm wave take me. Then another, lapping gently over me, submerging me, drowning everything out.

I felt my arms being pulled as they tried to remove my dress. I cried out in pain.

'No...' I resisted. 'Please?'

'Let her sleep in it. It doesn't matter. Not tonight,' my husband muttered.

'It's filthy, Mr Langdon. It's covered in blood and grass stains.'

'She doesn't know or care,' he replied. 'So why make her more uncomfortable?'

'I would advise changing Mrs Langdon out of that dress. But, as you wish,' she conceded.

Relieved, I fell back down against the pillows. I could feel the weight of the duvet now covering my body.

It was dark. The curtains were closed, shutting out the approaching night. There was no light in my room. However, the lamp on the table in the hallway outside accounted for the warm glow filtering into the room. It was enough for me to see them – my husband and his housekeeper standing over me. The light sneaking into my room cast an eerie shadow over their faces, accentuating the appearance of expressionless white masks with black slits for eyes.

What terrified me was that I had no idea what they were thinking. Or what they were going to do with me.

'Doesn't Mrs Langdon have something to help her sleep through the night?' my husband questioned.

'Yes, but after the day she has had, I don't think she'll need anything to help her sleep. She will be exhausted. I don't expect she will stir. If she does, then I will give her something. I'm concerned she hasn't eaten anything since this morning. If Mrs Langdon does wake up, I'll bring her up some soup and bread.'

'I'll let you know if she does, as I intend to sit with her. This will be our last night together. Not that she'll ever know.'

I inwardly gasped.

Did he say that or have you imagined those words?

My eyes fluttered open. I tried to speak, but I couldn't move my lips. I looked up at the housekeeper and willed her not to leave me. Not alone with him. Not when it would be our final night together.

Not that she'll ever know...

But Mrs Taylor didn't hear my tortured thoughts.

'Shall I take the dogs downstairs?'

I shifted my eyes to his figure standing over me.

Can he see you? Does he know you are still awake?

'No. They're fine with me.'

'You know how Mrs Langdon feels about her bedroom and keeping it sterile?'

'She won't know. And anyway, what does it matter? This is the last night she'll ever spend in here.'

Oh God! What does he plan to do to you?

Unable to move or speak, I watched as he looked around the spartan white room.

'Why?' he said, shaking his head. 'I mean this is so... So clinical. So cold,' he stated.

Mrs Taylor didn't reply.

'Like her, I suppose,' he added, more to himself than for his housekeeper's benefit.

I heard a chair being dragged across the wooden floor.

'Here, Mr Langdon. Sit down. You're exhausted as well.'

I looked up as my husband collapsed down in the chair that normally sat by the table in the corner.

Your book... Did she take your book?

I remembered that it had all that was left of Isabella Langdon's life in those pages, torn from her diary. Or at least the beginning of a diary, cut short by...

By what? What happened to her? What did he do to Isabella? Where has he hidden her remains?

My mind recalled the ultrasound picture of her ten-week-old baby. So fragile with such tiny limbs, body and head.

Had Mrs Taylor found them in my book, the tattered, ripped pages documenting Isabella Langdon, his first wife's frantic, desperate thoughts? The grainy black-and-white image of the promise of a life yet unlived?

I tried to speak. To ask her. But again, my body failed my mind.

'Can I bring you something to drink?' Mrs Taylor asked him. 'Or something to eat? You haven't eaten either. And it's gone past seven.'

He shook his head. 'No, thank you. If I get hungry, I'll get something later. Just now, I want to sit with her.'

I watched, curious as he looked at his watch.

Why? What is he waiting for?

'The conservatory? I left the door open. Do you want me to lock it?' the housekeeper asked.

'No...' he muttered. 'I'll do it, later. I want to see what's left. If there's anything I can salvage that hasn't been destroyed. I want to take something of Isabella's with me. For... for...' His voice broke off.

Again, that familiar, twisty feeling returned – *jealousy*.

My husband was still thinking about her.

I couldn't recall him ever coming to my room, let alone sitting with me. And yet, here he was, and still, it was her – Isabella Langdon – whom he obsessed over.

Why are you not enough for him?

But I knew why. I had gazed upon my reflection. His first wife and I were the opposites of one another. Isabella Langdon was beautiful, passionate and filled with life. Whereas I didn't belong in this world, not any more. I was wasting away, neither living nor dead, barely existing, waiting for the chaos and confusion to end.

Is this your final resting place? This bed? Will he be the last person to witness your final breath?

But I didn't want that. I didn't want to die here alone with him. I wanted to leave this unfamiliar and godforsaken place and return to my previous life.

Who were you before?

But I couldn't remember.

'You know the irony of this evening, Mrs Taylor?' he began.

I looked up at him. He seemed lost to me. In as much as I was lost to him.

Not that he registered me staring at him.

Has he ever seen you? Or has it always been her he desired? Is that why he can't bring himself to touch you as his wife? To sleep with you. Why is he always in London with... With whom?

His words came back to me when Mrs Taylor had asked if he was returning to London:

'Yes, as early as possible. I want to get back to—'

To whom? Whom was he going back to?

'It was two years to this night when it happened,' he mumbled. 'Ironic, eh?'

His Adam's apple bobbed up and down as he swallowed. He took his large hand and wiped at his eyes.

'If only I hadn't reacted the way I did, then she'd still be here,' he said to no one in particular.

Mrs Taylor didn't respond.

I lay there listening to the oppressive silence.

Neither of them moved. They both continued watching me as I watched them.

'Do you think she realises?' he eventually asked her.

'Who realises?'

'My wife?' he questioned, his gaze never leaving mine.

But his eyes were unfocused, not seeing that I was staring straight back at him.

'That it happened on this date. Do you think that's why she destroyed the paintings? I even noticed she had smashed her cup... The one I had never washed because it still had Isabella's lipstick imprint around the lip. God! If only I had locked those conservatory doors. I didn't know they were unlocked... After the storm, I had tried to salvage what paintings I could. But I must have forgotten about the doors...' He faltered.

'I'm sorry, Mr Langdon. I was only minutes in the kitchen preparing something for Mrs Langdon. I had no idea that she could get out of the library.'

'I know... I know... I'm responsible. I left the key in the door from when the dogs had gone out to do their business,' he said, shaking his head. 'I made a mistake bringing her here. I should have realised that she could never be Isabella. You understand, don't you? I tried... God, how I've tried...'

Mrs Taylor remained silent.

I tried to swallow, couldn't. My mouth was unbearably dry.

'Do you think she cut herself intentionally because she remembered what tonight means?' he asked her.

Unblinking, I stared at him. Still, he didn't see me.

It felt as if he was seeking absolution.

For what? What did he do to her? To his first wife?

'My honest opinion?' Mrs Taylor finally replied.

'Yes,' he answered.

'I don't think she remembers anything. I don't think she even knows who Isabella Langdon is, or what happened that night. I think she cut herself because she suffers from bouts of manic depression. It's dangerous to read into these situations, otherwise you'll drive yourself mad. Mrs Langdon isn't who you think she is and that's part of your problem. You've been trying to convince yourself that she could even remotely be like her. But, you must know after two years, Mrs Langdon will never be Isabella. She's gone, Mr Langdon. She's dead. You can't bring her back.'

'I know. I see that now,' he muttered.

She's dead... His first wife is dead.

The housekeeper's words replayed over in my head.

'She's dead...'

But Mrs Taylor was wrong; I knew about his other wife.

And I knew something terrible had happened to her, and that my husband – her husband – was responsible. Just as I knew that something was going to happen to me tonight if Mrs Taylor left me alone with him.

My mind screamed at me:

Get up! Get out! RUN!

But I couldn't move.

All I could do was lie there and wait for the inevitable.

I knew that, when the housekeeper left, my husband would kill me.

And he would get away with it, just as he had when he killed his other wife two years ago on this night.

Then, I felt the weight of my fate pressing down on me. The fear that had kept me awake was dissipating.

No... Please... You might never wake up...

But it was too late. Numbing blackness surrounded me.

18

'Mr Langdon?'

I stirred from somewhere deep within.

'Mr Langdon?'

It was Mrs Taylor's voice.

My eyelids twitched as I willed myself not to react, not to open them.

I tried to move my fingers, to see whether my mind had resumed control of my body. Relief coursed through me when I felt them flex ever so slightly.

'Is everything all right with Mrs Langdon?'

As I listened, I questioned whether I could hear a trace of fear in her voice.

It was then I felt his breath lingering on me.

Why is he leaning over you?

'I dozed off. Then I noticed Mrs Langdon had ripped off her bandages in her sleep,' my husband replied. 'I was just reapplying them.'

I felt him straighten up.

'Do you want me to check the wounds and replace the gauze dressing and bandages?'

'No... Leave it until the morning. I don't want her disturbed,' he answered. 'She's slept without stirring for the past four hours. Hopefully, she's so exhausted, she'll sleep straight through the night.'

'There was a call for you in the library. I said you would ring back,' she said.

I kept my eyes closed, not wanting him to know I was awake. Otherwise, they would give me a sedative to make me fall back asleep.

Never waking up...

'It's late. It's after eleven?' His voice sounded perturbed.

'Yes,' she answered.

'Who was it?'

'They wouldn't say,' Mrs Taylor replied. 'A woman,' she added as an afterthought. 'She said it was important. That you were supposed to speak earlier this evening.'

'Oh God! I was supposed to call her hours ago. Christ!' he muttered. 'I got completely distracted.'

'Is she taking care of—'

'Yes,' he hurriedly answered, cutting her off.

I didn't need to see him to know he was watching me now. Perhaps nervous that I had overheard them.

'Does she know about Mrs Langdon?' Mrs Taylor ventured.

I presumed she had remained standing in the open doorway as her voice drifted over me from that direction.

'No. No, she doesn't know about her.'

'Will you ever tell her?'

I heard him sigh.

What happened to the carefree man in the photographs with her – Isabella Langdon?

I expected that the whites of his eyes were bloodshot and dark stubble had taken over his face. He sounded close to the point of breaking.

Or close to the point of committing murder? Your murder?

I silenced the thoughts from taking me somewhere I didn't want to go. I needed to hear who he was talking about. Who it was that had called him.

'I'm not sure. Maybe one day, when I think she'll be able to understand. But I mean, how do you explain something like this? Or how it ended so—' He abruptly stopped.

'Mr Langdon? Are you all right?'

'No,' he mumbled. 'But then, what man would be, faced with the choice I have to make?'

'You knew it might come to this. Remember, I warned you,' she whispered.

'I know...'

'And now?'

'I see the night through and go back to London and live my life with the knowledge that I killed her.'

I tried not to react, but I felt my eyelids flutter as my eyes darted in panic beneath them.

Killed who? You or his first wife?

I lay there in the darkness for what felt like hours. In reality, I suspected it was only minutes. My husband had dared to leave me alone. His current obsession, some new woman back in London, had called him away. Her existence was confirmation of my greatest fear: he had someone else. And now he wanted to replace me. But first, he had to get rid of me, just as he had with his first wife, whom I had unwittingly usurped.

I overheard Mrs Taylor suggest she sit with me. He had declined her offer, insisting she retire for the evening. It was late. She, like him, had experienced quite an eventful day. And anyway, he wouldn't take long, and I was asleep and presumably would remain so until the morning. He had reassured Mrs Taylor that I would be fine unsupervised for a few minutes.

I slowly sat up, trying to be as quiet as possible. I pulled the duvet back and swung my legs over the bed, wincing as it creaked. Light seeped in under the door from the hallway. The caller – *potentially his next wife* – had given me the opportunity to escape.

Whether what I had contrived would lead to me being able to abscond from this castle and its proud, ancient land was questionable. But at least I had to try. And I knew I would die in my attempt to get out rather than await my fate at his hands. Their mistake was not to give me my usual sleeping drugs, which would have knocked me out until the morning. And by then, it would have been too late – for me. I would have slept through whatever my husband was psyching himself up to do as he sat in the chair by my bed, waiting, contemplating. I doubted he had expected to be distracted by a phone call.

I seized my chance and felt under the mattress for Isabella Langdon's hidden possessions. My fingers found them, still where I had left them, undiscovered by Mrs Taylor's routine checks. I dragged the contraband out. The red lipstick, brass key and the final, most important one: the heavy gold-plated Cartier lighter. My bandaged right hand throbbed, and even in the darkness I could see the traces of blood seeping through the gauze underneath. Then my eyes caught sight of further bandages stained with blood, binding my—

No... How? What happened to you? To your wrists? Why are they bandaged with blood seeping through? Did he do that to you?

I pushed the troubling questions away. I needed to focus. I

didn't have long before my husband would return to see this night through.

I glanced at my wrists: evidence he had already begun.

Remember? Remember the plan!

I swallowed, my hand trembling with the weight of the importance of the lighter I held – her cigarette lighter inscribed from my husband to her. My fingertips delicately traced the loving words he had etched into the metal for posterity. Touching her name, I found myself questioning whether I could do it.

You can do this... You have no choice.

You know that this is your final night here.

I recalled his terrifying words:

'This will be my wife's last night here... I intend for every trace of her to be gone from here by the morning.'

It wasn't his first wife, Isabella Langdon, he had been referring to – it was me.

I looked at the other evidence in my hand of his first wife's existence here in Dunstrafne Castle before me: her red lipstick, her wedding ring and the key to her bedroom in the west wing.

I curled my fingers around them.

I knew what I had to do. Whether I had the strength to see it through was another matter. But I had to try.

Fate had intervened. If my husband's new woman – his next wife – hadn't rung, I wouldn't have even been able to attempt anything.

Attempt what? Retribution? For whom? You or Isabella Langdon?

It was a moot point now. We were one and the same, sharing the dark fate of being married to him. But I had witnessed in the photographs in her bedroom and on my husband's desk in the library, evidenced by what I held in the palm of my hand, that he had been a different man with her. He loved her in a way he could never love me. I had nothing: no jewellery to speak of, no wedding ring engraved with our names. And where were our wedding photographs testifying our love – his love for me? I couldn't recall ever marrying my husband, let alone falling in love with him. Photographs would have helped me remember and presented me with empirical evidence that everything he and his housekeeper told me was the truth. But no photographs existed, or if they once had, he had removed all traces of them.

Just as he plans to destroy all trace of your existence here.

Remember what he said?

'*I intend for every trace of her to be gone from here by the morning.*'

The thought prompted me to act and not procrastinate, dwelling on what had or hadn't existed.

I shoved the other wife's items in the left pocket of my dress.

Why are you still wearing your dress? It's disgusting. Look at it! At all the blood and other stains.

I struggled to recall why.

Maybe because this is your last night here. If so, why would they bother changing you into your nightdress?

I turned and padded to the door and pulled it towards me, allowing light to seep into the room. I listened. Nothing. The castle was silent. It was as if it knew that something terrible was about to happen.

I looked back at the table.

Your book...

It was still there. I couldn't leave without it. I headed over to it, picked it up and opened the faded tea-stain-coloured pages.

Oh...

She still existed. Her raw words were so elegantly written on the ripped-out pages from her diary tucked inside my book.

I held my breath for a moment as I gazed again upon the ultra-sound scan picture.

They both existed as one... And now?

I shut the pages of the book, and put it in my other pocket. I needed to go before my husband or his housekeeper returned.

But for some reason I was compelled to check the wardrobe and drawers. To see whether I had imagined my husband instructing Mrs Taylor to strip my room of all my personal effects.

Surely you imagined it. Or did you?

I walked over to the wardrobe. There was no white linen summer dress, identical to the one I was wearing, hanging on the door in anticipation of the morning.

I trembled as a cold breath lingered on the back of my neck, making the fine hairs stand up in alarm.

I prised the door open and dared myself to look. It was empty.

Oh God...

I moved over to the drawers and carefully pulled them out. One by one, they all proved to me that I hadn't imagined my husband instructing his housekeeper to remove what little possessions I had here. Not one item had been left behind.

Panicking, I looked over at the wall with the whiteboard to see whether it was still there. Not that I could trust the words and numbers on that whiteboard. I was sure that Mrs Taylor repeatedly added days and changed them around to jumble my thoughts, gaslighting me into believing I couldn't trust my mind.

It's them you can't trust. Your husband and his housekeeper.

I gasped when I saw that it was still hanging there. But it was blank.

Where have all the prompts gone? Your memories? They're... they're...

I stared in shock.

I walked over to it, hoping the darkness had obscured the content. But there was nothing there. I reached up and touched the blank space. Nothing was left, not even a shadow of what had once existed. My fingers trailed over the whiteboard, seeking out something, anything from my past. But it was all gone. He had erased every trace of it – of me.

What has he done?

I snapped my head to the chair, watching guard over my bed as if expecting him to be there. But, of course, the chair was empty, aside from his Barbour jacket. I imagined he had taken it off after carrying me upstairs to bed, too distracted by what he had found in the conservatory to realise he was still wearing it after being called in from searching for me in the castle grounds.

I walked over to the chair and picked up his jacket.

What are you doing? You need to go! You have a plan! Implement it. Don't let yourself get distracted because he'll be back soon, and then—

My mind threw me back to what he had said to his house-keeper: that he wanted everything gone from my room. That he would remove every trace of me, and that was exactly what he had done.

I rummaged through the pockets, searching for his mobile phone.

You could call the police. Tell them... Tell them what he plans to do.

But reality struck me. If he had a mobile phone, it wasn't in his jacket. I assumed it would be on his person. But I had the key to Isabella Langdon's bedroom. I could call the police from the vintage candlestick telephone on her writing bureau. I then remembered the two officers who had responded to my 999 call earlier today. The police might suspect it was another hoax call. After all, my husband had gone to great lengths, with the aid of his housekeeper, to discredit me.

I felt all hope slipping through my fingers as I groped for some-thing, anything, that could tell me what was happening, what he planned to do with me.

I gasped as my left hand found it and pulled it out. I tiptoed to the doorway and held it up to the cascading light streaming in from the hallway.

I gazed at it. I had seen him use this. I was sure of it. I turned it over in my fingers, luxuriating in the feel of the smooth juniper-wood handle. It was a pocketknife, but it also included a corkscrew. Had I watched him take it from his pocket and open a bottle of red wine with it? The memory was so fragile, so tenuous, but I was certain of it.

I unfolded the slim stainless-steel blade. I stared at the little bee. I recognised it as the manufacturer's iconic signature Laguiole bee.

How do you know that?

Perhaps I had asked him when he had used the pocketknife with the corkscrew to open the wine. But I couldn't remember.

Why can't you remember?

Why?

I shivered as a cold breeze brushed over my skin.

Her words to him were engraved there on the blade below the bee.

To my love, forever yours, Isabella x

Oh God...

But it wasn't her words that made my stomach lurch.

There was a sliver of something dried on the blade's edge. Something dark red.

It was at that moment I forced myself to look at the bandages on my wrists and the blood seeping through. The dressings that I had refused to acknowledge earlier, too fearful it would distract me from my plan to escape.

What did he do to you?

It wasn't only my right hand that had been bandaged, both my wrists were covered in dressings. I didn't need to tear off the discoloured material to know that my wrists had been cut. I could now feel the burning pain as if the blade was still slicing through my flesh.

I heard myself give out a strangled sob.

Oh God...

How was this possible?

He did this to you.

When? In the conservatory when you were alone? Or here, in your bedroom? Could that be why he was so insistent he sit with you, dismissing the housekeeper for the evening?

Then he bandaged your wrists and waited. He sat there waiting for you to die. Then he could claim you had killed yourself. That you had suicidal ideation and it was inevitable that you would eventually succeed.

He threw you off the rock into the ocean with the knowledge you couldn't swim. But Mrs Taylor witnessed him there. So he had no choice but to dive in and save you and later claim that you threw yourself into the water.

But he pushed you. Remember? REMEMBER!

And now? I stared in horror at my wrists.

Is this why he asked Mrs Taylor to remove your belongings from your bedroom, so he could cut your wrists while you were alone in the conservatory? Then bandage them before she returned?

My eyes darted to the bed. There were drops of blood on the duvet.

Oh God... It was here he did this to you... While you lay sleeping. And if Mrs Taylor hadn't walked in, perhaps he would have succeeded.

I remembered his words again:

'This will be my wife's last night here... I intend for every trace of her to be gone from here by the morning.'

19

I gripped the pocketknife as I crept out of my room. I waited, listening for someone approaching. Again, silence was my only answer. I could feel the anticipation in the very air of Dunstrafne Castle as if it knew my desperate plan. I looked up at the proud and defiant portraits of my husband's ancestors. I knew they had fought valiantly to keep this castle and the surrounding land. And now, I planned to destroy the last of their lineage – James Buchanan Langdon.

I avoided their damning gazes, condemning me as an imposter. I could hear them whispering to one another that I was a Sassenach: deriding me for being English. And that I deserved to die for what I was contemplating. And if I didn't reach the conservatory before anyone found me, I was under no illusions: I would die at my husband's hands tonight. No one was coming to save me. Unless, I—

I stopped myself. I had to get there first without being caught.

I remembered Mrs Taylor had asked him if he wanted her to lock the conservatory door. He had said no – I was sure of that. Or at least, I hoped I hadn't imagined it because that was where I was heading.

Perhaps he planned not only to eradicate me but to raze the castle to the ground in the process. It would conveniently hide his crimes, and he could simultaneously blame me for the destruction of his ancestral home. My body would perish in the flames, as would his first wife's remains. He would claim, substantiated by his housekeeper, that I was a threat to myself. And now it had escalated, and I was a threat to others, despite assuring the two police officers earlier today that wasn't the case. But now—

I looked down at the blood-splattered white dress I was still wearing and the crimson-stained bandages on my wrists. Then the unfolded pocketknife, clutched in my hand. The blade that had traces of my blood on it. My husband would cite that I had already tried to kill myself by throwing my body off the rocks into the wild waters of the north Atlantic Ocean, witnessed by his housekeeper. That he had saved me – *of course.*

But now, I was too disturbed, too twisted to trust. I was deceiving my husband and his housekeeper, and they were finding it impossible to keep me safe. Or those around me safe. For I was becoming dangerous, uncontrollable and a liability. At least, that was what he would tell people.

I had played right into my husband's hands. Even calling the police and claiming I was being held against my will and in danger had worked in his favour and gone against me. For who would doubt his word when he reported I had taken my life?

Hadn't I evidenced myself to be unhinged when talking to the police officers?

You walked right into his trap.

Even Mrs Taylor would substantiate that I was a danger to myself – and others – citing I had smashed a mirror to use the glass to cut my hand. And now I had stolen my husband's treasured pocketknife from his Barbour jacket to—

What are you going to do with his knife?

Had he second-guessed I would go through his jacket and find it?

Was that why he left his jacket there on the chair, for you to discover his pocketknife?

I dropped my gaze to my bandaged hand. I noted that it was trembling as it held the open blade.

It has his prints with your blood on it.

But it's his pocketknife. The police would expect his prints to be on it. But as for your blood?

Oh God...

I realised my mistake had been going through his jacket and handling the pocketknife. Taking it out; keeping it. It now had both my prints and blood. Damning evidence that I had cut my own wrists.

I had lain in bed with the chilling knowledge that my husband wanted me dead. The question was, how did he plan to get away with my murder? And now I knew. He had cut my wrists. Perhaps he had only begun, interrupted by Mrs Taylor approaching the room. So he had claimed I had ripped off my bandages, and he was reapplying them. Would he return and finish what he had started?

I knew the answer.

Terror scorched through me, driving me forward.

I strained to hear the boys, Henry and Jack. Nothing. I suspected they had faithfully followed my husband and were lying by the fire in the library. I assumed he was still on the phone, otherwise he would have returned to my room. He wasn't foolish enough to leave me for too long. But it was imprudent not to have locked me in. Mrs Taylor, who kept the master key to all the castle rooms, would never have left the door unlocked again.

I crept along the first-floor hallway. I glanced across at the darkness that beckoned, leading to the west wing. To her room. It called to me like a siren, lulling me to join her, his first wife. I felt the weight of the key to her bedroom in my pocket, with her lipstick. I looked at my left hand, which held on to her gold-plated lighter as if it were some religious relic and was surprised to see her wedding ring on my fourth finger.

When did you place it there?

I couldn't remember slipping it on. It was a couple of sizes too large and subsequently could fall off without me realising. But for some reason, I couldn't take it off. It was as if it connected me to her. She had worn this ring for the seven years she was married to Laird James Buchanan Langdon. And now...

Where was she? What had he done to her?

I had survived two years with him. A time that I couldn't recall, aside from snatches of stolen memories from them – my husband and his housekeeper. I couldn't trust what they told me was true. I had nothing comparable to challenge them with. I possessed no knowledge of myself. Other than, at times, a knowing, like déjà vu or a recollection, that I couldn't be sure belonged to me. And now my husband had wiped every trace of my past from the whiteboard. I had nothing to reference, no map to navigate my mind.

And your mother? Where is she? Does she even know they stripped you of your memories of her? Flooded your body with a mind-numbing cocktail of sedatives to keep you from her?

I recalled that he didn't want me to remember something.

His other wife? Her murder?

For he had said he had killed his wife. His words earlier tore through me:

'I see the night through and go back to London and live my life with the knowledge that I killed her.'

But was he talking about his first wife?

Or was it you?

I caught sight of the blood-stained bandages binding my wrists, too tight.

I had my answer.

I held my breath as I inched my way down the sweeping central staircase. I didn't feel the cold on my bare feet or arms, too preoccupied with the fear of being caught. The grand hallway, with its stone columns, cast eerie shadows below. I avoided eye contact with his ancestors lining the walls. I could feel their vengeful eyes, indignant, filled with fury, as I made my way undetected by their only heir. I reached the last step, turned, and looked back up as if expecting to see Isabella Langdon at the top of the staircase, breathtaking in her elegant emerald-green ball gown, her wild, long, tight blonde spiral curls cascading down her beautiful bare shoulders, her full red lips, half-turned in a wicked smile as if delighted at my rebellion.

But she wasn't there, just a figment of my imagination. I turned my back on the warm, appealing glow of the lamps burning on the first-floor landing. Ahead of me, shadows lurked in the dark corners. For some reason, the lights were off. Neither the overhead lights nor the hall table lamps were on. It was oddly disconcerting. Unless Mrs Taylor had turned them off on her way to bed? I turned, looking at the entrance hallway. The chinoiserie longcase clock caught my attention. It struck me how silent it was, its hands forever stuck at 11.11.

Why? What was the significance of that time?

Did I know? I felt I should know, but the memory eluded me.

If it ever existed.

Wait... Something terrible happened to you at 11.11. Or was that to his other wife? Did the hands stop at the precise moment he took her life from her?

W. H. Auden's poem, 'Stop All the Clocks', came to mind again.

Stop all the clocks, cut off the telephone,
Prevent the dog from barking with a juicy bone,
Silence the pianos and with muffled drum
Bring out the coffin, let the mourners come...

He Is Dead...

At that moment, I knew what I had to do. I somehow had to convince the police that he had tried to kill me, just as he had killed his first wife, Isabella Langdon. I needed to expose him for the man he was and prevent him from hurting this new woman he seemingly spent most of his time with in London. The one he was talking to now.

For I could now hear his deep, low voice resonating from the library as he spoke untruths to her, offering her whatever it took to bring her back here to Dunstrafne Castle. And when he succeeded, I would be erased as if I never existed. My room, and his first wife's room, would be locked forever from prying eyes and inquisitive minds.

I walked past the silenced longcase clock in the direction of his voice, lured by curiosity and –

Jealousy or revenge?

Spurred on, I clenched the handle of his pocketknife tight.

What are you doing? Stick to the plan! Remember?

I needed to expose him, but first I had to make sure the police would come. My life didn't warrant police protection, but I knew that *his* was worthy of their attention. After all, he was the laird of Dunstrafne Castle.

I would prove to the police that he had tried to kill me and that he had killed his pregnant first wife, Isabella Langdon. I needed to expose him for the man he was, and that meant—

I stopped.

I glanced down at the blade as it glinted in the darkness. I felt myself wavering, unsure whether I had the strength to follow through with my plan. Then I remembered her – Isabella Langdon. It was as if she were pressing me on. I touched her wedding ring with my thumb as a reminder of why I was here.

You can do this... Bring the police here.

Let them find out what he did to her.

20

I pressed my body against the wall and, not daring to breathe, listened.

I could hear his voice slipping out from the gap in the library door. I suspected that he hadn't secured it behind him in his rush to call her. Not that there was anyone else here to hear him. He believed me to be asleep in my room and Mrs Taylor to have retired to her quarters.

I looked at the empty reading chair opposite, anticipating some apparition materialising in front of me. Beside it was a table with a large lamp. I resisted the urge to switch it on so the light would chase away the spectres and ghosts seeking me out. I felt wretched. I was tired and presumably cold as my body was trembling. Not that I felt it. I had other more pressing concerns occupying my mind than my body's ailments.

The brutal words that had chilled me to the core came back to me:

'I see the night through and go back to London and live my life with the knowledge that I killed her.'

I couldn't dispel the irrational feeling that I wasn't alone out here. I snapped my eyes shut, trying to ignore the shadows lurking in the corners while others hid behind the tall antique vase and other Victorian ornaments adorning the panelled hallway. The ground floor was a maze with passages sneaking off in multiple directions. I had followed my husband's voice, memorising my steps, terrified I would forget how to find my way to the main entrance hall and the imposing centre stone staircase. I could visualise how to reach the conservatory from when he, with Mrs Taylor following, had carried me upstairs to my room as I begged him not to.

I swallowed, trying but failing to dislodge the knot of fear lodged at the back of my throat. I pressed the wedding ring against my flesh, willing myself to be brave. *For her.*

I forced myself to open my eyes and listen. I needed to know that I wasn't imagining everything that was happening to me before I—

I glanced down at my bandaged right hand. I felt no discomfort from the pressure of gripping the pocketknife, only relief that it was there. I assumed that whatever painkillers Mrs Taylor had administered would still be blocking my pain receptors.

Will you really be able to stab—

Then I heard him speaking. I had unconsciously picked up on the sudden change in his tone. It sounded so unfamiliar, as if someone else was in the library with him, that it had managed to penetrate through my dark thoughts. His voice was soft and gentle, more of a whisper, as if fearful of waking someone.

You?

'I'll be home tomorrow. I promise. Night, my darling. I love you more than life itself.'

His gravelly voice was low, the words delicate and adoring. I felt a poisonous knot of jealousy twist inside me. He hadn't declared his love to me. Instead, he had shared his unadulterated hatred and his desire for me to be dead. To have died when he had pushed me off the rocks into the waiting, watchful waves.

I heard myself let out a low hiss of air at the realisation I wasn't losing my mind. He did have someone else. And he loved her. He had just uttered those precious words to her.

'I love you more than life itself.'

And conversely, he hated me, his wife, enough to desire my life to be over.

I felt a tear slip silently down my cheek. Then another.

And now? What do you do?

I breathed out slowly and waited, trying to navigate through my thoughts that had disintegrated into blind chaos. My mind was in free fall as everything I had once believed dissipated around me.

I had suspected he was seeing someone else. It was the only logical explanation for his frequent trips to London. His presence here at the castle became less and less as his absences became more pronounced.

It's true... It's all true... This is your last night here.

Terror consumed me at the realisation at what would happen to me. He had replaced me, just as he had replaced his first wife. I could feel Isabella's ring against my skin, consoling me, reassuring me. I curled my fingers around her cigarette lighter, pressing it against the wedding ring.

You know what to do. Remember the plan!

I swallowed.

Then I heard his voice cut through my pain. It was louder, more assertive than before as if he was talking to someone else.

'Yes, I know it's late...' He paused.

Did he know I was out here, or was he gathering his thoughts?

I waited, not daring to breathe.

'I admit that you were right. I made a mistake.' He sighed before repeating himself, 'I made a terrible, terrible mistake.'

I felt trapped, unable to move.

You need to go! While he's preoccupied!

But I couldn't go. The compulsion to know what he was about to say was too great for me to override.

He was silent as he listened to whomever he had called speak to him.

Talk him down.

'No... No. I... I don't know! I don't know what to do any more,' he admitted.

His voice scared me. He sounded desperate. As if he was being driven to do something against his will.

'I fear for her safety. I'm worried about what she could do to herself or to others. I can't cope any more...' He paused, waited. 'I know I said I would let you know within the week after our meeting, but things have deteriorated.'

I inwardly cursed as the furious pounding in my ears intensified, threatening to drown out his words.

'Yes... I'm thinking as soon as possible.'

I could hear his breathing, heavy and ragged as he listened to the other speaker.

'Ahuh, yes. I know... I thought being here would have helped... But I was wrong... Yes... I made a mistake thinking this would help. I wanted to make things right. Guilt, I expect, for what happened. In hindsight, I realise you were right and I was wrong. My reasons were selfish. I understand that now. I mean... She's so different from Isabella. I can't cope with seeing her now... God! I can't believe I've just admitted that to you.'

I squeezed her cigarette lighter hard, to stop myself from gasping out.

I wanted to run. To get as far away from him as possible.

I didn't want to stay here and listen to whatever twisted thoughts were troubling him. He had committed enough atrocities against me – and his other wife – to have him committed to purgatory in perpetuity. If not hell forever.

I thought of the Elizabethan tragedy by Christopher Marlowe, *Doctor Faustus*, and Faustus's final monologue when he is dragged down to hell by Mephistopheles's demons. Throughout the play, Faustus has ample opportunities to repent and save his soul, which he repeatedly defers until it is too late. I thought of my husband now and whether he was fearing such an end for all the sins he had committed and was yet to commit. Conflicted, he was confiding with someone on the phone about what he planned to do next – to me. Was it permission he was seeking or absolution?

Then it struck me. Who was he talking to? Who had he called at such a late hour?

A priest? Is he calling to confess?

I didn't know whether he was religious. It was then I realised I knew nothing of this man I called my husband.

'I can't cope with her. I wish I had never brought her here. I mean... What was I thinking?'

He was silent again.

I found myself paralysed, not wanting to be here, but unable to prise myself away.

You need to go! Remember! GO!

But I couldn't. I needed to hear my husband say her name. Admit that he had killed her – his first wife. Only then would I be released from whatever sorcery was keeping me here. I knew it was cruel and masochistic, but still, I couldn't leave.

It was as if Isabella Langdon's ghost held me captive, until her murder was finally acknowledged – *admitted*.

'Why did I think she could be Isabella? Why?' he murmured.

I held my breath.

He's talking about you...

'The woman I love is dead. I can't bring her back,' he explained in response to the person he had called.

Silent, he listened to their answer.

Isabella Langdon is dead...

I shivered as an icy chill caressed my face, an acknowledgement I wasn't alone. It was as if she was here with me, urging me to act now, to take some form of requital for her death.

'Yes, I know that. But how can I continue on, knowing that I was responsible? I killed my wife that night two years ago. Me! No one else. And no matter how hard I've tried, I can't bring her back. She's gone. Lost to me forever. And God... Oh God, I miss her...'

He killed her... But he loved her. Why would he kill her? What drove him to kill the woman he so loved?

I couldn't breathe. His confession had paralysed me. I knew she was dead. Felt it deep within me. But now...

Now you know for definite he killed her.

I had promised her I would avenge her death. My husband – *her husband* – had killed her and I intended to force the police to come to Dunstrafne Castle and find her remains. I would risk my life for the egregious wrong committed against her and her unborn child. Her wedding ring with their initials and wedding date nine years ago on my fourth finger and the cigarette lighter engraved to her from my husband evidenced she existed.

Had existed...

I felt her with me, beseeching me to act now. To avenge her death.

The pocketknife in your hand... NOW!

I crept to the door and peeked through the gap. I could barely make him out sitting at the desk as he hadn't switched the reading lamp on or any other light. The glow of the fire lit his face, making him appear ghoulish and tormented as if he had sold his tortured soul to bring his first wife, Isabella Langdon, back.

His head was resting in one hand while the other held the phone to his ear.

I could see a crystal glass with the remnants of a rich honey-coloured liquid: whisky. The quarter-full bottle was on the desk.

'I... I loved her and miss her so much. If it wasn't for...' He faltered as his voice cracked as he gulped in air.

Is he sobbing?

I stared at his defeated figure as he wiped his eyes before reaching for the glass beside him. He nodded at whatever was spoken to him – not that the caller could see him nod – and took a gulp.

A few moments later he managed to speak: 'No... I accept that the marriage is over. I should never have tried. It was too soon after what happened...' He paused again. Listened.

I felt sick as my stomach twisted and contracted. He never loved me. It was her – Isabella Langdon – he loved. And it would always be her.

But he killed her...

And you? You mean nothing to him. Nothing... All you are is a reminder of what he has lost... What he destroyed.

'I... I killed Isabella that night. I know it, and you know it. And now I'm being punished. Living with her is like... Christ! I can't even put it into words. It's unbearable... I can't even bring myself to look at her. Her physical appearance couldn't be more different... Even the way she talks to me... Her voice, personality and everything else about her couldn't be more unlike Isabella. What was I thinking these past two years? That I could make it work with her? She's... she's not Isabella... And never will be. I accept that now.'

I heard myself gasp. I put my fist in my mouth to stop myself from betraying my presence.

'I know... I know... If only I could change that night... Change what I did, how I reacted,' he mumbled as if to himself at whatever the other person said to him.

I watched as he listened, staring intently at the photograph on his desk.

Of her. It's the black-and-white photograph of Isabella and him.

I bit down hard on my hand as tears, hot and salty, trailed down my face.

'Yes... I know. As for her, well, her behaviour has been more erratic these past few days... No, I can't say why. She... She cut her wrists earlier this evening with a piece of broken mirror that she smashed...'

My body turned cold.

He's lying... LYING.

'I know... I... We just can't keep her under control. She's devious. Always trying to escape and... And she's intent on taking her life. Then, of course, she never remembers. Claims it's me trying to hurt her... If I'm honest with you, I'm so close to losing it, to... to actually hurting—' He stopped himself, as if aware of what he was admitting.

I wanted to scream that he was lying. That he had cut my wrists. Instead, I continued to sink my teeth into my flesh to prevent myself from being discovered.

'I've cleaned the slashes and sealed them, then bandaged her wrists,' he replied.

He was silent for a moment before answering.

'For all the reasons I've outlined, it's over. I have to accept that Isabella is dead. And as for...'

I watched, horrified as he dragged his trembling hand through his hair.

'I tried... God knows how I tried to make it work. You know that?'

He waited.

'I'm sorry. I should have listened to you. I realise that now. After tonight, I accept I have no wife... She's gone. I need to live my life and move on without her. I'll be back in London tomorrow... Yes... Yes, the necessary arrangements need to be made.' He paused, waited. 'If you can send private transport. I... I can't bring myself to do it... Yes, Mrs Taylor will stay with her until... Until...'

He cleared his throat.

'I'll make sure I do that. And, I'm sorry for calling you at such a late hour. I... I just needed to talk to someone I trusted. And I needed your perspective as a woman. As my... Yes... I... I... just can't go on any longer pretending she's someone she's not. It's better for her it ends this way. You understand, don't you? Tell me I'm not some monster for what I'm about to do. Please?'

Oh God...

He's talking to another woman about what he plans to do to you. Who? Who is she?

But I didn't have time to worry about who she was.

RUN! YOU NEED TO GO!

It was as if Isabella Langdon was beseeching me to flee and hide. To save my life. For she knew better than anyone what our husband was capable of. But there was nowhere left to run. No place to hide. This was his ancestral castle and grounds. He would find me sooner or later, and then?

He's going to kill you... Just as he killed his other wife.

You have no choice now.

I retraced my steps, careful not to alert him of my presence. I didn't have long before he would discover I was missing. And then...

It will be too late... He will be too late.

21

I reached the entrance to the conservatory, gasping for breath. Not from the exertion of running, once I was out of earshot of his library, but terror.

Fear scorched through me, blocking any pain I should have felt as I ran. I had sliced my feet with the shattered mirror fragments scattered across the conservatory floor. I recalled Mrs Taylor cleaning my soles with antiseptic swabs and sealing the worst cuts with butterfly stitches before covering them with plasters. Not that I could feel the superficial wounds.

Or were my bare feet too cold to feel pain? Or was it that I was now immune to feeling physical pain?

Where are your shoes? Or socks even? Why have they hidden them?

Not that it mattered now. My only concern was carrying out my plan.

But I was terrified I wouldn't be able to exact it. That my husband would find me first, ending my hope of bringing Dunstrafne Castle and its laird to the attention of the police.

I stared in disbelief at the partially open door, left unlocked, just as Mrs Taylor had said. Why hadn't my husband returned? I recalled he had said he would personally secure it. I presumed the phone call in the library had distracted him. But when he ended it, surely, he would come straight here.

I pushed the door further ajar and peeked inside, wary of who was waiting for me in there. The wind was whipping up a frenzy outside, stirring the tall native pinewoods into a cacophony of disquieting sounds. Creaks and groans surrounded the conservatory as unchecked, overgrown tree limbs tapped at the glass panes as if in a desperate bid to warn me.

I hesitated, filled with trepidation, unsure of what they were warning me against.

Your husband?

I looked behind, to see whether he had followed me. But no one was there, only shadows clinging to the corners of the castle corridors.

I turned back to the conservatory.

Then I saw her through the open doorway. I gasped, startled as she stared back at me from between the hanging vines and brittle, twisted twigs.

Isabella Langdon. His first wife. She's here…

It took me a moment to realise the beautiful, mystical shadowy form was her doppelganger and not her. She had immortalised herself here in this place. Perhaps she knew what was going to happen to her. Some kind of presentiment of her death? The paintings and sketches left behind were her legacy, her proof of her existence here in Dunstrafne Castle.

I questioned how I had missed it. Or had my husband selected it from the canvases stacked against the wall while Mrs Taylor had tended to my injuries?

His words came back to me:

'I want to see what's left. If there's anything I can salvage that hasn't been destroyed. I want to take something of Isabella's with me.'

Was he planning on taking this self-portrait of his other wife with him back to London?

Remember! Remember what you are here to do... Don't get distracted.

The disjointed limbs continued tapping and scratching to get my attention, goaded by the wind, piercing my thoughts and adding to the prescient feeling that this was my last night here. And that what I was about to do would be the death of me.

I had reconciled myself with that fact. I would rather die by my own hand than those of my husband's. And if doing so would prove he was a murderer and that he had killed his other wife and hunted me to my death, then I would have succeeded in righting a terrible wrong.

I felt for her wedding ring again, pressing it with my thumb into my skin, as if to reassure myself that it was still there. I was fearful of losing it, for it was as if it linked me in some mystical way to my husband's first wife. The knowledge it had once pressed against her flesh, and now mine, made me feel connected with her.

You haven't got long before he discovers you're not in your room. That you've gone...

The voice in my head cut through my thoughts. Her voice, perhaps, prevailing on me to act. For there was a reason I had come here. I was seeking what my husband so desired: Isabella Langdon's eternalised image created by her own hand.

Hurry! You need to act before he finds you.

It wouldn't be long before he concluded his phone call, downed his whisky and came here to search for what he had lost. For he was seeking all that he had left of his first wife: her beauty and form perpetuated in one of her self-portraits. But a painting wouldn't bring her back to him. No matter how much he pleaded for redemption and to change the past, undo the grievous act he committed against her, it wouldn't return her from the dead.

Nothing could bring her back and he knew that. And he didn't deserve to take anything of hers. He had no right to some trophy, some keepsake.

Why? To remind him of what he did to her? Or to remind him of the dichotomous relationship between you and her? That Isabella Langdon was beautiful, brilliant and bold. And you are? You are incomparable. The opposite of her in every way. The darkness to her light.

You mean nothing to him...

I felt the familiar toxic feeling of jealousy as the words I had heard him utter as if confessing some heinous secret to the woman on the phone poisoned my mind.

'I can't even bring myself to look at her. Her physical appearance couldn't be more different... Even the way she talks to me... Her voice, personality and everything else about her couldn't be more unlike Isabella. What was I thinking these past two years? That I could make it work with her? She's... she's not Isabella... And never will be.'

I felt the pocketknife, clutched tight in my right hand, forgetting the bloodied bandages and gauze dressing protecting the deep cut, as I willed him to come here and end it – for both of us. I was tired, and suspected that I physically didn't have the strength to continue fighting. They, my husband and his housekeeper, had slowly starved me, depleting my body until it resorted to catabolysis: breaking down what fat was left, and then muscle tissue in a desperate bid to survive.

Mentally, they had tried – and succeeded, until now – to destroy my mind. To break it down into tiny pieces, shattered like slithers of glass fragments from a broken mirror. What had once reflected and shone was now destroyed, and all that was left was blackness. There was a void where my memories should have been, leaving me to scrabble around in the darkness for the billions of pieces that were my life: a scattered jigsaw puzzle that was too large to comprehend, too complicated to piece together.

Remember! Remember why you're here!

I felt a jolt of adrenaline course through me as I reminded myself.

I stepped through the doorway into the conservatory, hearing the brittle shards of organic material disintegrating under my bare feet. A sense of disquiet overcame me. Death was everywhere in this room. Baleful, resentful and unforgiving, forgotten about. I barely breathed, terrified that whatever was in here with me would sense my presence. The wind rattled the loose panes of glass, alerting me to some approaching threat. Or was it me that had alarmed it so?

Are you the threat?

Again, the glass panes threatened to crack under the duress of the wind's rage at my audacity. I felt sure now it knew why I was here. What I had planned.

I strengthened my resolve and tightened my grip on what I held in my hands.

I looked at the self-portrait of his other wife that my husband, I assumed, had selected to take with him. I stared at her – at Isabella Langdon's beautiful face, so perfect, so radiant and filled with life. Her intelligent, compelling brown eyes looked upon me with such pity and surprise that I had usurped her. That I was her husband's second wife, and he had chosen me over her. And now she was gone, our husband yearned to be with her, and it was her bed he wanted to share rather than mine.

But he killed her! Why? Why, if he so loved her? Still loves her...

I hated her for looking at me in that way. It was the stupefying sneer that I could have succeeded her. My hatred was murderous as I glared back at her. I wanted to kill her. In that bitter moment, I forgot she was dead, no longer a threat to me. But that was a lie. She was a threat and always would be. And I hated him more, my husband – her husband – for desiring her above me. For regretting ever being with me and not being able to forget her – his other wife. Filled with remorse for ever choosing me over her.

Without thinking, I raised my husband's pocketknife and slashed at her red, seductive, smiling lips. I twisted the knife into the taut canvas, stabbing at her again and again, but the effect was a sinister sneer as if she were now mocking me for my attempt to destroy her. I stabbed and stabbed, panting with exhaustion. But it was futile. I was hurting myself, not her. She didn't exist any more.

You're wasting time by misdirecting your rage. Your hatred should be at your husband – her husband – not at her. She was his victim. Let her go.

She's gone. A ghost from a past that doesn't belong to you.

But still, I cut and hacked furiously at her alluring features. Unabated and unsated, I took the knife to her neck, unable to appease the toxic jealousy that spurred me on, desirous of revenge. I hated her for representing everything I wasn't and could never be, for being the epitome of my husband's desire.

Conversely, I was abhorrent to him. He had whispered as much in the darkness of his library to whomever he had bared his soul to on the phone at this late, godforsaken hour. It then struck me that someone else knew about me. He had admitted that he was keeping me here at Dunstrafne Castle with his housekeeper. I remembered him saying that 'the necessary arrangements need to be made'.

What did that mean? Who else was involved with his plans to erase me from his life? Could it be someone within the police, which would explain why they hadn't helped me. Why they had left me here to—

I jumped, startled as the wind howled outside, shaking the double glass doors to the conservatory as if trying to get in to cause more destruction in this place and join me in my frenzied attack. Surprised at the wind's fury, I looked at what I had done to Isabella Langdon's proud and elegant face. Her smooth, supple skin abundant and unblemished, unlike mine. Her blonde, tight, curly hair fell around her shoulders and down her back, wild and luxurious, making me hate her all the more.

I looked down at my white dress, stained with blood, and at my lower legs, covered in bruises and welts. Then my marked arms and bandaged wrists.

Who did that to you? And why?

But I knew whom: my husband and his housekeeper. And why: because he hated the fact I wasn't her – his first wife.

I looked at her, at Isabella Langdon's face covered in ugly, long slashes, her features completely unrecognisable. I knew that when my husband saw this painting, the one I suspected he was going to take with him to London tomorrow, it would break him. I had destroyed all there was of her. There was nothing left for him to take when he left here to join his new woman: the one I had over-heard him talking to, telling her he loved her; the one whom he would be with the next day.

And after tonight, you, like Isabella Langdon, will no longer exist. Erased as if you had never been here. Your room has been emptied of what few belongings you possessed and the whiteboard with your memories, your means of navigating this terrifying world, erased.

It was then that I remembered why I was here.

I was going to erase everything he – my husband – owned: all his memories of her, his other wife and his past, just as he had wiped my mind of mine.

I felt her gold-plated cigarette lighter secure in my left hand. A reminder of what I had to do. Again, it was as if she, my husband's first wife, was with me, persuading me to hurry, to do what was necessary. That she would forgive me for destroying all that was hers in here. That I had to implement my plan before he found me. Stopped me.

I ran over to the large wooden filing-style cabinets. I already knew what was inside – bottles and bottles of turpentine. I put the pocketknife in my pocket, next to the brass key to his first wife's bedroom and her lipstick for safekeeping, aware I would need it later. I felt the reassuring weight of my talisman in the other pocket – the book my mother had given me that had once belonged to her mother. Spurred on, I grabbed the bottles, carrying them in my arms, and placing them on a long, scratched and tarnished wooden table covered in brittle paintbrushes and hardened tubes of paint. I returned to the cabinet and carried another armful back, placing them with the others. I stepped back and stared at the bottles. So many of them. Some were half-empty, others had dregs of liquid inside, but the majority were full. There was enough here to fulfil my promise to her – Isabella Langdon – to bring the police to Dunstrafne Castle so they would know about her. And they would discover what our husband, the laird of this land, had done to her: that he had killed her. I could hear his damning admission to whomever he had spoken to on the phone in his library, seeking absolution for ending her life.

The glass doors to the conservatory started rattling again as the wind forced itself against them, trying to get in by any means to stop me. Or perhaps to help fuel the flames of revenge I was about to ignite. The brown, shrivelled leaves covering the dusty surfaces and the floor scattered in anticipation as the wind gusted through the cracked and broken glass panels. I placed Isabella Langdon's engraved, gold-plated lighter on the wooden table and picked up a bottle of turpentine. I unscrewed the lid and doused the liquid over the remaining undamaged sketches and paintings. I took another bottle and repeated it again and again until only two bottles remained.

I looked around at all that was left of her. There was nothing here he could take with him when he began his new life, without us, his first wife and me. I stared at the self-portrait of Isabella

Langdon, not that you could discern it was her any longer. Her features now too fragmented and damaged to ever repair. She was unrecognisable, just as I was unrecognisable to myself. My memories too fragmented, too damaged, scattered and lost to me.

Forever? Perhaps.

Why? WHY? Why can't you remember anything? Not even how you met your husband. Or if you are the other woman, the charity worker he had an affair with and the woman he killed his wife to be with. Is that you?

I didn't know. I couldn't remember turning thirty-two. Or the past two years – longer even. Nor could I recall my wedding day. Or even, when we got Henry and Jack.

Why can't you remember anything? WHY?

It was terrifying not to know my life. And my mother? Why couldn't I remember when I last saw her? I couldn't even remember her phone number correctly.

WHY?

I wiped at my damp cheeks. Perhaps, I conceded, I would never find myself again. Perhaps there were some things that couldn't be undone.

I reached for the penultimate remaining bottle, took the piece of cloth next to it and doused it in the liquid. I then shoved half of the rag into the bottle with the remaining turpentine. I took the lighter, clicked it and watched as it instantaneously sparked into life. I held it to the soaked rag and waited, fascinated, as it burst into flames. I then threw it at her. At the self-portrait I had cut at, again and again, gouging out her eyes so she couldn't mock me any longer. I gazed on as all that was left of her erupted into a blaze of glory. Flames – orange, blue and yellow – then devoured what was left of her, licking and consuming the pieces of her flesh that I had left intact.

The crackling of flames intensified as it spread, rampant

through the conservatory, consuming everything in its wake. I could feel the heat of its intensity as the panes of glass started to complain and crack under the pressure of its roaring rage. I curled my fingers around the lighter, then turned and walked out, carrying the last bottle of turpentine. I unscrewed the lid and turned the bottle upside down, leaving a trail of the flammable liquid behind me.

Empty, I dropped the bottle. I reached for the pocketknife in my pocket and clutched it in my bandaged right hand. I could feel the brass key for Isabella Langdon's bedroom – his bedroom – brush my skin, reminding me where I had to go.

Now run... Run to her room.
And wait. Wait for him.

22

I looked down at the pocketknife in my hand. I unfolded the blade, and in doing so, the metal reflected the hypnotic, redemptive blaze behind me. The light from the voracious flames spread in and out of the dry debris, engulfing all in its frenzied greed. I imagined them licking the powdery, parched vines, encouraging them to come to life. I could feel the intensity of the heat as the fire took hold, claiming the conservatory as its own, intent on razing it to the ground. I felt warm now for the first time in this doomed castle.

You know what you have to do. You wait for him and then...

I looked up at one of the auld lairds who had once ruled Dunstrafne Castle and its ancient lands and dared to hold his outraged glare.

Did I see panic in his eyes? Perhaps.

For I planned to prove to the police once and for all that his kin, Laird James Buchanan Langdon, was intent on murdering me, just as he had murdered his other wife. And I knew exactly how to prove it.

I felt the tight constriction of the bandages binding my wrists. My husband had already lied to whomever he had spoken to in his library, telling them I had cut my wrists earlier in the evening, laying the seeds for when he returned to me to finish what he had started – killing me and staging it to appear like a suicide. After all, he had left his jacket with his pocketknife in it. He would claim I had found it, and that, when he returned from the library, he was too late. I had cut my wrists and bled out. He had lied to the woman on the phone, telling her I had slashed at my wrists with a shard of broken mirror. So, it would come as no surprise that on finding his pocketknife, I would have finished what I had started. Then, he could return to London to his new love and begin again as if I had never existed. Or his first wife.

But he has underestimated you. And her – Isabella Langdon.

I crept along the corridor and waited when I came to the main hallway, hiding in the gloom. I listened for movement. But all I could hear was the crackling and hissing of the flames behind me as they devoured all of her paintings and sketches in the conservatory. All my husband would find left of her would be ashes.

Then I thought I heard approaching footsteps. Heavy, oppressive and heading in my direction. I took my chance and darted from the protection of the shadows for the stone stairs, running up them, too fearful to look back.

I reached the top and headed for the darkness of the west wing, avoiding the glowing lamps of the east wing and my bedroom. I pushed my body against the wall and listened. I tried to ignore my ragged breathing so I could hear my husband. I covered my mouth so as not to give myself away when the sound of his foreboding steps echoing on the stone staircase reached me. Panic scorched through me, blinding me. I was paralysed with doubt, unsure of myself.

You can do this... Run... NOW.

I felt for the reassurance of his first wife's wedding ring, twisting it round and round on my finger to soothe me and allay my fears.

I moved quickly, running down the hall, retracing my steps from this morning when I had followed Henry.

Was it really this morning? Or has more time passed by without you realising? Days, weeks, months even...

Not that it mattered. Not any more.

I finally reached the door to the principal bedroom – their bedroom – that belonged to my husband and his other wife.

I sought out the brass key from my pocket. I swapped the pocketknife into my left hand, so I could open the door. I hadn't realised how badly I was trembling until the key escaped from my grip.

Oh God...

I crouched down and felt in the darkness for the fallen treasure.

No... No... Please...

I gasped with relief when my fingers groped it. I straightened up and exhaled slowly, trying to steady my nerves. I didn't know what awaited me behind this door, and whether I would ever leave this room alive.

You haven't got time to indulge in fear! You need to hide. He's coming for you!

I held my breath as I tried to hear whether he was closing in on me. But it was difficult to discern anything above the thundering blood as it pummelled recklessly through my veins.

Then I heard his voice, so loud that it reached my ears on the other side of the castle: 'MRS TAYLOR! MRS TAYLOR!'

Frantic, desperate – *murderous.*

I imagined he had found my room deserted, or was it the fire in the conservatory? Had he gone there first? I assumed it must be after midnight by now and Mrs Taylor would be deep asleep.

Not for long...

I inserted the key, turned it, releasing the lock. I twisted the handle and pushed open the door.

A cold chill rushed at me.

Is that a warning?

I stood for a moment, unsure. Blackness enshrouded the vast room. The air was cold, and dampness clung to it, adding to the feeling I had entered a crypt. I contemplated flicking the light switch to bring the centre ceiling crystal chandelier to life, dispersing the spectres that hid in here, but decided against it. I would brave the portentous darkness and shadows that dwelled here, waiting for their true mistress to return.

I forced my legs to move forward, stepping inside her bedroom. I couldn't bring myself to look over at her portrait above the fireplace. I was thankful it was too dark to see it – to see her – too fearful of what I would encounter. After all, I had set fire to all her paintings and sketches in the conservatory she had used as her art studio. Jealousy had spurred me on. I hated the fact my husband – her husband – still desired her. That I wasn't enough. I never would be. At that moment I hated her more than I hated him.

Remember! Remember why you're here.

I breathed shakily out as I tried to focus.

Too scared to look around the room for fear of what I would see, I looked over at the windows rattling in the wild wind as the storm whipped itself up into a frenzied hysteria. I walked over to the lead-paned windows, now battered by driving rain, hearing the call of the ocean crashing ever higher up the stone walls to reach me. I looked out at the bleak darkness far below before a glowing light caught my attention off to the right. I watched and waited as it grew brighter and more defiant, undeterred by the rain. Hissing sparks were now rising, intense and furious as it spread. Hypnotised by what swiftly became a raging ball of blue, red and orange within the large Victorian conservatory, I watched with delight.

I knew what I had to do when he found me. I had the proof of his other wife's existence in my pockets: empirical evidence that something terrible had happened to her, ready for when the police arrived. I was in no doubt that the fire would bring the emergency services. I gripped his pocketknife, prepared to expose him for the murderer he was. I touched the white-gold band of her wedding ring, a reminder of why I was going to do what would soon follow.

It wouldn't be long before the fumes from the conservatory triggered the smoke alarms in the main castle, alerting my husband and Mrs Taylor. Then the emergency services would be notified and would have to attend the situation at Dunstrafne Castle. But the firefighters and police wouldn't only find the castle in flames when they arrived. They would discover my body in his missing first wife's bedroom, holding her diary and other belongings, with Laird James Buchanan Langdon's Laguiole juniper-handled pocketknife, a present from her, stabbed deep into my abdomen.

I was prepared to wait until he came at me, to have the pocketknife ready to stab myself, using the force of his body to impale the tip of the blade deep into my stomach. My blood would be all over his shirt and his handprints were already on the handle. To all intents and purposes, it would appear as if he had stabbed me. And why not? I had given him motive enough for I had set fire to his beloved ancestral castle, home to his clan for centuries. Hadn't he admitted to whomever he had spoken to in the library in the darkest of hours that he was so close to losing it? His chilling words seemed to fill the room, endorsing my desperate plan:

'If I'm honest with you, I'm so close to losing it, to... to actually hurting—'

Hurting whom, I wondered. But I knew the answer: me. And I would prove it. I would show the police who my husband was and what he was capable of. I had nothing to lose. He had already admitted he had killed his first wife and that I would be gone by the morning. By taking control of my murder, he couldn't claim it was suicide. When the police arrived, they would know he had stabbed me. Especially after it became evident that he had attacked me and I had struggled to get away from him.

Now, all I had to do was watch as the fire took hold and wait for my husband to end my life. And there was no more apt place than her bedroom – his first wife's.

No more running or hiding. Expose him as the murderer he is...

Then the police will have to believe you. Even if it is too late...

But first, I wanted to surprise my husband.

I walked over to the fireplace and dared to look up into the shadowy gloom that concealed her portrait. I dragged one of the brown leather Queen Anne armchairs and positioned it directly in front of the middle of the mantelpiece. I climbed onto it, and with the blade of the pocketknife extended, I slashed again and again at her beautiful face and voluptuous body as I gave free rein to sheer, unadulterated hatred. And pleasure.

Sated, I turned and felt my way in the darkness for Isabella Langdon's walk-in closet. I had destroyed all paintings of her. All he had left was me... I would strip off this white, bloodstained summer dress. I would replace it with her beautiful emerald-green ball gown and smear her seductive, bold red lipstick over my flesh as we became one. I would avenge her death – his other wife – and my own slow, cruel, painful demise at the hands of my husband and his housekeeper and watch his horror as his ancestral castle burned to the ground.

23

I could hear faint whispers buzzing around me. I tried to open my eyelids, my eyes beneath moving frantically like a trapped butterfly as the whispers intensified. I kept trying to wake up in an attempt to break out of whatever prison I had found myself in. A wave of exhaustion took me hostage. Then another wave and another until, finally, the irritating whispering dissipated. I had no concept of how long, until again I found myself aware of a low hum. I eventually discerned it to be people talking around me. It was as if I didn't exist. But I was here, and I could hear them. I tried to flex my toes to see whether they were still a part of me. They jerked sporadically. I then tried to make my fingers move, making them twitch.

The murmuring around me became louder, encouraging. I assumed it was in response to my attempts to move my extremities. I willed my heavy eyelids to prise open, cajoling them, begging them to let me see who was with me. To find out where I was and what had happened to me. I gasped, blinded by the light when my eyelids succeeded in parting. They fluttered, shut, then opened and shut again against the brightness that flooded my pupils.

'Close the blinds,' a low voice suggested.

I heard the whoosh of curtains sealing out the world beyond.

The light became more subdued, less intrusive and invasive. Bearable.

My eyes were dry and uncomfortable, as if the surface layer was pebble-dashed by grit, some of it embedded. I could feel the rheum or mucus surrounding these foreign objects, trying to force out the discomfort, seeping into the corners of my eyes. I attempted to wipe away the irritating sleep that had formed while I had slept, but my arms refused to comply. I sighed, a breathless low and wounded hissing sound, as I struggled and failed again to move them. It felt like they were strapped down to...

My fingertips touched tentatively a soft sheet, then the firm mattress below.

To a bed.

I blinked again, trying to relieve the scratchy discomfort as the corner of the white ceiling started to come into focus. Then the walls, the door, until finally I understood I was in a white room with low beeping machines.

'Hey, there. I'm Adam and this is my colleague, Jodie. We're both ICU nurses.'

I stared up at him as he came into view.

'How are you feeling?'

His voice was gentle, inquisitive. Unfamiliar.

I swallowed. Failed. My throat hurt. My tongue was swollen, my mouth parched, desperate for water.

'Here,' he offered. 'This might help.'

I felt something pushed in between my cracked lips.

'Water,' he explained in reaction to my confusion.

It took me a few moments to catch up. I then understood and sucked greedily at the straw, desperate for the tasteless, lukewarm liquid offered to me.

'Slowly... Yeah? Take your time or you'll gag,' he advised, smiling at me.

I did as he asked, and tempered my desire to gulp it all in one go.

'That's enough for now,' he said before removing the straw from my mouth.

I relaxed against the pillows behind my head.

'So, do you think you can tell me how you are feeling?' he asked, still smiling.

I blinked. Tried to test out the question. I wasn't sure how I was feeling.

Exhausted, in pain and... confused.

'Where?' I mumbled, my hoarse voice cracking under the force of the word.

'You're in the intensive care unit,' the female nurse replied, leaning over me. 'In hospital,' she added for clarification.

I noted that she was dressed in blue scrubs with a lanyard around her neck.

'Where?' I heard myself repeat.

'QEUH. Glasgow's Queen Elizabeth University Hospital,' she explained.

'Oh...' I muttered.

I struggled to swallow and started choking.

'Slowly this time,' the male nurse suggested as he replaced the straw between my lips again.

I did as he instructed, and took my time sucking up the water.

'Good,' he said before removing the straw.

'How? How am I here?' I mumbled as my mind tried to fill in the blanks.

But it was all blank. There was nothing there.

'You were helicoptered here to QEUH.'

I blinked up at him. 'Why?'

'You...' He hesitated. 'You were injured and flown here.'

'When?' I asked.

Not that the knowledge would make a difference. The void in my mind was too vast for that one minuscule piece of information to explode into life, a memory of what had happened to me. To help me understand how I had ended up in a hospital.

And crucially, who was I?

I must have looked troubled, because he smiled reassuringly at me.

'Don't worry. You've been unconscious for nearly a week now. It's normal for things to be confusing to begin with. It will come back to you,' he promised.

'I... I'm...'

But before I could finish the sentence, I lost the word or words to convey the fear I felt at not knowing who I was or what had happened to me. My eyelids started to close. I struggled to keep them open, blinking repeatedly, but it was futile. I was losing myself again. His smiling face and that of his colleague with the blue scrubs and lanyard were fading away.

'Do you think she'll remember what happened?'

'Maybe, with time. You know her medical history?'

'Yeah. That's why I asked if you think she'll remember.'

'I don't know whether it's a good thing or not, if I'm honest. I mean, she's had enough trauma in her life. But to add the memory of your husband stabbing you as well...'

The voices drifted off.

I thought to myself, *I have a husband?*

A husband who stabbed you...

* * *

'Hey, you. How are you feeling this morning?' Adam asked.

I stared at him as I thought about how I felt.

'That good, huh?' he replied with a smile. 'The police are here. Do you think you feel up to talking to them?'

I didn't reply. I wasn't sure whether I wanted to talk to anyone.

'My husband?' I questioned.

Adam's smile slipped. 'Huh?'

'Is he here? Has he come to see me?'

'No. Remember, I explained to you that he can't visit you.'

'Oh,' I mumbled, struggling to remember.

I watched as Adam turned to the doorway. It was open and two police officers were watching us.

Watching you.

'I'm not sure that this is a good idea,' Adam said to them.

'Just a few minutes. That's all. If Mrs Langdon starts to get upset, we'll stop,' one of the officers assured him.

Adam turned back to me. 'Do you feel up to talking to the police?'

'About?' I questioned, confused.

'What happened to you?'

'Oh...' I mumbled. 'I had surgery,' I answered, noting the drainage tube was still attached to my abdomen.

'Yes. You suffered a knife wound to the upper part of your abdomen, known as the epigastrium, just below your ribs. The knife penetrated your liver and small intestine, and you required immediate surgery. Remember?'

I shook my head.

'Ms Anderson, your surgeon, came by yesterday to see how you are doing.'

I stared at him. I had no idea who he was talking about.

Adam turned back to the officers and shrugged. 'I don't think you'll be able to get much information about what happened. She is still very confused and doesn't remember much from that night. Trauma, I suspect, and—'

'We've got all the facts we need,' the male officer interrupted.

'We just want to hear from Mrs Langdon,' the female officer added. 'Like I said, if Mrs Langdon starts to get distressed, we'll stop.'

I looked at Adam, who sighed. He shook his head and turned to me. 'If this is too much for you, just say. Okay?'

I nodded. I liked Adam. I believed he liked me as well.

The officers came into my room.

'Remember, she gets tired very quickly. And, she doesn't know about her husband. We're waiting for her consultant to tell her,' Adam instructed.

'We won't mention anything,' the male officer asserted.

'Mention what?' I asked. 'What about my husband?'

But Adam had disappeared and the two police officers acted as if they hadn't heard me.

'Do you mind if we sit down?' the male officer asked as he approached my bed.

'I don't know,' I replied.

'I'm Officer Ferguson and this is my partner, Officer Murray,' he introduced before bringing over one of the two chairs sat against the wall.

I watched as his female colleague, Officer Murray, also grabbed a chair and positioned it next to his by my bed.

I realised in that moment that no one had visited me – until now.

'Where's my husband?' I asked them.

A look passed between them before the female officer turned her gaze on me and replied, 'He's tied up at the moment. I'm sure he'll visit you when he gets the opportunity.'

'Did he stab me?' I questioned. 'Is that why you're here?'

'We wanted to see what you remembered from that night,' she replied, avoiding my question.

'When he stabbed me?' I asked them.

'When you were stabbed, yes.'

They were both watching me.

I tried to recollect what had led me here, to this hospital room with two police officers waiting to take my statement.

'Do you remember the fire at Dunstrafne Castle, Mrs Langdon?'

I shook my head. 'No. I don't remember any fire,' I replied.

'You don't know how it started?' she asked me.

I had the vaguest of feelings that I should know, but it was a tenuous thread that snapped as soon as I pulled on it. 'No.'

'I see. Do you remember staying at Dunstrafne Castle with your husband, Mrs Langdon?'

I looked at her. It was odd. I couldn't read her expression. I didn't know whether she suspected me of something.

Of what? Of starting a fire, perhaps.

'You think I started the fire?' I asked.

'Did you?' she asked.

'Did I what?'

She gave her colleague a sideways glance. 'Did you start the fire or maybe you know who did?' she continued.

'I... I don't think so. Why would I start a fire?'

'That's what we're trying to establish,' she answered.

'Oh...' I mumbled.

None of it made sense to me. My head was starting to hurt from the pressure of answering their questions, of trying to remember.

'Did my husband start the fire?' I asked.

'Not as far as we believe,' she replied.

'Did you ask him?'

'Yes,' she answered.

'What did he say?' I asked her.

'That you started the fire,' her colleague answered.

Startled, I looked at him. 'Me?'

He nodded. 'Your hands,' he noted.

I looked down at my hands. They were both bandaged. As were my wrists.

'Why are my hands bandaged?' I muttered more to myself than them.

I didn't recall Adam telling me I had burned my hands.

'We believe from when you started the fire in the conservatory at Dunstrafne Castle.'

'Is there a conservatory?' I questioned.

'Yes. That's where the fire was intentionally started and it was your—'

'I don't remember,' I said, cutting him off. 'And I'm tired and my head hurts.'

Neither one of them said anything.

'My husband, where is he?' I repeated.

'Thank you for your time, Mrs Langdon. We hope you feel better soon,' the female police officer said as she stood up.

'My husband?' I repeated.

I watched as, ignoring me, she replaced her chair against the wall.

I looked at her colleague who had also risen. He was staring at something on the cabinet by my bed. I followed his gaze. It was my book. The one my mother had given to me years ago.

'Who brought you the book?' he asked.

'Mrs Taylor,' I answered without thinking.

Mrs Taylor...

He nodded as if what I had said made perfect sense.

She had left the book for me. I was unaware she had brought it as I had been unconscious at the time. Adam had told me that she explained to him that the book meant a great deal to me and that I would want it when I woke up. She was right.

'Have you spoken to her? To Mrs Taylor?' I asked.

'Yes, we interviewed Mrs Taylor after the fire.'

Then I remembered.

The boys... Henry and Jack.

'Henry and Jack?' I questioned.

Neither of them understood me.

'My dogs. Are they all right?'

'Yes, your dogs are fine. Mrs Taylor made sure they were safe.'

I reached over but struggled to pick up the book with bandaged hands.

'Here, let me,' the male officer offered, handing me my book.

'Thank you,' I replied as he laid it down on the bed beside me.

As he did so, some loose pages with writing on them fell out.

I picked them up and stared at them.

They were her diary entries.

Isabella Langdon?

Your husband's other wife. The one he killed.

I stared from the pages up to the police officer. 'Isabella Langdon? Where is she? Did you find her? My husband killed her, just as he tried to kill me.'

I could hear the panic in my voice, felt it in my expression, but for some reason the two officers didn't react.

I watched as they both stepped back away from me.

'Here!' I shouted at them, holding up the few pages that documented her last days. 'This is hers! She disappeared two years ago! Look! LOOK!' I yelled. 'This belonged to Isabella Langdon! His wife before me!' I cried, desperate for them to take me seriously.

'Mrs Langdon,' the female officer began, 'there is no first wife.'

'There is!' I fired back. 'Look at this! And I found her wedding ring, her cigarette lighter—'

'Look at the whiteboard,' Adam interrupted. I hadn't seen him come back into the room.

'NO!' I screamed at Adam. 'This is important! It's about what my husband did to her. His first wife, Isabella Langdon. They need to believe me!' I pleaded as tears of frustration slid down my face. 'Adam? Please? Tell them, they have to believe me.'

'Sure,' he said as he approached my bed. 'I will, if you calm down and look at the whiteboard for me.'

Breathing shallowly, I did as he asked and looked at the wall in front of me.

'When did you put that there?' I questioned, confused.

'It's always been there,' Adam assured me. 'Now read the first line. Remember, we do this every time you wake up.'

'No,' I mumbled, shaking my head. 'We don't.'

'We do. Now read the first line for me. It will help you understand what's happening to you. Please?'

I forced myself to focus on the bold black words written on the whiteboard.

'No...' I mumbled. 'No... How? That's not possible. Adam? Please? Don't make me.'

'Read it out for me,' he repeated in a firm but gentle tone.

'Who am I?' I read out, swiping at the tears that blurred the words together.

'Who are you?' questioned Adam, placing his hand on top of my bandaged left hand. 'Do it for me,' he encouraged gently.

But I couldn't. I couldn't say those terrifying words. How could I? How could they possibly be true?

Q: Who am I?
A: I am Isabella Langdon.

24

'You have a visitor,' Adam announced, walking into my room. 'No visitors and then two visits in two days!'

Surprised, I looked up at him.

'The police yesterday and now—'

'My husband?' I questioned.

'No. But you do know her.'

'Who?' I asked.

'Mrs Langdon?'

I didn't recognise the voice. Nor did I recognise the owner of the voice who had followed Adam into my room.

Or do you?

I had a feeling that I should know her.

'Right, I'll leave you to it, Professor Walker,' Adam said as he moved towards the door.

'No... Adam, no. Don't go...' I pleaded.

'You'll be fine. Professor Walker's your... your doctor. She's known you for a long time.'

Without waiting for an answer, Adam stepped out of the room, leaving me alone with her.

'I'm Alex. Alexandra Walker. Remember me?'

I shook my head as I looked at her. She wasn't dressed in scrubs, like the nurses and other doctors here. Instead, she was wearing a dark grey, wool Prada pinstriped trouser suit. Her long, sleek auburn hair was pulled back from her attractive, oval face. I looked at her eyes, the lightest and brightest blue eyes I had ever seen. They shone with a sharpness, an intelligence that seemed to penetrate my mind.

Is she studying you? Appraising you?

I couldn't be sure.

She smiled, making the fine lines around her eyes crinkle. 'You'll remember in time.'

I watched as she took a chair and placed it beside my bed.

'Why have you come here?' I asked, fearful.

She didn't answer me immediately. She took her time getting seated. I watched as she placed her traditional black Prada leather work bag on the floor. It was as old-school as her fitted white shirt and tailored suit.

My eyes drifted to her socks. They were pristine, as if worn for the first time. I imagined they wouldn't have any traces of laundry detergent scent but that new-clothing aroma. They were grey wool ribbed socks. I noted the black Christian Dior signature and bee on the side as she crossed her leg over her knee. Her black Dior loafers with the gold-tone Christian Dior Paris signature on the leather tag on the front.

She folded her slender hands as she looked at me, as if weighing up how to respond to my question. Her hands looked young for her late-forty-something years. Her fingers were long, delicate even, with manicured nails, as if the hands of a surgeon. I noticed the gold band on her left fourth finger.

'It's time for you to come back,' she said slowly, as if allowing me a moment to absorb the impact of those words.

Come back? Back where? Back from where?

I shook my head. 'No. I want to stay here.'

'You can't stay here. It's time you were moved, so someone else can have this room. You're improving every day. And we can take care of you properly at Sanderson Hospital,' she assured me.

'Sanderson Hospital?'

She nodded as she watched me absorb her proposal. 'It's not like here, at Glasgow's Queen Elizabeth University Hospital. We offer specialist care for injuries like the one you sustained. It's private residential care. It's a rehabilitation unit for patients such as yourself.'

I looked at her. 'Do you know where my husband is?'

'Yes... We'll get to James in time, Mrs Langdon. After we've gone over a few things first,' she replied.

I shook my head. 'No. I want to see my husband.'

She smiled at me with her azure-blue eyes. 'I know. And you will.'

Can you trust her?

I didn't know. All I knew was I wanted to go back home.

Home? Where?

I gasped.

Your mother...

'What did you remember?' questioned Alex.

I looked at her, startled that she could read my mind.

I shook my head.

'You can tell me. It's important that you tell me what you can remember and then...' She paused, smiled. 'I'll fill in the gaps for you.'

Do you trust her?

My eyes instinctively looked at her Prada work bag waiting on the floor next to her.

'I was about to get to that,' she said, following my gaze. She bent down and opened the large black leather bag. 'Ready?' she asked me as she pulled out a substantial folder with the name 'Isabella Langdon' written across the front.

The folder contained her life – her memories.

They're not your memories; they are hers. Otherwise, you would remember them.

'You can trust me,' she assured as if I had spoken my suspicion about her, about the contents of that folder, out loud.

Can you trust her? Can you trust what is in that folder?

I shook my head. 'No... I don't want to know what's in there...'

I turned my head away from her and the folder now resting in her hands and stared straight ahead at the whiteboard.

No... NO!

The bold black words stared straight back at me:

Q: Who am I?
A: I am Isabella Langdon.

The name on the thick folder that Alex Walker, the woman Adam claimed was my doctor, was holding in her surgeon-honed hands with the same name, 'Isabella Langdon', written in black ink across the front.

Your name?

NO! It can't be... You can't be Isabella Langdon...

I heard her snap open the folder, followed by her reassuring, soothing voice: 'I know you're scared. But it will all make sense. I promise... Look.'

I shook my head as I squeezed my eyelids shut against those terrifying words:

Q: Who am I?
A: I am Isabella Langdon.

I didn't want to know... Not now. Not ever. I didn't want to know what terrible thing had happened to me.

What did he do to you? Your husband? How did he make you forget who you are? Even your name? How did he take your essence away so all you have is chaos and fear: fear of the blank, blinding spaces where your memories once were?

25

'Mrs Langdon?'

She was still there.

'Please go... I'm tired,' I whispered, keeping my eyes closed to block out the whiteboard.

To block out her.

'I travelled from London to see you,' she replied.

'Go away,' I repeated.

'No. I promised your husband I would check on you.'

I opened my eyes to look at her. 'Do you know my husband?'

'I have known him for some time. James is a friend of mine. And I have known you for two years. I met you when—'

'At our wedding?' I interrupted. 'I can't remember my wedding,' I shared. 'And there's no photographs of us getting married. I think my husband destroyed them all because he regrets marrying me. He doesn't want to be with me. Did you know that? I heard him say that he can't bear to...' I faltered, unable to actually articulate it.

I could hear the fragile tremor in my voice as the pain of that acknowledgement blindsided me.

He can't tolerate you. He can't abide even looking at you. You disgust him. That's why he's not visited you.

Alex smiled as she shook her head. I couldn't tell whether it was a sad smile or not.

'No... No, I wasn't at your wedding. I met you when—'

I cut her off again. 'He keeps photographs of her. His first wife. Did you know that?' I asked as tears, hot and wet, slipped down my face.

'That's you, Mrs Langdon. You are James's only wife,' she stated, still smiling.

'No! I'm not! I... I look nothing like her!'

She looked at me with an expression I didn't understand. The smile had slipped.

I used the back of my bandaged right hand to swipe at my damp cheeks.

'I found her...' I paused as I tried to force the tenuous memory. 'Her...' I struggled, trying but failing to pull something out of nothing.

My brain was filled with an aching void. Everything that I wanted to know, needed to know, had been erased. Gone in the blink of an eye. All that was left was a blinding light that hurt when I tried to look at it. To get past it to see whether anything was left inside of me.

I dropped my eyes, letting them fall on her hands resting on top of the folder waiting to show me whatever she had travelled from London to...

I tried to recall my location. I couldn't. I looked around the white room and at the continuously beeping machines monitoring my vital signs. The room and sterile equipment told me I was in hospital.

But where? And why?

I frowned, as I tried to retrieve the information as the thin gold band that she was wearing glinted in the light from the window as she moved her fingers.

It acted as a prompt.

'Her gold ring... I found her wedding ring,' I exclaimed with a gush of relief that the memory had come back.

She nodded. 'The staff have kept it safe at the nurses' station until you're discharged. You were wearing it when you were brought in.'

'I don't want it. It's not mine. Give it to my husband,' I fired back. 'It belongs to his other wife!'

Why would she want you to have her ring? Why is no one concerned about her? About what happened to Isabella Langdon?

'It's your ring, Mrs Langdon,' she replied.

'It's not! How could it be? He married her nine years ago. We have only been married for two years. And you know what?' I questioned, feeling the heat spread up my neck.

She shook her head and waited.

'That's when she disappeared. What happened to her? Do you know? If you have known my husband before me, then you must have met her.'

I watched as the smile slowly returned. 'I've only ever met you.'

Can you trust her?

I felt nauseous as the familiar knot in my stomach twisted and turned.

'Adam?' I shouted weakly. 'Adam?'

I then found the buzzer lying on my bed sheet. I pressed it. Again, and again.

'Adam can't help you,' she said. 'But I can. That's why I'm here.'

Her voice was calm. Reassuring even.

Can you trust her?

'Adam?' I repeated. 'Adam?'

The ICU nurse popped his head around the door. 'Hey, what's up?'

'I want her to go now.'

Adam looked from me to the visitor who claimed to be my doctor. The woman with the impeccable clothes and surgeon's hands.

'Mrs Langdon is feeling overwhelmed. It's understandable. I won't stay for much longer,' she stated.

Adam nodded. He then looked at me. 'You need to listen to Professor Walker. I know it's challenging for you. But you can do it. You need to do it.'

I stared at him, confused. I didn't understand why he wasn't making her leave as I had requested.

'No! Please, I'm tired,' I insisted.

'I know you are,' Alex intervened. 'And I won't stay for much longer. You have my word.'

Do you trust her?

I didn't know...

'I'll be back in five minutes. All right?' Adam assured me.

I shook my head. 'No,' I mumbled as he left.

But it wasn't Adam's disappearance that distressed me. I watched as her long, precise surgeon hands removed photographs from the folder she was holding.

I forced my eyes shut. I could feel the explosive pressure building up in my head, a forewarning of ensuing pain. A tsunami that would wipe me out, forcing me to retreat into myself, hiding from my body, unable to cope with the debilitating pain that even the act of breathing would cause me.

'Please, Mrs Langdon, open your eyes,' she requested.

'No,' I replied. 'I don't want to see what you have there.'

'The photographs?'

'Yes.'

'They won't hurt you. They'll help you understand what is happening to you. So, you can make sense of all the confusion. Don't you want that?'

I hesitated. Then nodded. 'But I don't want to see them... The photographs,' I insisted.

'All right. We'll leave them for now.'

'Thank you,' I mumbled.

'You can open your eyes,' she said.

Can you trust her?

'You can trust me,' she assured.

Can you?

I opened my eyes and looked at the folder. She hadn't returned the photographs to the folder, but she had covered them with it. For now.

'Isabella?'

'That's not my name!' I hissed.

'What is your name?' she asked.

'It's... It's...' But I couldn't find it. It didn't exist any more. 'Mrs Langdon,' I finally answered.

'Your first name?'

'I... I...' I didn't know. 'It's not Isabella,' I stated.

'It is Isabella. You are Isabella Langdon and—'

'I'm not!' I argued.

'And you have been married to James Langdon for nine years.'

'NO!' I raged. I started to hum to block out her disruptive voice.

'You were involved in a car crash,' she continued, unabated, in a firmer voice so it would penetrate through my humming.

I stopped. Silent, I stared at her.

Do you trust her?

She held my gaze. 'Two years ago,' she continued, 'your husband was driving you both back to Dunstrafne Castle from dinner.'

'With whom?' I asked.

'Oh, I think James said they were old family acquaintances. He felt duty-bound. Otherwise, he would have cancelled given the circumstances.'

'Circumstances?' I mumbled.

'Yes, the pregnancy,' she explained. 'Remember?'

I nodded. 'Yes, her diary. Isabella wrote about it in her diary.'

'Your diary,' she corrected.

I stared at her. She kept getting it wrong and I didn't know why. Maybe she was misremembering.

But I remembered. I remembered the words Isabella Langdon wrote about my – her – husband's response to the pregnancy. For I had lain in this hospital bed rereading those final entries of hers before she—

I stopped myself and focused on her fearful words:

I told James I was pregnant. I was so excited when I surprised him with the ultrasound scan picture, but instead of being happy, he was angry, claiming I shouldn't have made a unilateral decision. That he had explained to me his reservations about having children.

'Why wasn't he happy about the news? The pregnancy?' I asked her.

She nodded at me. 'You recall he wasn't happy?'

I failed to respond.

'Well,' she continued, 'he had concerns that any children of his would inherit the same genetic disorder as his older brother, Thomas. He had—'

'Adrenoleukodystrophy,' I cut in.

She nodded, her smile broadening as her eyes lit up.

'A simple guess,' I explained. 'The charity he worked for?'

'Ah, I see.' Her smile faded. 'Yes. James's older brother died at the age of eleven when James was only seven. His mother, Moireach Buchanan, never got over her eldest son's death. Neither did your husband. Thomas started showing neurological symptoms at the age of eight. These were the first signs of childhood cerebral ALD. He began to regress, losing concentration at school, followed by convulsions and seizures. Eventually, he lost most of his neurological abilities: sight, hearing and voluntary movements. Unfortunately, children with this type of ALD typically pass away within a few years of diagnosis, which is what happened to Thomas.'

'That's terrible,' I mumbled.

'Yes. ALD is a rare genetic condition affecting more males than females and one in fifteen thousand people worldwide. James didn't want to risk a child inheriting ALD. He had witnessed what this condition had done to Thomas and his parents. So when you told him the news, he was shocked that you had discounted his genuine concerns and became pregnant while he believed you were still taking the oral contraceptive pill.'

'Isabella,' I corrected her. 'Isabella told him she was pregnant.'

She studied me for a moment.

I wasn't sure whether I saw a flicker of disappointment cross her face. I couldn't tell.

'What happened? You said James was driving?' I questioned.

'Yes. It was late at night, after eleven—'

'Eleven minutes past eleven,' I interrupted.

'You remember?' she questioned, a note of surprise in her voice.

I recalled passing the tall, chinoiserie longcase clock in the grand hallway. I had paused, mesmerised, and stared at the brass face with its black numbers and hands, waiting for them to move. Only, for some reason, time had stopped in Dunstrafne Castle at precisely 11.11.

Why?

I had always had a feeling that this time was significant – to me
or to Isabella Langdon.

Alex waited for me to elaborate. When I failed to, she continued: 'As I was saying, from what James has told me, you were having
a heated argument on the drive back.'

'Over his affair?' I guessed.

She nodded at me, smiling. 'He was having an affair with a
woman he had met as a board member of the adrenoleukodystrophy charity in London.'

'Was that me?'

She stared at me.

'Was I the woman he was having the affair with?' I questioned.

'No. Not you,' she answered. 'You are Isabella Langdon.
Remember?'

I shook my head. I didn't remember.

'Becky, that was her name. James had ended it that same day
when you told him about the pregnancy. But you didn't believe him.
It then escalated to an argument about the pregnancy. James was
furious at you for disregarding his genuine concerns, and you were
equally angry at him about the affair and his reaction to your news.
He said that you were screaming at him to pull over, that you
wanted to get out of the car. He regrets his decision not to drive the
Range Rover, but instead, the classic Mercedes-Benz sports car.'

'Why?'

She stared at me as if assessing whether I had any recollection
of that night.

'The Range Rover has an airbag, unlike the classic sports car. He
walked away virtually unscathed while the impact threw you
through the windscreen and—'

'How? How did he walk away unhurt and I... I...?' My voice
faltered.

It made no sense.

'You unclipped your seat belt, wanting to get out of the car, just as a deer shot out into the road. James lost control of the car and crashed head-on into a tree—'

'That can't be true,' I interjected, cutting her off. 'It's either at dusk or dawn that deer are active, not late at night.'

'I don't know, this is what James told me. It's detailed in the police report if you want to read it.'

'You have it with you?' I asked, surprised.

She nodded. 'In here,' she said, tapping the folder.

'Why?'

'Because you can't remember and I know you won't trust what I tell you. So, I brought what evidence I could to show you who you are,' she explained.

'Why? Why bother?'

'Because James, your husband, asked me to see you.'

'Is he coming to see me?' I asked. 'He hasn't come.'

'That's because he's currently being questioned by the police.'

'Why?' I asked.

'Because he's helping them understand what happened to you.'

'Me?' I mumbled.

She nodded. 'I'll be seeing the police later, and James. They want a statement from me as your clinician.'

I stared at her.

'You told the police that James stabbed you with his pocketknife in your abdomen,' she added for clarification.

I followed her gaze and looked down at the drainage tube snaking out from under my bed sheet.

'Dunstrafne Castle? We were in Isabella Langdon's bedroom. And... and...' I stopped. I couldn't recall what had happened. 'Did he? Did he stab me?' I whispered. 'I heard him talking to someone on the phone about how much he hated being with me and not her.'

'It was me that James was talking to that evening,' she shared.

'You?' I murmured. 'Why?'

She looked at me for a moment, as if deliberating before answering: 'He was scared. Scared of what he might do to you. He had been pushed to his limit and couldn't cope. He had thought it was a good idea after the car crash—'

'Crash?'

'Yes, the car crash. We were just talking about it. Remember?'

I shook my head.

'You sustained a serious head injury,' she explained.

I instinctively touched my short hair. My fingers sought out the truth as they fumbled through my aggressively cropped hair. I ran my fingers over my head, digging into my scalp in frustration at all that was left. I heard myself exhale – a low, wounded sound – when I touched thick ridges of scarring.

NO... No... Oh God...

What happened to you?

Horrified, I snatched my hands from the gnarled knots of skin stapled together like a jigsaw puzzle. But someone had sealed it while the pieces were still missing inside my head, too complicated for them to complete.

'I was your surgeon. You sustained a great deal of trauma which has affected your memories. That's why you can't remember before the accident, being married to James. Or being Isabella Langdon.'

I stared at her. None of it made sense. Her words were making the building pressure in my head intolerable.

'I don't have a brain injury. I suffer from migraines. They affect me for days and strip away my memories. But they return. Eventually. That is what my husband's housekeeper told me.'

'Rachael Taylor? Yes, she worked with you and was involved in your recovery at the neuro rehabilitation unit at Sanderson Hospital. She's outside, waiting to see you.'

'No, Mrs Taylor's my husband's housekeeper,' I corrected.

'She's a psychiatric nurse who specialises in acquired brain injuries,' she informed me.

'No...' I mumbled. 'Why are you lying to me?'

'You refused to accept you had a brain injury and so, James decided to let you believe you only suffered from migraines. Which you do, can I add. You have light and sound sensitivity. It's a side effect of the brain trauma.'

'No...' I whispered, not wanting to believe her.

Do you trust her?

'If what you say is true, then why am I not still there at this...'

'Sanderson Hospital?' she suggested.

'Yes. There! Why would I be living with my husband at... at...' But I couldn't retrieve the memory. I raised my bandaged fists and started thumping my head. 'Remember! Remember!'

She stood up and reached over and held my arms, forcing me to stop. 'You're tired. It's worse when you're tired,' she explained as she gently rested my hands on the bed.

Terrified, I stared up at her. 'I can't remember...' More tears escaped, blurring my perception of the world, of her.

'Trust me. It will get better.'

I shook my head. 'How can you know that?'

'Because I am a brain surgeon, Mrs Langdon. Your surgeon. You were in a coma for six months after the surgery. When you did wake up, it was a long recovery process. You had to learn to eat, walk, talk again. But you did it. You worked hard,' she told me.

'What happened? Why haven't my memories come back?'

'Because your brain suffered extensive trauma, which has disrupted your long-term memory. That is why you can't remember being Isabella Langdon, those seven years of marriage before the car accident. As for your short-term memory, conversion to long-term memory requires time, but you have suffered a disrupting factor. An injury which is preventing a significant number from being consolidated. But, as you have proven to me in our conversation, some short-term memories are being converted to your hippocampus, which is promising news.'

'I don't understand.'

'We have daily experiences which our brain files away over a period of time as a permanent record in our memory, to the hippocampus. Patients who have a neurodegenerative disorder like Alzheimer's disease, have what we call anterograde amnesia—'

'Do I have that?' I cut in.

She shook her head, smiled at me. 'No, but you do have a brain injury with the same outcome as Alzheimer's, which is the inability to form new memories. This is because your long-term memory—'

'The hippocampus?' I questioned.

'Yes, that's correct. The hippocampus can no longer connect to the neocortex to access the consolidated short-term memories. Typically, hippocampal damage affects memories post-trauma: patients can remember details before the injury, but unfortunately for you, the accident also impaired what long-term memories you had already stored.'

'No...' I mumbled. 'I don't believe you. Mrs Taylor and my husband were drugging me to make me forget. To make me sleep.'

She again smiled at me. 'They were giving you the same medication that you've received here. The medication that you have to take is because of your brain injury—'

'What? Drugs for epilepsy? That doesn't make sense. Or Valium? I know she was giving me Valium tablets,' I insisted, feeling the agitation, fuelled by fear, making my skin feel hot and itchy, and my scalp was burning as if it were on fire.

'Yes, you're prescribed anti-epileptic drugs because of your brain injury and medication for your migraines. As for the Valium, that is to help stabilise your mood when you are feeling over-whelmed and agitated.'

Like now?

I closed my eyes, struggling to comprehend the enormity of what she was telling me.

I could feel myself drifting. I didn't want to know any more.

I heard the treacherous sound of her removing the photographs and laying them on my bed to force me to see them. But I didn't want to face my past or my future: both lost to me. For what good would it do as I would no doubt forget again? All she was going to cause was pain.

NO... No... you don't want to see them. If you do, it might make it all real. And you don't want this to be your reality.

You don't want to be her – to be Isabella Langdon. To know all that you have lost. To realise your husband took it all from you. He caused you to be like this – he crashed the car because he was angry and wasn't thinking about the tight, bending country roads leading up to the Dunstrafne estate.

I thought of Isabella Langdon's last diary entry the night she was killed. That she was worried for... her safety.

Why?

Then the memory hit me so hard, I gasped for breath...

...an uneasy, bad feeling about tonight...

That had been her last night with him. The night he crashed the car. Intentionally?

There was no deer... He swerved and braked so hard your body went through the windscreen. He unclipped your seat belt... Not you. Or did you unclip it in a fit of pique? Angry at him for not wanting the baby? For cheating on you after everything you had given him? And now he didn't want your child. His child... He wanted her – this other woman.

I felt a thousand hornets stinging me, darting and stabbing in all corners of my brain in a desperate, furious bid to escape.

Her final diary entry forced its way up from the mythological River Lethe of forgetfulness that coursed through my veins, flooding my mind, submerging all my memories, drowning my thoughts.

What if he doesn't want me any more... What if he wants a new life with her? What happens to me?

I could hear her voice, Isabella Langdon's, as if she were in my head screaming at me.

Why did he choose to drive his 1954 classic Mercedes-Benz sports car that night? Why was he speeding around those single-lane roads on the blackest of darkest nights?

The night he tried to kill her – you.

Or did you try to kill yourself?

26

I opened my eyes and was surprised to see someone sitting by my bedside watching me.

I blinked a couple of times as I tried to focus.

'Who are you?'

She smiled. 'I am Alex. Remember? Professor Alex Walker, your clinician.'

'Oh,' I mumbled.

Perhaps...

Her name was familiar. I noticed her hands holding—

I stopped myself. I didn't want to think about what was inside that folder.

'How long have you been sitting there?' I asked, suspicious.

'I left you sleeping for the day. It's just after six in the evening now. I came back to see if we could finish our conversation, before I see you again at Sanderson Hospital.'

'I've been there before?' I questioned, confused.

The memory was hazy, shrouded in pain. And fear.

'Yes. You spent twenty-two months at the rehabilitation unit after the car accident. The first six months in a coma and then sixteen months relearning fundamental skills.'

'And then where did I go?' I questioned.

She nodded, smiling again. 'Then your husband, James, asked to take you back to Dunstrafne Castle with a full-time residential psychiatric nurse who specialises in brain trauma.'

I stared at her, unsure of what it had to do with me.

'Mrs Taylor?' she prompted. 'Rachael Taylor?'

'My husband's housekeeper?'

'The nurse he hired to look after you,' she answered.

'Where is she?' I asked. 'I need to see her!'

'She's been sitting with you this afternoon as you slept.'

'Is she coming back?' I asked. 'I need to talk to her!'

'Yes, she said she would call by briefly again this evening.'

I slowly breathed out and relaxed back against the pillows.

'Why? Why did you let him take me away?' I suddenly questioned, the agitation returning.

She sighed. The smile was gone. 'Because your husband persuaded me that it might be beneficial for your recovery. Dunstrafne Castle was so close to your heart: a location and home you loved, filled with your past there. James hoped it would act as a prompt and remind you of who you were before the accident. You painted there in the conservatory, and you had your horses and dogs.'

'I didn't see any horses,' I stated.

She nodded, the smile returning.

Why?

Because you remembered that detail perhaps.

'I recall James saying only Rachael, Mrs Taylor that is, would be residing at the property while you were there. I assume he stabled the horses somewhere else as he didn't want the stablehands or other staff bothering you.'

'She starved me!' I cried. 'They starved me. They locked me up with bars on my window. They kept me isolated. I couldn't get out.'

She looked at me. Her expression was now blank, blocking me from ascertaining what she was thinking. Or whether she believed me.

'They starved me,' I repeated, wanting a reaction.

'You're starving yourself,' she explained quietly.

'No! How could you say that? I wanted to eat but the food she was giving me was tasteless. It was like chewing soggy cardboard. The Earl Grey tea she claimed to be giving me tasted of nothing. That's why I couldn't eat. They were starving me so I would fade into oblivion.'

She took her time before replying as if meditating on her words. 'You suffered a life-altering brain injury which impacted your sense of smell and taste. Without prompting, you forget to eat as your senses aren't there to entice you, to remind you.'

I swallowed, trying to dislodge the knot at the back of my throat.

No... No, it can't be true, can it?

'The bars on my window? They kept me a prisoner. She would lock me in my room. They even locked all the external doors to prevent me from leaving,' I heard myself repeating.

'They did that to protect you,' she answered.

'Protect me from whom?' I demanded.

'Yourself.'

'No! They were the threat to me. My husband tried to kill me!' I fired back.

Your wrists...

I looked down at my wrists.

You didn't imagine it...

'He did this to me!' I said, holding out my bandaged wrists to her.

'No, Isabella—'

'Don't call me that! My name is Mrs Langdon!'

She nodded. 'You did that to yourself with the mirror you smashed in the conservatory. Remember? And you cut your hand quite badly. It's lucky you didn't sever your flexor tendons. Thank goodness Rachael was there to clean you up and stitch the wounds.'

'I didn't do that. I didn't cut my wrists. He did it!' I argued.

'Remember we discussed your medication?'

I shook my head. 'No.'

'We did this morning. You also take antidepressants because of your brain injury—'

'Why?' I interrupted. 'I'm not depressed. You said I had a car accident.'

'Depression is prevalent in brain injuries. The antidepressants you take enhance your serotonin neurotransmitter. Female patients who have suffered brain trauma are particularly susceptible to suicidal ideation. You have made multiple attempts to take your life.'

'No! NO! That's not true. You're lying to me,' I exclaimed.

'I've spoken to James,' she said. 'Your husband,' she added as if for clarity.

'My husband? When?' I demanded, shocked.

Why hasn't he visited you?

'This afternoon while you slept. He explained what happened that night and how you had repeatedly tried to take your life. James and Rachael, Mrs Taylor, found you in time hiding in the conservatory after you had cut your wrists—'

'Conservatory. She used the conservatory as her art studio,' I stated.

She smiled at me. 'Yes.'

'And the rocks? He pushed me off the rocks into the ocean,' I said.

'That was you. You escaped and ran down to the rocks. You

jumped off and if it hadn't been for your husband, you would have died.'

'I can't swim,' I replied. 'He knew that. He knew that I couldn't swim.'

'No, you can swim. You chose not to,' she clarified. 'You're a champion swimmer. You competed for your county and with your university swimming team.'

I shook my head. 'No, I can't swim. Maybe she can, Isabella Langdon. But I can't swim and he knew that when he pushed me into the water. If Mrs Taylor hadn't witnessed it, he would have left me to drown.'

'No. James loves you. Your husband has tried everything in his power to aid your recovery. He spent two months caring for you at Dunstrafne Castle, trying to help you remember.'

'He spent his time in London,' I spat. 'He left me with his house-keeper. He hates me.'

'No, he loves you. He doesn't hate you. What makes you say that?' she asked.

I couldn't tell if she was curious or not.

'Because...' I left the word hanging. I couldn't explain how I knew, I just felt it.

'You might not be aware, but because of the brain trauma, your perception of emotion from facial expression has been affected. Facial expressions are a key component of non-verbal communication. It's how we decode what someone is feeling from their face. Expressions such as animosity, happiness and sadness help give us feedback and are an essential indicator of how we interact with that person.'

I shook my head, not understanding what she was saying. 'I can see when you smile,' I said, trying to refute her.

She smiled at me.

'See! I can see that you are smiling at me,' I said.

'And now?' she asked me. 'Can you tell me what I am feeling now? Am I angry or sad?'

But I couldn't discern her emotions. 'You're trying to trick me!' I argued.

'No, I am trying to explain to you that your husband doesn't hate you. And even if his face showed that emotion, your lack of facial-expression recognition means you wouldn't be able to tell. That's why you need full-time care as it places you in a vulnerable position. If you can't read someone's expression, then you can end up behaving in a way they find inappropriate or offensive.'

I shook my head. 'No...' I murmured.

I didn't want to live indefinitely in some rehabilitation unit with strangers. I wanted to go home.

'Will it ever return? My...' I stopped, unable to remember what she had said.

'Your perception of emotion from other people's facial expressions?'

I nodded.

'No, I'm sorry. Facial emotion recognition does not appear to be regained in brain injury patients.'

'What does that mean for me?'

'A lack of accurate emotion perception can lead to increased levels of altercations, misunderstandings and subsequent loss of social connections,' she answered.

'You're very blunt,' I stated.

'I have to be. You need to know precisely what has happened to you and the prognosis.'

'I don't want to live in a rehabilitation unit. I want to live independently,' I asserted.

She nodded. 'You said that often to James. That was why he took you back to Dunstrafne Castle. But it didn't work out. I don't believe your husband realised what was involved and how much care you need.'

'What? To stop me from killing myself?'

'In part, yes.'

'So why don't I remember trying to hurt myself? All I remember is my husband trying to kill me.'

'What you are experiencing is typical for the brain trauma you have suffered. Psychotic symptoms are common in one in twenty people with a brain injury. More severe brain injuries and trauma to certain parts of the brain, such as in your case, have a higher risk of developing psychotic symptoms.'

'Such as?' I asked, unsure whether I wanted to hear the answer.

'Delusions. Such as the false belief that things are true that no one else experiences as reality. Paranoid delusions, for example, people talking about them, watching them, or trying to kill them.'

'And?' I asked.

'Confused thinking and changed emotions. Some people become withdrawn or isolated, and others become more extroverted, the antithesis of their behaviour before sustaining a brain injury.'

'And me? Have I changed?' I questioned.

'Maybe your husband should be the person to ask.'

'If you say I was married for nine years, why did my husband and Mrs Taylor say I was married for two years? Why lie to me?'

'You resisted the facts so vehemently. You refused to acknowledge your husband or that you were married to him prior to your accident. So, he constructed a truth that he thought you could accept and would allow you to trust him to take you back to Dunstrafne Castle where he hoped you would recover your memories.'

'That I was married to him for two years?' I mumbled.

'Yes. He took photographs of your recovery and put them

together in a scrapbook for you to look at. You would look at that
and accepted his word when he said you were married. But he
dated the marriage to directly after the car accident.'

'And that's why there's no wedding photographs from two years
ago?'

She nodded.

'Or wedding ring?'

'He did have a new wedding ring fitted for you after the accident, but you somehow misplaced it.'

I stared at her. 'He lied to me? Why do that?'

'He did it out of love because you couldn't accept the truth. So,
James gave you a version of the truth you could tolerate. He showed
you photographs of you and him, your wedding day, for example,
before the accident, but you managed to destroy every copy as it
distressed you so much. You couldn't and still can't reconcile that
you are Isabella Langdon. That the woman in the photographs he
showed you is really you.'

'Why? Why is that? Why don't I recognise myself? Why recognise the person after the accident as being married to him and not
before? That makes no sense,' I argued.

'I think you know the answer,' she replied.

'I do?' I murmured, feeling tired again.

She tapped the folder.

'The photographs?'

She nodded. 'Your mind wasn't the only part of you affected by
the injury, your body has also physically changed. That's why you
can't recognise yourself.'

My fingers instinctively touched my scalp and my cropped hair.

'She had long, curly blonde hair and I...' I faltered as I tried to
remember the colour of my hair.

'Your hair was all cut off for surgery. I imagine it was dyed
blonde as it grew in dark. Your scalp was shaved for some time to

allow the surgery incisions to heal. You've also undergone numerous operations due to complications.'

I exhaled slowly. I let my eyes drift down to the two photographs laid side by side on my bed. I had been avoiding them this entire time.

'Her?' I questioned, picking up the photograph of Isabella Langdon.

'You,' she replied, 'before the accident.'

'She's beautiful,' I murmured to myself.

I dropped the photograph and forced myself to touch the second one with my fingers. I couldn't hold it. Not that I needed to, as I recognised the image from the reflection in the mirror in Isabella Langdon's bedroom and walk-in closet.

'Me?' I questioned as I looked at her.

She nodded. 'Yes, that's you now.'

'It's not the same person. Isabella Langdon's heavier, much heavier. And, her face is different,' I stated.

'You've lost a considerable amount of weight. I mentioned earlier, you need to be prompted to eat. And as for your face, well, again it is weight loss, but also you suffered trauma to your features. But if you look closely enough at the two photographs, you'll see a similarity.'

I did as she said, then shook my head. 'You're lying. They're not the same person. They're not remotely similar.'

She sighed.

I looked at her. 'They're not. You can't make me believe something that isn't true.'

'No,' she conceded. 'You're right. But I'll leave them with you. They might help you remember.'

'No,' I said, swiping them off my bed. 'Take them away.'

I watched as she bent down and picked up the scattered photographs from the floor.

'Why were there no mirrors in Dunstrafne Castle? Why? Why didn't they want me to know what I looked like? Why are you showing me what they wouldn't let me see?'

She tilted her head up to me, still crouching. 'Because you broke the first mirror and tried to use a piece of it to harm yourself.'

'I... I don't remember,' I mumbled.

She didn't reply.

She straightened up and replaced the photographs into the folder and then into her Prada work bag.

'My husband... When is he coming to see me? You said you had seen him. Does he know I am here?'

She didn't answer me.

Then I remembered. 'He's with the police? He stabbed me?'

'No. He's not with the police. He gave a statement, as did I, as your clinician. He didn't stab you, Mrs Langdon. You stabbed yourself.'

'No...' I whispered. 'That's not possible.'

Or is it?

'The wound to your abdomen is on the right-hand side, indicative of self-infliction. You are right-handed as is James. If your husband had stabbed you, your injury would be on the left-hand side.'

'So where is he?' I asked, confused. 'If he's not been detained by the police, then where is he?'

A coldness descended upon me. There was something very wrong. Why wouldn't he come and see me? I was his wife, wasn't I?

'Why didn't he come with you this evening?'

I waited for a response as she bent down and picked up her bag.

'Where is my husband? Why doesn't he want to see me?'

Oh God... He's with her...

I realised I hadn't imagined it. The conversation I overheard when he was on the phone in the study.

'He's with her, isn't he? He's in London with her.'

I watched her face, trying to discern her reaction. But I couldn't read her expression.

'He's chosen her over me...' I mumbled more to myself than her.

'Yes, he's returned to London.'

'He's with her?'

She looked at me, unsure of whether to answer.

But her silence confirmed my worst fear.

'And me? What happens to me?' I whispered.

'That's why I am here. To arrange your return with me to Sanderson Hospital.'

'No... Please? I want to speak to my husband. I want to speak to...' I faltered, lost.

I looked up at the whiteboard as Adam had instructed when I felt myself becoming disorientated, losing track of my thoughts – my life.

'James,' I murmured as I read the prompt on the whiteboard.

A: Your husband is James Buchanan Langdon.

But for how long?

How long before he replaces you with another wife?

'Mrs Langdon? Shall I continue reading?'

I broke away from the whiteboard and turned to the softly spoken voice.

Mrs Taylor?

'Where is Alex? Alex was here.'

Mrs Taylor was now sitting in the same chair as Professor Alex Walker, holding my book.

'Professor Walker left some time ago. Remember?'

I shook my head.

'No matter. You're exhausted.'

'You're reading my book?'

She smiled at me, nodded. 'I'm reading it to you. I did this every evening at Dunstrafne Castle.'

'You did?'

I couldn't recall.

'Her diary? Is it—'

'Yes, it's safe. See?' she said, showing me. 'It's lodged between the pages.'

'And the ultrasound scan? Did you take it? It wasn't with the pages from her diary.'

Mrs Taylor shook her head.

I stared at her, noting that her hair was still pinned back from her pale, thin face. She smiled at me. 'Shall I continue?'

'Did he take it? My husband?' I asked, ignoring her question.

'Yes. Mr Langdon decided it was best he kept it.'

I nodded. It made sense. After all, he had nothing else left of Isabella Langdon.

'The fire? Did it destroy the castle?' I questioned, hoping the answer would be yes.

'There was considerable water damage, to be expected, of course, from extinguishing the fire. But it's not beyond repair. I believe Mr Langdon has had a report that restorations will take at least a year before Dunstrafne is habitable again.'

'And where... Where is he living now?'

'I believe Mr Langdon will be staying at your London residence while the repairs are carried out.'

With her... His new woman.

'Is he coming to see me?' I asked, hopeful. Even though it was a rhetorical question.

Mrs Taylor cleared her throat first before replying: 'I am sure once he's got settled, he will visit you,' she assured me.

I looked at her. We both knew she was lying.

'Shall I continue reading?'

'You'll still visit me, won't you? When Alex... Professor Walker takes me to Sanderson... Sanderson Hospital?'

I heard the quiver in my voice. It was fear.

She reached forward and rested her hand on top of my bandaged one. 'Of course, Mrs Langdon. Who else would read to you?'

I smiled at her as I wiped at the tears with the back of my other hand. 'My mother used to read to me,' I shared.

Mrs Taylor nodded.

'Does she know I'm here?' I asked.

'The whiteboard, Mrs Langdon. Remember. Everything about your mother is there on the whiteboard.'

'No. Not now. I'm tired.' I rested my head back and closed my eyes.

I felt Mrs Taylor gently pat the back of my bandaged hand. 'Shall I continue reading then?'

'I'd like that,' I said, wanting to fill my mind with something familiar. Something that made me feel safe. 'Will you begin at the beginning again?'

I heard the rustle of pages as she flicked back to the opening page.

A smile played on my lips as her soft, quiet voice drifted over me, luxuriating in the words that spoke to me of home.

'Last night I dreamt...'

27

THREE MONTHS LATER

I lay back on the grass and closed my eyes, luxuriating in the feel of the sun.

Time had passed, but I had no concept of how long. I cast my mind back to the whiteboard in the kitchen, but couldn't recall the date scrawled on there.

'What month is it?' I asked.

Tabitha, who was beside me, answered, 'You know. We wrote it down on the whiteboard earlier.'

'I can't remember,' I said.

'Try. Try to remember what I said this morning.'

I tried. Failed.

'It's still warm so it has to be... September?' I guessed.

'It's early November. But it is warm because of the sun today.'

'And the day?' I asked as my fingers trailed through the blades of green.

There was an excited, glowing, bubbly feeling in the pit of my stomach. I thought of it as a fizzy, sweet lemonade feeling pre-empting what was going to be a good day: the best of days.

'Sunday,' she replied. 'And what happens on Sundays?'

My faint smile broadened to a grin in anticipation of the day's events. My lemonade feeling intensified, sparkling and popping inside me. I twisted my head to face Tabitha. She was lying on her side, propped up on her elbow, watching me. She was smiling. It made me feel good because I knew why – I remembered.

'He visits.'

'Who's he?' Tabitha asked.

'My husband,' I replied, feeling the excitement intensify. 'I like Sundays. It's my favourite day.'

'I know. You tell me all the time.' She laughed.

I liked it when Tabitha laughed. Her laughter was as brilliant and nurturing as the sun on my skin.

'And the boys? He's bringing Henry and Jack? Yes?'

'Doesn't he always bring the dogs?' Tabitha replied.

I plucked a blade of grass and stuck it between my teeth. 'Ahuh. He knows I love the boys. I miss them. I want Henry and Jack to stay here, Tab, with us.'

'I know. And we've been through this. They're better staying with James. You know that.'

'Maybe…'

I trusted Tabitha. She made sense of the world when I felt confused and forgot things. But she was also kind and funny and made me laugh when I couldn't remember.

'But we have this garden. They could stay here with me. I have lots of room in the house,' I said, sitting up. 'Mummy wouldn't mind.'

'They have a big garden where they are. Remember? It was the house you used to live in with your husband and the dogs before the accident.'

'In Hampstead Heath?'

'Yes, that's right.'

'We live in Hampstead Heath as well,' I stated.

She smiled at me. 'I know. We can go and visit them at your old house for a change,' she suggested.

'No. No, I prefer them to come here.'

'Maybe one day.'

I shook my head. I didn't want to ever leave this place again.

I looked back at my mother's large house.

'I grew up here,' I then said.

'I know,' answered Tabitha. 'It's a beautiful home.'

'It is, isn't it? I love it here.'

'So do I,' Tabitha replied.

I grinned at her. 'And this evening, is Mrs Taylor visiting me? She promised she would read to me again.'

'Yes. That's right. That's what's on the whiteboard.'

Happy, I turned and faced the brightest of blue skies. There were no clouds overhead, just a ball of intense golden fire set against a sea of tranquillity. I closed my eyes and listened as the tall oak trees whispered to one another above me, their brittle brown leaves rustling ever so faintly with promises of what was to come. I ran my hands through my short, thick, dark brown, tight curls, luxuriating in the knowledge that my hair was finally growing back.

I adored it here. The sprawling, private garden with its high walls covered in wild roses, climbing higher and higher, intertwined with ivy. There were trees everywhere, protecting and sheltering me not only from the elements but from the world. Not only in the garden but all around the house. At the bottom of the driveway was a narrow road, and opposite, an old stone wall which acted as a border with centuries-old trees conspiring together, hiding my favourite place – Hampstead Heath. This was home. My home. My safe place. I had the vaguest of memories that where I had been before was some kind of hospital.

Had I been ill?

And where was I before that? I couldn't remember.

I just knew I never wanted to leave here. I never wanted to leave my mother's house.

'Where's my mother, Tab? I haven't seen her this morning. Is she rehearsing? You know, she doesn't like to be disturbed when she's rehearsing. We'll have to be quiet if we go inside.'

I looked at Tabitha. She was still smiling. But it wasn't her big, infectious smile. It was different.

'Where's my mother? You know she's a classical pianist. She's travelled the world playing.'

'Yes, I know. I've listened to her recordings. She's extraordinarily talented.'

'She is, isn't she?'

The doorbell rang. It was a distant chime, but I had been waiting for the cue.

'It's him, Tab! He's here!' I leapt up to my feet.

'Hey, slow down,' Tabitha said, getting up off the grass, laughing at my enthusiasm.

I ran to the French doors that led into the sitting room. I opened them and darted past the stunning walnut Steinway & Sons grand piano, and out to the hallway and the front door, followed by Tabitha, calling for me to slow down.

'Hurry, Tab,' I yelled back over my shoulder.

I reached the front door.

'Tabitha!' I cried. 'They're here!'

She caught up with me.

'I know, let me get to the door,' she said.

I moved out of the way and watched her take the front door key out of her pocket and then unlock the heavy wooden door. She opened it and was greeted by two red fox Labradors who bounded past her.

Henry threw himself at me, knocking me back against the wall, while Jack weaved around my legs, whacking me with his wagging tail.

'Hey, Henry! Jack!' I cried out.

I pushed Henry down and then crouched close to the floor so I could fuss over them.

'You missed me, huh? Well, I missed you guys as well,' I cooed.

'Hello, darling.'

I looked up.

I saw him – my husband. He was smiling down at me.

'They miss me,' I said.

'I know they do,' he agreed. 'But they're here now. And so is...' He paused and looked at the young toddler squirming in his arms as she managed to force her red wellies off, so she was only wearing cream ribbed tights on her kicking feet. 'Bella.'

I could see from the smile he bestowed upon her that she was his world now. Not me. If I had ever been.

He placed the wriggling toddler down on her petite feet. Her head was covered in platinum-blonde spirals of curls tumbling across her face. Her deep brown eyes fixed on me. I watched as my husband took her padded red coat off.

'Ohh, what a pretty red dress,' I said to her.

'Red's her favourite colour this week. Can you tell?' My husband laughed.

I looked at him as he pulled off his scarf and removed his Barbour jacket.

'It's hot in here,' he noted.

'Mrs Langdon feels the cold,' Tabitha replied.

Not that I was listening, I was watching the toddler, worried she might fall.

I quickly scooped her up in my arms before Jack's overly enthusiastic tail knocked her over.

'Careful,' warned my husband. 'She's getting more and more difficult to hold as she's a world-class wriggler now. Aren't you Bella Boo? Eh?' he said, tickling her tummy.

She gurgled and squealed in delight, babbling what sounded like 'Da Da' in response.

'I know,' I replied. 'I am careful with her.'

He didn't hear; my words lost to him as he held his arms out for me to hand her over.

'She's safe. I'll put her down,' I said, not wanting to give her back.

I placed her down on the original wooden parquet hallway floor as the boys shot off in the direction of the sitting room, heading for the garden.

I took hold of her tiny, chubby hand and knelt down to her level. 'Do you want to sit with me at the piano?'

She tilted her head to look at me. Smiled and then babbled something.

'Come on then,' I said, straightening up.

'Do you want something to drink for Bella or for yourself?' Tabitha offered.

I turned back to her, but she was asking my husband.

'We have that organic, unsweetened apple juice that you give Bella in the fridge. Mrs Langdon insisted we keep some for her.'

'Maybe before we go. Bella's just had a drink and a snack.'

I led the little girl down the hallway while Tabitha and my husband followed us, talking amongst themselves.

I believed that sometimes they didn't think I could hear what they said. But I did.

'She still won't let you call her Isabella?'

'No,' answered Tabitha. 'I repeatedly use the flash cards and the whiteboard, of course, but Mrs Langdon still won't accept that she is Isabella. She won't let me use any other name than Mrs Langdon.'

'Maybe one day,' I heard my husband say.

Wistfully, perhaps.

'She's really happy here, though. So, yes, maybe one day,' Tabitha conceded.

'Yes, I did the right thing taking her out of Sanderson's residential unit. And I know she is so happy with you, Tabitha,' he said. 'It's self-evident. I mean, look at her. She's even gaining weight. You're doing wonders with her.'

'Well, for what it's worth, I like working with her. As does Clemmy. Mrs Langdon likes her as well.'

Clemmy?

Clemmy for Clementine, I thought.

'Without you and Clemmy looking after her, well, I don't know what I'd do. It's a relief. It means I can focus on Bella. She's a handful! However, what else should one expect with a nineteen-month-old toddler?'

'You still won't consider getting a live-in nanny to help you? I mean, it's a lot to cope with bringing up a toddler on your own.'

'I'm fine. I have Mia during the weekdays, as you know. She's great. And I couldn't have taken my wife to Dunstrafne Castle for those two months if Mia hadn't been looking after Bella for me. But I want to make up for the time I lost with my daughter when I would return to Dunstrafne Castle and my wife. She of course didn't understand I was looking after...'

I heard him pause.

I wondered who he was looking after.

'Her mother...'

Her mother?

'Without her,' he continued, 'I don't think I could have coped. She means everything to me.'

Me?

Or her?

I automatically looked down at the flouncing mop of wild flaxen-white curls and felt compelled to kiss her small head. I stopped and crouched beside her, pulling her in for a bear hug. I buried my face in her soft baby curls as she struggled to get away and inhaled, seeking out the comfort of her scent. But there was nothing. Whatever connection or solace I was seeking didn't exist.

'After what happened to Isabella and the injuries she sustained, it's a miracle that Bella survived. But, against the odds, she did and was born seven months later by caesarean section while Isabella was thankfully still in the coma. Can you imagine waking up from a coma to find you are heavily pregnant? Odd, isn't it, that the day after Bella was born, she came out of the coma?'

'Yes, that is bizarre,' I heard Tabitha reply.

'Careful, darling! Bella doesn't like to be held too tightly. Remember?' my husband stated.

I turned and looked back up at him and Tabitha. They were both watching me.

It was as if they were expecting me to accidentally hurt her. Not that I would ever do that. I was careful with her. So careful.

'She's fine. Aren't you?' I questioned as I released her squirming body. 'Come on. Do you want to play my mummy's piano? She won't mind.'

She stared at me with her large, beautiful brown eyes and thick, lavish dark eyelashes.

For a moment I was frozen. She reminded me of someone.

Her. She reminds me of Isabella Langdon...

How? How is that possible? How can she look so like her?

I smiled at her. She was beautiful. So beautiful.

I thought of Isabella Langdon, his other wife, the one before me, and I felt nothing. Gone was the toxic jealousy I had so often suffered at not being as beautiful or engaging as her. I realised it was because I was happy. I was back where I belonged, and she hadn't followed me. She couldn't. After all, I had razed her tormented ghost to the ground when I had set fire to Dunstrafne Castle.

The toddler tugged my dress and tried to pull me forward.

'Okay, then,' I said enthusiastically. 'Let's go make some music!'

I straightened up and continued leading her by her hand down the hallway, turning into the sitting room.

Behind us, my husband and Tabitha resumed talking as they followed. Their words drifted over me as I lifted the toddler up and sat down on the stool at the piano, placing her on my lap.

'She still believes her mother's here?' I heard him say.

'Yes,' Tabitha replied. 'She keeps asking where she is.'

'How often?' he questioned.

My mother? Where is she?

My eyes rested on the black-and-white photograph of her with me as a baby in the silver frame on top of the piano.

This is her piano...

'A lot. She can't remember. Regardless of how many times I have told her she's gone. She just can't retain the information.'

'Is it on the whiteboard?' I heard him ask.

'Yes. Every morning we go over what happened to her mother.'

'I can understand why. Her mother died of secondary cancer while Isabella was in a coma. So, she has no memory, no reference point to tell her that her mother has died. Her breast cancer returned after being in remission for years. It was so aggressive. I sometimes wonder if the accident caused the cancer to come back. The stress of not knowing what would happen to her daughter and whether she would pull through and...' He faltered.

I watched as the wild-haired toddler pressed the keys with her podgy fingers.

'See? There's me with my mummy,' I whispered into her blonde curls as I stared at my mother's beautiful face. 'You might meet her.'

'Darling—'

'No,' interrupted Tabitha. 'She's fine. Give her time. Bella doesn't understand.'

'Not yet. But one day… What do I tell her?'

'I don't know. The truth? That her mother had a serious accident that—'

'Exactly!' he cut her off. 'That it changed her personality. That it makes her irate and unable to tolerate her own daughter for no longer than a few minutes.'

'It will get better,' Tabitha assured him.

I heard him exhale. I could feel the heat of his body as he stood directly behind me.

'I am being careful with her!' I retaliated.

'I know, darling. I know you are,' he replied, placing his hand on my shoulder.

I shrugged him off. 'Don't! Don't touch me!' I snapped.

'Darling?' he replied.

'No! Let me be with her. I am being careful!'

I waited for a response. He remained silent.

The unruly-haired toddler lurched forward and, with a clenched fist, started banging at the keys.

'Shh…' I said to her as I grabbed her dimpled fist. I planted a big, wet kiss on her cheek.

She turned and looked up at me with those huge, familiar eyes.

'Why don't I take Bella now, darling? Play for her. Play the piece your mother played to you when you were little.'

'Yes,' I said. 'Yes, she will like that, won't she?' I kissed her cheek again and whispered, 'Let me play what my mummy would play for me when I was your age. Maybe your mummy will teach you how to play the piano like my mummy did with me.'

My husband bent down and lifted her out of my arms. He smiled at me, but I felt as if something was missing. What that was, I couldn't pinpoint.

He raised the toddler in the air much to her delight, before securing her in his arms. She babbled as she attempted to grab at his nose, making him laugh.

I let my fingers float over the keys as they stood behind me. I couldn't remember what it was that I was playing, but I intuitively knew it.

'I'm sure at some point she'll want to spend longer with Bella,' I heard Tabitha say.

'Maybe,' my husband replied. But he didn't sound convinced. 'She just won't accept that she is her daughter no matter—' His voice broke off as Bella babbled at him.

I heard her gurgle in delight in response to some action of his.

I continued playing.

'It's so beautiful. So haunting,' I heard Tabitha murmur from behind me. 'What is it?'

I shook my head. I didn't know.

'It's Chopin's Prelude in B Minor Op twenty-eight,' answered my husband. 'It was Isabella's favourite piece of music.'

'I didn't realise Mrs Langdon could play like that,' Tabitha said to him.

'She couldn't... At least, not until after the car accident. She's playing that piece with a level of competency and fluidity of movement she never had before.'

'How is that possible?' I heard Tabitha question.

'My friend and her neurosurgeon, Alex, explained to me that it's known as acquired savant syndrome. It's a result of the head injury. She can't remember who she was before the accident, particularly her time married to me, and yet she can recall this piece of music and play it as if she were a professional pianist.'

'Mrs Langdon told me her mother was a classical pianist,' Tabitha said as I continued playing.

'Yes,' he agreed. 'Isabella was never talented like her mother, never had that *je ne sais quoi* to follow a career in music. But,' I heard him sigh above the melancholic notes, 'she was the most gifted artist. She had exhibitions at art galleries here in London. She was making a name for herself and then...' He faltered. 'She can't even remember that she was an artist. She's lost the ability to paint. She doesn't even attempt to. No desire. And yet here she is playing the piano. Something she was never interested in until after the...' His voice faltered again.

They then remained silent, even the toddler, until I finished playing.

'Darling, that was beautiful,' he said.

I turned around to see him smiling at me.

It felt as if his smile caressed my cheek.

'Thank you,' I murmured.

'Say, bye bye, Bella! See you next Sunday!'

'The boys? Let them stay. Please?'

'Darling, they need to come home with me.'

'Oh,' I mumbled. 'I miss them.'

'I know. Maybe one day they can stay.'

I beamed at him. 'I would love that!'

I then turned away from him and the beautiful child with the huge brown eyes in his arms and resumed playing. My eyes sought out my mother's photograph, holding me as a baby. Next to it was the beloved book she had given me when I had been ill in what felt like another life. Isabella Langdon's torn diary pages were still hidden within the pages. I smiled at the title, *Rebecca* by Daphne du Maurier. I had read it so many times that I felt like Manderley was mine. Not that I read it now. I didn't need to, not any more. I had dreamt of

Manderley and of returning home. Again, and again. And now, here I was.

'I love you, darling. Always will,' I heard him say.

I smiled and continued playing.

ACKNOWLEDGEMENTS

Thanks to my wonderful mother and sister for their unending support and for being my most valued readers. A special thank you to Francesca Rosalind Dempsey for inspiring me to write this book and sharing her academic research. Thanks always to Charlotte, Gabriel-Myles and Ruby. Thanks as well to Ellie Kane and Kai Benjamin Debbonaire. Thanks to Peter Dempsey for all your much-appreciated support.

Thank you to Kirstie Long for your fabulous support.

As always, thank you to my fantastic literary agent, Annette Crossland.

Thanks to all at Boldwood Books for your brilliance and for being such an amazing team. Thank you to both my exceptional copyeditor, Ross Dickinson, and proofreader, Susan Sugden. And, in particular, Caroline Ridding, for yet again being such an exceptional and fabulous editor and for sprinkling her special magic all over this book – thank you.

A final special thank you to Tom McRae, whose music inspired me as I wrote.

ABOUT THE AUTHOR

Danielle Ramsay is the author of the DI Jack Brady crime novels and other dark thrillers. She is a Scot living in the North-East of England.

Sign up to Danielle Ramsay's mailing list here for news, competitions and updates on future books.

Visit Danielle Ramsay's Website: https://www.danielle-ramsay.com

Follow Danielle Ramsay on social media:

 x.com/danielleramsay2

 facebook.com/Danielle.ramsay.author

 instagram.com/danielle.ramsay.author

ALSO BY DANIELLE RAMSAY

The Perfect Husband

My Best Friend's Secret

The Other Wife

THE

Murder

LIST

**THE MURDER LIST IS A NEWSLETTER
DEDICATED TO SPINE-CHILLING FICTION
AND GRIPPING PAGE-TURNERS!**

**SIGN UP TO MAKE SURE YOU'RE ON OUR
HIT LIST FOR EXCLUSIVE DEALS, AUTHOR
CONTENT, AND COMPETITIONS.**

SIGN UP TO OUR NEWSLETTER

BIT.LY/THEMURDERLISTNEWS

Boldwood

Boldwood Books is an award-winning fiction publishing company seeking out the best stories from around the world.

Find out more at www.boldwoodbooks.com

Join our reader community for brilliant books, competitions and offers!

Follow us
@BoldwoodBooks
@TheBoldBookClub

Sign up to our weekly deals newsletter

https://bit.ly/BoldwoodBNewsletter

Printed in Great Britain
by Amazon